The Wicked

THE
WICKED

A Novel

Douglas Nicholas

EMILY BESTLER BOOKS

—

ATRIA

New York   London   Toronto   Sydney   New Delhi

ATRIA PAPERBACK
A Division of Simon & Schuster, Inc.
1230 Avenue of the Americas
New York, NY 10020

Copyright © 2014 by Douglas Nicholas

First Emily Bestler Books/Atria Paperback edition March 2014

EMILY BESTLER BOOKS / ATRIA PAPERBACK and colophon are
trademarks of Simon & Schuster, Inc.

For information about special discounts for bulk purchases,
please contact Simon & Schuster Special Sales at 1-866-506-1949
or business@simonandschuster.com.

The Simon & Schuster Speakers Bureau can bring authors to your
live event. For more information or to book an event, contact the
Simon & Schuster Speakers Bureau at 1-866-248-3049 or
visit our website at www.simonspeakers.com.

Manufactured in the United States of America

10 9 8 7 6 5 4 3 2 1

Library of Congress Cataloging-in-Publication Data

Nicholas, Douglas.
  The wicked / by Douglas Nicholas.—First Emily Bestler Books/
Atria Paperback edition.
    pages cm
  I. Title.
  PS3614.13375W53 2013
  813'.6—dc23

                                        2013004311

ISBN 978-1-4516-6024-1
ISBN 978-1-4516-6026-5 (ebook)

for Theresa

The wicked plotteth against the just,
and gnasheth upon him with his teeth.

—Psalm 37

this dead butcher and his fiend-like queen

—*Macbeth*, V. viii.

Pronunciation of Irish names:

Maeve = MAYV

Nemain = NEV-an

A glossary of Irish terms is to be found on page 339.

A glossary of archaisms and of North England dialect terms is to be found on page 341.

Part I

THE GRAVEN HAND

CHAPTER 1

BENEATH THE HUM AND CHAT-
ter of the lower hall, the bang of
wooden dishes and the clink of
pewter, the crackle of flames in the fireplace, Hob
could hear the tick of Sir Jehan's bronze fingertips
against the arm of his chair.

The lad sat at the high table in the great hall
of Castle Blanchefontaine. The castle, high in the
forested ridges of the Pennine Mountains, had been
built by Sir Jehan's ancestors a hundred years ago in
the twelfth century. Around Hob were his adopted
family: Maeve, called Molly, and her granddaughter,
Nemain, both out of Ireland, and the strong-bodied
Jack Brown, Molly's lover. They were here at the
invitation of Sir Jehan, the Sieur de Blanchefontaine,

and they awaited another knight that they were to meet this chill spring evening. Sir Jehan, never one to sit quietly, was fidgeting in his impatience.

He lifted his chin to indicate one of the diners in the lower hall, a young man-at-arms with new-washed hands, but with a thin gray layer of road dust in his hair and on the shoulders of his leather gambeson. "That man there, madam," he said to Molly, "is one of Sir Odinell's outriders; he says their party will be here within the hour. I had messages from him this winter past, and when I knew you were to visit us, I sent for him. I believe that you will be of much benefit, one to the other. We are old friends. He has family—he is one of the De Umfrevilles, although a minor branch, and he has connections with the De Lucys and the Nevilles as well. You are perhaps familiar with them?"

"I have heard somewhat," said Molly.

"These are magnates of the North," said Sir Jehan, "and have lands here and in Scotland and in Normandy; their influence, or even patronage, would be no small matter. Sir Odinell has wealth, he has knights; when you are ready to return to Ireland, he can be as a stout shield to you. As will I, as will I—but he has greater kinfolk, and . . ." With his left hand he toyed with his trencher for a few heartbeats, then pushed it aside; drew his goblet toward him, but did not drink. "But he is much vexed; has a burden upon him; strange neighbors have come to him, and his people are plagued with horrid doings. He has written to me, entreating me to advise him. . . ."

He looked at Molly, a heavy but shapely woman, with startling blue eyes and a thick mane of gray and silver hair, a handsome woman a few years past her half-century mark, sitting calmly across the wide table, hardly a daunting figure, and said, "I believe you to be, madam, the one person I would commend to him in this . . . this *odd* and perplexing trouble. . . ." He took the stem of his goblet between the thumb and forefinger of his left hand and, twirling the stem, turned the goblet round and round on the tabletop. "I will let him tell you of his woes, and I will try to explain to him why he must trust you so fully. He may disbelieve at first; still, he has seen so much that is . . ." His voice trailed off; he turned a little in his chair so he could see the fire, and lapsed into silence as his gaze was drawn toward the flames.

The firelight played over his rather lupine features: the prominent cheekbones and strong chin that formed a triangle, accented by a broad brow and deep-set blue eyes, a carrot-colored widow's peak. The Sieur de Blanchefontaine stretched his long legs out before him, then drew them back. Hob had the sense that the knight—active, lean, athletic—was restive; this waiting, this enforced idleness, chafed him, which seemed a kind of proof that he had recovered from the terrible events of a year and a quarter ago.

Sir Jehan was in no wise so restless as he had been when first Hob had encountered him last year, but there was yet an abundance of energy that would express itself now and again in fretful movements, as at this moment, when his beautiful, immobile right hand tapped lightly and persistently, Sir Jehan himself all unaware of it.

The hand was hollow: the knight's ruined real hand fit inside as in a glove, the fingers that remained to him slipping into the hollow bronze ones, the rigid metal supporting his hand. The fingers of the hollow hand bent in a slight natural curve; the fingernails, the wrinkles of the knuckles, even the veins on the back, had been delicately fashioned by an Italian, a master craftsman from that land of cunning master craftsmen. A hinged bracelet proceeded from the back of the bronze glove, clasped Sir Jehan's wrist, and helped to secure the hand. Were it not for the color and the rigidity, it might be thought a true hand, though perforce a bit larger to accommodate the living hand within.

Sir Jehan had had his secretary and chaplain, Father Baudoin, write out, in the priest's angular Norman characters, a motto for the Italian to copy. Graven across the back of the hand, just behind the knuckles, facing the observer, the grooves of the letters filled in with green gold, was the legend *Cave Sinistram*: "Beware the Left Hand." And indeed Sir Jehan had become, by dint of the force of his will and a near-frenzied devotion to practice, as dangerous with his left hand as he had been with his right.

He had another metal hand that he wore on campaign: this was of iron, and the fingers hinged, so that he could close and lock them on a shield's bracket, and the iron hand's bracelet was reinforced by stout straps that ran up above his elbow. The motto was the same, *Cave Sinistram*, but picked out in silver letters. It was, however, unlikely that a foe of Sir Jehan would have the leisure to take advantage of the warning—one who had survived an encounter with him said that engaging the Sieur de Blanchefontaine was like finding oneself in the midst of a four-dog fight, a storm of blurred sharp-edged danger.

Hob looked around at the whitewashed plaster of the great hall, stained above the huge hearth by swirls of pale gray, dark gray, and carbon-black soot. He felt happy and secure here in Blanchefontaine's high-ceilinged hall, with its lattice-screened balcony for musicians to play unseen, its two hearths, its wide-planked floors spread with rushes, the rushes freshened with sprinklings of lady-of-the-meadow and germander. The walls were adorned with the brightly colored escutcheons of the household knights; with displays of battered and age-darkened weapons, including a spray of angons and other ancient throwing spears; and with adroitly made tapestries.

Some of these tapestries depicted the hunt and some depicted martial scenes; three others illustrated certain songs of the troubadours. These last were the work of blithe little Dame Aline, the wife of Sir Balthasar, Blanchefontaine's stern castellan. Dame Aline, ever eager to hear the latest song or poem from the continent, had woven the large tapestry that now hung behind the pages' bench, a favorite of Hob's: a scene from an *alba* of Guiraut de Bornelh, in which the lovers embrace in a shadowed garden, while their accomplice, a watchman in a tower, calls down to them that dawn approaches, with its danger of discovery.

Over the last year Molly's little troupe had returned to the castle at intervals, staying a few weeks at a time. During these visits Molly tended to Sir Jehan's injuries, physical and otherwise, from the disastrous winter of the year before. Her deliverance of the castle from an evil invader had made fierce partisans of Sir Jehan and everyone else in the castle, high to low.

Hob himself was under the tutelage of Sir Balthasar: both that fearsome knight and Sir Jehan had promised that Hob would be trained in the Norman fashion, and would be made a knight, and addressed him now as *Squire Robert*. Whenever Molly's troupe sojourned at Blanchefontaine, the two subjected Hob by night to intricate instruction in castle etiquette, and by day to brutal lessons in weaponcraft, horsemanship, and the destruction of one's enemies. The intense exercise when they were at the castle, along with Jack's insistence on activity designed to increase Hob's strength whenever they camped along the road, had wrought a change: Hob was no longer a boy, but a sturdy muscular youth.

Some of Castle Blanchefontaine's junior knights—including Sir Tancred, who had by sheer good fortune escaped the events of last year unscathed—shared the high table. They had withdrawn to the far end, for there are no secrets in a castle's community, and it was known that Sir Jehan was to conduct a matter of some grave import that night, and was not to be intruded upon.

From the hall led four archways: one that gave onto the steps that went down to the guardhouse and so out to the bailey, and three that gave access to interior stairways. From one of the latter came a burst of high-pitched laughter, and a moment later a party of women appeared: the wives of two of the married knights, as well as Dame Aline, and Lady Isabeau herself, Sir Jehan's wife.

Sir Jehan and the other knights stood; he greeted his wife and murmured something to her. She nodded, and swept Dame Aline and the other women down to the far end of the table, there to preside among the castle's resident knights, for Sir Jehan was to excuse himself as soon as Sir Odinell arrived.

Hob, who was beginning to grow bored as well as hungry, took the occasion to contemplate Lady Isabeau and Dame Aline. He was now well into his fifteenth year—he had turned fourteen last October, and here they were, halfway through April—and betrothed to Nemain, whom he adored. But in his newly awakened manhood, he found himself acutely aware of the appeal to the eye that women—more beautiful than flowers, more graceful than cats—presented. These two women, close friends, presented a contrast in appearance, each with her own virtue.

Lady Isabeau was tall and slim. Her hair, black and lustrous as raven-feather, her dark eyes, her dark brows, all were set off by her ivory skin; the long and very thin scar that interrupted her left eyebrow and curved to the corner of her mouth only enhanced an expressionless, almost eerie beauty. Dame Aline, pretty rather than beautiful, was short and sonsy, lightly freckled, with features that, lit from within by a sweet and merry nature, achieved a kind of radiance.

As Hob watched, the two women gathered all attention to themselves and, by dint of question and comment, drew every knight and lady into the circle of banter and discussion. Soon their end of the high table was alight with jest, conversation, even snatches of song, while the other end, where sat the Sieur de Blanchefontaine and his party, seemed somber by contrast.

At the opposite end of the hall from the dais where Sir Jehan and his guests sat at table, there was a stout wooden screen. For all its decorative carving, it was thick, and securely fastened, and several feet wider than the doorway it concealed. This doorway, with its two heavy leaves, led to the top landing of an external closed stairway, which descended one storey to the ground, and doubled back on itself, and ended in a strong guardhouse. The whole was intended to slow attackers and so prevent surprise attacks, and to make entrance as difficult as possible. There was even a pitfall on the stairway that could be uncovered. The screen itself obliged anyone who sought entrance to turn and walk a few feet in the narrow space between the carved wood and the plaster of the wall. Sir Jehan stationed guards at all times within the hall, clustered down by the screen, and in the doorway behind it as well.

Among these guards now arose a stirring: murmured questions, men standing up and drawing nearer to the entranceway, loosening weapons; a gradual increase in the noise down-hall silenced those on the dais; then the detail commander stepped around the end of the screen and announced, crisp as a trained herald: "Sir Odinell de Umfreville, Sieur de Chantemerle." And around the screen came a burly knight of medium stature, clean-shaven, hard-eyed, his broad forehead continuing on to a head quite bald in front and crowned with a horseshoe-shaped fringe of salt-and-pepper hair. Behind him came three of his knights, and twice that many of his household guard, surrendering their swords to the door-watch.

Sir Jehan stood to receive him; then, impatient as ever, lithe as ever, sprang from the dais and strode to meet him. They embraced like kinfolk in the middle of the hall. A moment's private greeting, then they turned and made their way to the dais, the common folk of the castle turning on their benches, leaning across their trestle tables, to watch the visitors' progress: welcome matter for observation, analysis, gossip.

A very small girl, clad only in a blue smock and pulling a large patient dog along by one ear, had wandered into the center aisle between the tables, and stood barefoot on the rushes, staring openmouthed at the oncoming knights. Sir

Jehan nimbly detoured around her; with his metal hand he waved Sir Odinell and his people to the high table on the dais, with the other he pointed to the child and called into the crowd of people at the tables, "Edith! Come get this strayed lamb!"

There was a burst of laughter from the folk who sat near, and a young woman, flushed, wiping her hands on her apron, came quickly from among the diners. "My lord," she said apologetically, and scooped up the child. Sir Jehan nodded, not really vexed, and jumped lightly onto the dais.

The six men-at-arms joined the outrider on the benches of the castle folk; the three knights followed Sir Odinell onto the dais. Sir Jehan indicated chairs, and the four knights disposed themselves about the main table, while Sir Jehan made brief introductions. Molly he styled as *Queen Maeve,* and Nemain as *Queen Nemain,* and both were correct, were they back in Ireland, and at the head of their clan.

Molly, biding her time to return to Erin, to revenge, and to the resumption of her status as clan chieftain and queen, traveled in obscurity through England as musician and healer, and used the Christian pet name *Molly* rather than the pagan *Maeve.* Sir Odinell had been told somewhat of this, and was not taken aback by the introduction, although he was not sure that he completely understood Molly's status.

Now Sir Jehan turned to the pages' bench behind him and gave them a significant look before resuming his seat.

Two of the older pages had leaped to their feet as the guests arrived, and now they moved quickly along the line of younger boys, assigning this one to bring fresh flagons of bragget and that one to set out more goblets, a third to fetch a platter of oat cakes, and four to wait individually upon the visitor knights.

Sir Jehan had recently replaced the Irish wolfhounds he had lost, on the selfsame night that he had lost much of his hand, with two litters sent from Ireland. A wolfhound pup, wheat-colored, black-muzzled, a bit plump but already beginning to show length of leg, got up from the heap of its fellows dozing by the fire. It ambled over and sat down on Sir Jehan's foot.

"A handsome young fellow; he will be huge," said Sir Odinell.

"He will that," said Sir Jehan. He reached down and thumped its side with his good hand. "Rollo," he said absently. The puppy was named after the giant Orkney Norseman who had founded Normandy. Sir Jehan turned back to his guest. "I have a male and a female for you, Odinell, one from each litter, that you may breed a tribe of your own."

Sir Odinell gave a little seated half bow. "My thanks." He smiled politely, but Hob thought to see a shadow about his eyes; Sir Odinell's heart seemed so troubled that he was not fully aware of his surroundings.

There followed a period of idle chatter, mostly on the part of Sir Jehan: courtesy dictated that he at least give the travelers the opportunity to recover somewhat from the dust and fatigue of the trail. Hob noticed that it was not long, though, before the bronze hand began to tap gently upon the lion's head that terminated Sir Jehan's chair arm. A short while thereafter the knight rose, excused himself, gathered up Sir Odinell and Molly and her party, and led the way from the hall, leaving Lady Isabeau and Dame Aline to preside at table.

CHAPTER 2

U P THE ECHOING, WINDING turret stair with its slice-of-pie stair treads, the puppy scrabbling on the stone, determined to keep up. The party entered a solar that had been prepared for them: three rectangular rooms, not overlarge, with whitewashed walls; a small fireplace with a merry blaze against the cool evenings here in the mountains; a floor carpeted with the ubiquitous rushes, here mingled with lavender and hyssop. A table was set with brightly colored cloths, and on the sideboards was a simple meal, less ornate than that about to be enjoyed by Lady Isabeau and the others at the high table in the hall below. The food was adequate—pigeon stewed in garlic and herbs, bread, flagons of bragget and of barley beer, of wine and of apple wine, and so on—but not likely to be a distraction.

Pages waited to serve, but Sir Jehan shooed them out and bolted the door, saying, "Squire Robert, pray serve as page to all this night, that we may speak without fear of little ears and wagging tongues." Hob, who had served as one of the Blanchefontaine pages not so long ago, rose quickly and began to serve, placing trenchers of hardened bread to serve as plates; napkins; ewers of rosewater to rinse the fingers; a tureen heaped with satire, a mixture of beef and vegetables and dried apples. He began with Molly, then went on to Nemain, then Sir Odinell as a guest in the castle, then Sir Jehan. Lastly he set a trencher for Jack and one for himself, and thereafter was up and down, attentive to each diner, replenishing empty plates or drained goblets, pouring water over a diner's hands and providing a towel to dry them, bringing fresh supplies of food and drink from the sideboard.

Sir Jehan waited a bit out of consideration for his guest, but the subject to be discussed hung in the air, and at any rate, despite his long journey, Sir Odinell did not seem hungry, and ate some of his food and pushed more of it about on his plate. The Sieur de Blanchefontaine nodded at Hob, and said, "Our young man will gain—" Here he paused: it was his habit to pause in odd places, as his restless thoughts crowded in upon him, and he lost his thread for a moment, and then gathered it up again. "—gain his spurs, in perhaps three years. He has already slain a swordsman—" He fell silent; he looked at the graven bronze ghost of his own sword hand; then: "—a swordsman, one of two murderous gallants who were loose in the castle. This one had killed several of my best men; Sir Balthasar dealt with the other."

But Hob could not let this pass. "By your leave, my lord, 'twas not I. 'Twas Nem—, um, Queen Nemain who slew him."

Sir Odinell was looking from Hob to Nemain—small and pretty, with her mass of red hair and vivid green eyes—with an expression of mild confusion.

Nemain said fiercely, loyally: "But 'twas Hob who attacked that murdering *anmhas* first, and he trying to protect me; didn't he say to me, 'Run,' and he's giving me a wee push toward the stair, and then flying at that killer like a falcon, and Hob with only a torch in his hand and that grown man with a sword, and 'tis true I stabbed that *míolachán*, but wasn't I safe behind Hob the while, and myself leaning around him to strike."

Here she stopped, slightly out of breath. The three adults looked at her, and at Hob: Molly and Sir Jehan amused, proud, and striving to conceal both, while Sir Odinell's confusion slid toward bewilderment.

Slowly a blush began to bloom on Nemain's pale face, and then Hob reddened as well. Hob resumed serving with a certain intensity, while Nemain became interested in her trencher.

"They are betrothed," said Molly quietly.

Sir Odinell looked back and forth again. "She is a queen, and he but a squire?" he asked, very gently.

"Things are different in Erin," said Molly, "and he himself fated to be a great man, and to be her man as well."

Sir Jehan's hand began to tap against a silver ewer of wine, producing a dull *tunk, tunk* that he seemed not to hear, although the rest of the party looked to see its source. He cleared his throat.

"Odinell, brother," he began, but at that moment there were two thuds upon the solar door, heavy as doom, and without pause the door opened and Sir Balthasar entered. The company saw a tall and thick-built man, heavy-boned, dense with muscle: Hob had never encountered a man more powerful in body, except Jack. But where Jack Brown—so called for his dark hair and eyes—was calm, agreeable in pleasant circumstances and stolid in difficulty, Sir Balthasar was harsh and warlike, irascible, stern in demeanor. He was one of the foremost killers of the North, and Scottish raiders avoided Blanchefontaine lands on the strength of his name.

Sir Balthasar served Sir Jehan not only as castellan, but as mareschal, acquiring and training and maintaining the stable of mounts for the castle's knights. The castle's men-at-arms regarded him with great respect, admixed with a small tincture of fear. Nonetheless, Hob had seen little Dame Aline tease him mercilessly, and seen him soften in her presence. The forbidding castellan had become one of Molly's fiercest partisans on Fox Night, and had sworn to see Hob raised to knighthood. Hob had found him a fair if ferociously exacting teacher, and desired ardently to become such a man. Had he paused to think of it, or had someone asked, Hob would have surprised himself to realize that he was fond of Sir Balthasar.

Now the castellan, clad in his usual somber garb of green and pale gray and dark gray, and gray that was darker yet, almost black, took a seat at the table. He lowered his bulk carefully into a chair as though afraid it would break, which Hob thought entirely possible, and hitched his dagger in its green leather sheath forward to a more comfortable position. This was a war dagger, its pommel an iron sphere, rough-surfaced, gray-black, its hilt plain and wrapped in sweat-stained leather—like the knight himself, it was grim and heavy and perfect at destruction.

Sir Jehan turned to his castellan. "I was about to tell Sir Odinell of Fox Night."

Sir Balthasar nodded and said to Sir Odinell, "You may find it hard to credit; 'twas a night stranger than any I have seen, or even heard tale of." He looked back at Sir Jehan. "We do not speak of it often," he said pointedly.

"True enough," said Sir Jehan, "and we would ask that you speak with no one else concerning this: it is why we meet privily today."

Sir Odinell bowed slightly in his seat. "I will speak with no one else."

Sir Jehan regarded him with the utmost seriousness. "Swear to it, brother Odinell, swear to it."

DOUGLAS NICHOLAS

Sir Odinell looked startled. Then: "By my honor, I will speak of it with no one else, so aid me Christ and His saints." He drew his dagger, held it hilt upward so that the weapon made a crude cross, and kissed it at the juncture of quillons and hilt.

Sir Jehan cleared his throat again, tapped the wine ewer absently, looked into the distance somewhere, and began.

"We were confined in the castle by a snowstorm, and one other, trapped there with us by the gale, was a turnskin, and changed into a Fox. You must not think of a little thing, brother. This was an unholy being: a fox the size of a small horse." Sir Jehan spoke lightly, with his usual slightly mocking tone, but Hob saw that he had gone very white, and his good hand cradled his other wrist.

Sir Odinell, who might have been expected to laugh, or leave, at this juncture, surprised Hob by merely nodding, although he crossed himself a moment later. It was as though Sir Odinell had in some way become inured to monstrosity. Hob wondered as to the nature of his predicament, which Sir Jehan had not seen fit to describe, preferring to let the Sieur de Chantemerle explain it himself.

Sir Jehan resumed. "This Fox was strong even beyond its great size, strong beyond nature, and fast—you will recall I was accounted a fast hand, Odinell?"

"None faster," said the stocky knight. "In Ireland—" Molly's head came up, and he stopped, aware of the thinning ice before his feet. "Well, we were on several cam-

20

paigns together, in many places, and Sir Jehan here known throughout the camps as a paragon of speed: out with his sword, take your head from your shoulders, back with his sword, and sitting down to his meat and you not yet fallen to the ground."

"I would not have credited the speed of this—" Sir Jehan looked down at the tablecloth and his jaw tightened. Hob saw, like wind passing over a field of ripe barley, the feather-headed stalks bowing and straightening again, an expression of absolute rage sweep over Sir Jehan's features, and then vanish in a moment from the mercurial lord's face. The knight looked up again. "—this *abomination,* had I not fought it myself," said Sir Jehan. "I was accounted swift—I was *famed* for my speed—but, Christ for my refuge, it was swift beyond believing: you see the result." He lifted the bronze hand till it gleamed in the torchlight, a beautiful thing, the thick-and-thin strokes of the green-gold lettering catching the eye. He let his hand fall with a crack on the table, making the nearest dishes bounce a little and the wine slosh forward and back in the goblets.

He drew a deep breath and continued in a more measured fashion. "There was an attack: two swordsmen, and the monster. The swordsmen were excellent men of their hands, but their skills did not avail them; they perished as I have told you: these two young people did for the one, and the other—well, the other had the misfortune to encounter Balthasar.

"The monster went into a corridor with these four"—he indicated Molly, Nemain, Jack, and Hob—"and was destroyed. I may not tell you more of what happened, brother, for I too have sworn oaths, but it was utterly destroyed."

The Sieur de Chantemerle made no comment, but Hob could read Sir Odinell's features, his doubts as plain as rabbit tracks across a field of new-fallen snow. There was no question of doubting the honesty of his old comrade, but Sir Jehan might himself have been deceived in some way. Yet, if Sir Odinell had been told everything, Hob thought, he might not have stayed the night.

HOB WAS AN ORPHAN, raised by an old village priest, and Molly had taken him as an apprentice a year and a half before Fox Night, and till that night Hob had not fully realized the truth about his acquired family: that Molly and Nemain were queens away in the west of Ireland, although dispossessed at the moment; that they worshipped the Old Gods of Erin, and had surprising skill with weapon and spellcraft. Strangest of all, Jack Brown, plain sturdy pikeman Jack Brown, had been attacked when on pilgrimage to the Holy Land by some exotic Beast, for which none had a name, and had contracted a fever from the bite, and now was much more, and in a way much less, than he seemed.

The Beast, for so Molly called it, the creature being unknown in lands so far to the west of the Holy Land, so far to the north of the hot lands below Egypt, was manlike, but hugely made, with black-furred limbs and a naked leathery breast; it had great fangs, and moved at speed upon four limbs, the knuckles of its hands used as feet. It crushed Jack's ankle, so that he still limped, and it bit his throat so badly that he could barely speak today. It was destroyed almost by accident, trampled beneath the hooves of Templar war-horses. Jack lived, but found himself transforming into such a Beast, at ever smaller intervals; in this form he was driven to kill, and to eat of human flesh.

He sought out Molly at St. Audrey's Fair, the great fair held each year at Ely, and she was able to curb his changes, and to restore him to full humanity.

After Sir Jehan had been bitten, but not killed, by the Fox, he was himself susceptible to such change, and relied on Molly, with her knowledge of ways to control the change as she controlled it in Jack, for treatment—herbs, spells, amulets—to preserve him from losing his humanity, from shifting into a murderous Fox. He feared the loss of his soul: Hob had heard him say as much to Molly. The knight dared not even confess his plight to Father Baudoin, for fear the Church would burn him. Molly had shown him what herbs to take, and had said spells over him, and given him an amulet to wear such as Jack wore, and eased his physical pain and his worry at the same time. Molly and her family thus had a haven at Blanchefontaine, and promise of help when she went back to Ireland, to recover her position.

* * *

The brief silence that had settled over the table was now broken: Hob became aware that Sir Jehan had begun to speak again. "But tell these good people, Odinell, what it is that troubles you; as we are old comrades, so would I have you think of them."

Sir Odinell glanced once around the table, and then began.

"There is a castle, some miles down the coast from my own. There, somewhat less than a year ago, came to dwell a certain Sir Tarquin with his household. He was awarded this stronghold—Duncarlin; the name is older than the castle built there—when the former owner, who had been at court, offended the king in some wise, so badly that his lands and dwellings were stripped from him, and he imprisoned—what the exact tale may be, I know not, save that the king has settled this strange, this very strange, lord in his stead.

"He and his people are secretive; they are barely civil; none of us has had invitation to their hall, and though Sir Tarquin has accepted my own invitation, one that I now regret, so far he has not called upon us. This would be no great matter, save that, soon after their arrival, affairs began to go awry, in ways I hardly know how to describe, evil ways.

"This is how it first affected my household: two of my knights set out on the coast road, a simple errand down to Durham. They did not return in time; they were overdue a sennight, a fortnight. One night they came up to the gate after it was closed, and blew the horn. They declared themselves. The gatehouse guards looked through the postern wicket, but were uncertain; then they called the chief porter."

Sir Odinell stopped, drank wine. He looked at the table, not at the others, and Hob could see a slight sheen to his forehead, which might have been the wine. When he resumed, his voice was more quiet; he spoke more slowly: yet Hob thought he was if anything becoming more distressed. One hand gripped the goblet tightly; the other was in his lap, balled into a fist.

"The porter, the guards, could see these knights they had dwelt beside for years, yet could not decide if it were Sir Hugh and Sir Gilles, or no. The knights seemed the same in their features, or at any road similar, but with some . . . *difference* that the guards could not put tongue to. In the event they let them pass, but escorted them to the hall."

He drank again. A drop lingered in the corner of his mouth; he licked at it absently, then, as one coming awake, seized a hand-cloth from the table and scrubbed savagely at his lips.

"And I was no better! They stood before me in the torch-light, the firelight, and I wavered backward and forward, thinking *Surely it is they,* thinking *Surely it is not.* They were pale as wraiths or bogles, low-voiced, somber—they who had been among my merriest knights. You have knelt by a pond and seen yourself in the water? They were like that, shadowy, unstable: almost their features seemed to ripple, as when you trouble the water in which you regard yourself. When I asked them where they had abided so long, they seemed uncertain, and said something about the road being difficult, and the forest very dark, and it all ended in mumbles, and, Jesus and Mary be witness, *I did not want to speak with them further.*"

Sir Jehan stirred, made as if to speak, but Molly shot him a look and he subsided.

"And then there was the wife," said Sir Odinell. "One was married, the other not, and the married knight, Sir Hugh, went to his quarters with his wife after the two travelers had eaten. They spent the night together, and the next morning she went to her sister, and they left the castle by midday—they spoke of gathering herbs—and went straight to the convent at Whitby and sought asylum. Their cousin said that Dame Constance—she that is Sir Hugh's wife—told her that it was *not* her husband in her arms, but an evil spirit, and that she would not stay one more day with him. Sir Hugh did not seem distressed by this; indeed, he did not seem to notice. The two sat about the hall; they were courteous; but they were uncanny, and everyone heavy in spirit when they were near."

He made as if to drink, but then paused, the goblet held as if forgotten, halfway to his lips. He coughed a little. The six listeners sat very still: Molly with her usual calm, the quiet of a large and dangerous cat at ease; Nemain taut and intense, her green eyes fastened upon the knight's face; Jack and Sir Balthasar with the stolidity of old soldiers used to night watches, though the knight's large hand was clenching and unclenching about his dagger hilt. Hob himself was tense and uncomfortable, but afire with curiosity. Even the restless Sir Jehan was immobile for once.

"I gave them gold and freed them of their oaths of fealty; I said I could not have those near me who could not account for themselves. They made no objection, nor even scowled, but turned and went slowly from the hall. Of course I had them watched. They went quietly to the stables, saddled their mounts and led their spares, and rode out and away. Five years the one was in my service, and seven years and some months the other, and they did not so much as go to their quarters for their possessions. Nor did Sir Hugh seek out his wife at the convent. In time Dame Constance returned, she and her sister, for we are kindred, but she heard from him no more."

He drained the goblet. Sir Jehan reached over with his good hand and poured him another cup. Sir Odinell's face had begun to redden, and he stared at nothing; he did not seem to notice that his cup had been refilled, but drank again, mechanically, from the new-poured wine, hardly looking at it. *He is seeing something else,* thought Hob, *that is too terrible to ignore.*

"Then one day I saw them in the market square; they rode with three other knights from Sir Tarquin's household.

Their features had altered so much that, were it not for the devices upon the shields slung at their saddlebows, I would not have known them. Yet when I looked I could see them, or some trace of what they had been. How were they different? I feel that, that it was, it was . . . Nay, I cannot say. I remember they were so different, yet I cannot say. . . ."

He crossed himself twice, three times. His brow was moist; his breathing had begun to labor.

"Nay, give over, 'tis enough," said Molly kindly.

"Nay, 'tis *not* enough," said Sir Odinell. "Cattle disappear now and then, 'tis nought to speak of—I can defend against raiders. They drive off some cattle, and I mount with a few of my knights; we follow the tracks. . . . Sometimes we catch them and kill them, and recover the cattle. Other times they escape into Scotland. That is familiar work. But now . . . cattle began to disappear, and then they washed up on the beach, wizened, stringy, as though they were cattle made of dried beef. Some of it might have been from the seawater, but not all, not all.

"Peasants began to vanish. They went out to the fields, or to the pastures to watch their sheep, and a day or so later, their widows were in my hall pleading for help. We rode out, we scoured the manor from demesne lands to forest lands. We rode along the shore.

"Then they began to reappear, every one of them dead, and like the cattle their bodies were dried, shriveled—young men looked like old men, old men looked like those long dead. The folk are in a panic. The bodies were found behind a tree, in the midst of a field, washed up, like the cattle, on the strand. Never a sign of the murderers—more than one, because the peasants were vanishing at whiles in small groups. We suspected the new folk in their seaside towers, because they had come, and the evil had begun. But none had seen them at it, or indeed anyone at it. No one saw, save . . ."

He grew silent. Hob became aware again of the fire's crackle, and that he had been breathing shallowly, and that his left leg was asleep. He moved a little, and took a deep breath, but surreptitiously, so not to break Sir Odinell's concentration. But the knight said nothing, till Molly, almost murmuring, urged, "No one save . . ."

Sir Odinell looked from Molly to Sir Jehan to Sir Balthasar, and back. He seemed hardly aware of Jack and the younger people. Hob could see him gather himself, and could see how difficult he found it.

"There is a lad belonging to one of my people, a bit of a mooncalf. He has been a lackwit since his childhood, so. . . . He says he saw Sir Tarquin's wife, Lady Rohese, come from the woodland, it being dusk and he tending the miller's two draft horses that turn the millstones. She frightened him so—I am not sure how, but he spoke of her face, her walk— that he ran between the horses, where they were tied, and cowered there, and she made to come at him, but could not, and she circled the horses, around and about, but could not come in at him, he knows not why. The horses were agitated, but she did not seem afraid of them, only that she could not come at him. After a while—a very long while, he says—she went away and he crept out from between the horses and ran all the way to his home. His mother brought him to me the next day. I cannot say I believe him, he is such a knotpoll. Yet I cannot say I disbelieve him. Nay, I know not what I believe."

Molly and Nemain looked at each other. "The miller's horses are shod?" Molly asked Sir Odinell. He nodded. "And they shod with iron shoes, and not wooden?"

"Aye," he said. "The mill prospers, and they are shod with iron, and walk in a circle all the day on a stone path, and the shoes keep them from becoming halt."

"It may be 'tis the iron that holds her off, and that in horseshoes, and they on living horses at that, which may give them more power."

"Lady Rohese . . ." began Sir Odinell. He stopped. He indicated Sir Jehan, and began again. "We were on several campaigns together. He called me *Ironbrow*"—here Sir Jehan nodded, with a little smile—"because I was so hardheaded, and the least fanciful of men. Half of his daring schemes I put a halt to, and he said it was because I was too short of sight to see the advantage, and I said it was because I was a sensible man. But now . . . Lady Rohese, as my intent was to say, is a very beautiful woman, and yet somehow repellent. I cannot say how, or why, as I could not say what was different about Sir Hugh and Sir Gilles. Yet, when I see her, I find her beautiful and repellent in equal measure: my eye is drawn back and back to her, you understand, but my loins are cold. It is as though I grope in a mist—nothing seems safe now, nothing seems solid, and my people are frantic."

Sir Jehan, unable to sit quietly any longer, arose, paced to the fire, paced back to the table, paced to the fire. The wolfhound pup arose when he did, trotted after him to the fire, trotted back to the table close on the knight's heels, then followed him back to the fire. Sir Jehan paused, and the dog sat down, looking about him with a smug air: engaged in important business with his tall associate.

Molly was sitting calmly enough, but her air was preoccupied. Sir Jehan addressed her. "Have you any counsel for my brother knight, madam?"

"A thought there is to me," said Molly, then corrected herself: "I have a thought that I have heard some tale concerning a woman like this Lady Rohese."

Hob noticed her lapse into Irish phrasing, a sure sign with Molly that, however calm she appeared, she was distracted by some inner turmoil.

"I'm hearing—a while back, this is, and I a young lass myself—firelight tales of seeming women, killers, blood-drinkers; and they truly less than women, or more than women; and aren't they luring travelers, and dancing with them, and then rending them to pieces with the great strength that comes on them. And in one of the tales, there was a young man took refuge among the horses, and so he's keeping himself safe till the dawn came, and the night passing off, and the women departing. But his comrades all were slain. This other matter—the withered corpses—nay, I'm thinking that 'tis a new evil to me, but 'twould be curious if the one was not harnessed to the other."

Sir Odinell passed a hand over his brow. "Can you help me, madam?"

"It's my thought that I can help, though I'll be asking you to bind yourself to help me—when I'm to return to Erin, and myself needing help then to regain my place—with knights, or gold, or influence from your people. But why is it that you cannot have this evil knight removed, you working the while through the influence of your kin, the De Umfrevilles, the Nevilles, and the like?"

"My people are not negligible, as Sir Jehan will tell you, though I am the least of them. But this eldritch knight, it seems, may not be touched: on the one hand, he has letters and commissions from the pope, and on the other the king has granted him this castle that stood forfeit by virtue of its former lord's misadventures at court. Though the pope and the king be at each other's throat, he is the darling of both, and the messenger through which they may treat with each other privily, or so I am to hear. The bishop has given me no satisfaction. The parish priests, my own chaplain, all say masses for deliverance, but there is no deliverance. I am told by the magnates of my family that I am on my own in this, for fear of a misstep at court, or of excommunication. Sir Jehan alone has offered me hope, and you, madam, are that hope."

Molly looked at him coolly. "If it's unwilling the great men of your family are to help their own kinsman, why would they be helping me, and myself a stranger, and a widow, and nor am I even a Norman?"

"They will help you for my sake, and they will help you the more because they could not help me in this matter, where the most high and powerful men move against them. They are ashamed, and they will work to remove this shame in any other matter. But something about this man and his patrons has them helpless."

Molly sighed, and turned a bit in her chair to look into the hearth. There was a moment when no one spoke, and all Hob could hear was the crepitation of the flames biting at the wood. The knights watched her according to their natures: Sir Odinell stolidly; Sir Jehan with a tic twitching one corner of his mouth; Sir Balthasar scowling, his great body leaning forward somewhat as though he were a savage dog restrained by a leash.

Molly stirred herself. "*Bíodh sé amhlaidh,*" she murmured; then in English, louder, "So be it. We will help." She drew a great breath, turned to the table, and began to speak rapidly and clearly.

"We'll be taking our usual assortment of wagons, nor will we be dressing so grandly, either"—she gestured toward the gowns she and Nemain wore when guests at the castle—

"and as handsome an offer of a horse for Hob that it was" —here a nod to both Sir Jehan and his mareschal, Sir Balthasar—"he'll not be Squire Robert on the road, but Hob the prentice, and we all poor traveling entertainers. We'll be arriving as if by chance, and lodging at the inn nearby, and entertaining the folk, with music and suchlike, and ourselves listening, and watching, and myself seeking guidance from She who protects me."

Sir Odinell looked blank at this, but Sir Balthasar, fiercely loyal to Molly as he was, still was a follower of the Christ, and crossed himself, as he did whenever Molly spoke, however obliquely, of the Old Gods of Erin.

She looked at Sir Odinell. "You, my lord, will be hearing of us, and inviting us to stop in your stronghold, and we to remain a sennight, and you to hold a feast, and ourselves to entertain, in honor of Sir Tarquin and Lady . . . Roisín?"

"Rohese," said Sir Odinell.

"Rohese, that we may look on them, and all unmarked by them, ourselves being but poor traveling musicians and beneath notice."

"But . . . a sennight at the inn, and another at the castle, before you can do aught?"

"Nay, 'tis not a delay for a reaper to stop and sharpen the scythe," said Molly. She turned to Sir Jehan. "Would you ever give us writing materials?"

Sir Jehan said to Hob, "Robert, call in one of the men outside."

Hob went to the door and drew the bolt back. He looked out and beckoned to one of the two men-at-arms stationed there. The man came in and looked to Sir Jehan.

"Berengar, go you to Father Baudoin; give him my compliments, and say he is to give you a small amount of what is needful to write."

Berengar bowed and departed.

Molly turned to Sir Odinell. "My lord, you are to precede us, and that by no fewer than two days; tell us the path to take, and describe what we may see along the road, and I will make a map to follow. 'Twould not do for us to be arriving stirrup to stirrup with you, and Sir Tarquin and his witch wife taking note of it, and he concealing that which he does, or moving against us and we not ready for him."

When Berengar returned bearing a small sack with two rolls of parchment, ink, and quills, Molly set to work. She drew stylized mountains, streams, forests; she sketched out a path for them to follow. First north, then northeast, and then a gradual curve toward the east; down along what Sir Odinell said was a charcoal-burners' path through the forested slopes of the Pennines, into the long descending coombs that led toward the fells, and so finally to the coast, where Sir Odinell's castle, Chantemerle, stood with its feet in the cold waters of the German Sea.

Sir Odinell stood over her shoulder and described the landscape and the width of the path, pointing to the growing map with a scarred finger, while Molly, who could read and write where Sir Odinell could barely sign his name, jotted reminders of landmarks and indications of the quality of the road in her imperfect Latin.

For a time the only sounds in the room were the drone of Sir Odinell's voice, the scratch of the pen. At last Molly was satisfied, and she sat back and sighed.

"Do you leave tomorrow, my lord," she said, "and we two days after that, and ourselves being slower as well, we'll be coming to the coast some days after you, and none will be marking us together."

CHAPTER 3

OB WENT OUT INTO THE BAI-
ley to watch the Northumbrians'
departure. A gray morning, with
some low mist concealing the hard-packed earth of
the castle yard. The four knights and six mounted
men-at-arms were in the saddle, but not yet formed
into a column. They were awaiting hampers of the
pork-and-cheese pies called flampoyntes, packed
along with fired-clay bottles of bragget; these were
even now being put up in the castle's kitchens.

A small group of the castle's people, those with
no immediate business, had come out to see them
leave, a novelty to spice the daily round of work.
Each man-at-arms led a sumpter horse to carry the
baggage; one such horse had two large wicker bas-

kets, a basket to each side. In one was the male wolfhound pup, in the other the female, the Adam and Eve of Sir Odinell's future wolfhound pack.

Each knight led his huge destrier, roped to his saddle on the right. The Northumbrians' mounts, rounceys or saddle horses, eager to be moving, shifted position, tossed their heads, made water. The destriers, trained to ignore screaming men and clanging metal, stood like stone horses. Sir Odinell and his men sat quietly, their bodies swaying in the horseman's effortless compensation for a mount's fidgets, their faces masks of patient gloom, as they waited to take the trail back to their haunted home.

Sir Balthasar had initiated Hob's training as a knight: the lad had begun riding lessons last autumn, and he was keenly interested in the great destriers, one of which would, God willing, be his someday. He had tended some of them in the Blanchefontaine stables, big and powerful things in outsize stalls. He had practiced leading one while riding an ordinary rouncey, always keeping it on the right or dexter side, a standard practice that led to the term *destrier*. At these times it had cost Hob an effort not to keep looking back at the huge head, the shovel teeth, looming over his right shoulder.

Now he made his way around the packhorses to obtain a closer view of Sir Odinell's warhorse. The horse was an unusual gray, and the mist had settled along its flanks, giving its brawny haunches the sheen of steel. It was saddled, on the chance that Sir Odinell, making his way through bandit-sheltering forests, might have need of it in haste. Hob was admiring the ornate saddle cloth, with its scalloped edges, its elaborate embroidery, the colors standing out strongly against the gray hide, when he became aware of Sir Jehan's voice close by.

He looked up, past the horse's tall shoulders, to see Sir Odinell leaning away from him to speak with Sir Jehan on the other side. The reins of Sir Odinell's rouncey were in his left hand, and his right fist was on his hip; he bent from the waist to hear Jehan; the whole suggested an attitude at once tense, even uneasy, yet managing to convey the arrogance of the Norman.

"I feel that, dark as it may seem to you now, Christ and His saints will not abide this evil longer. If you need swords, send for us; Balthasar and I and half my knights are yours—but this business does not seem like sword-work. I do not know if we will even clear sword from scabbard before 'tis over," said Sir Jehan.

Hob moved a little, casually, to hear better above the whining of the puppies, who did not care for their new circumstances. From this angle, he could just see Sir Jehan reach up and rest his bronze hand on the saddle's high wooden cantle. "When you said you had someone who could aid me," said Sir Odinell, "I thought—well, I did not know what to think, but you are sending me one man-at-arms—a sturdy enough wight by the look of him, but not young—as well as a young squire, a damsel, and a grandmother. Should I be calm?"

Sir Jehan rapped lightly on the wooden face of the shield hung from Sir Odinell's saddle.

"A strong shield, Odinell. Could you make a seawall of such shields that would hold back the tide, were you to bury them side by side in the sands of the shore, away there by your castle beside the German Sea?"

"Could I make— Nay, brother, you have seen the sea and its movements: you know that nothing stands against the incoming tide. What is it that you tell me?"

Sir Jehan rapped again on the shield, but on the iron rim, and harder, the bronze clanking against the metal, the rouncey shying a little under Odinell.

"This grandmother is the sea, brother Odinell, the sea: she will go where she will, and nothing will stand against her, and she will wash your land clean of this filth."

CHAPTER 4

THE WAGONS TRUNDLED ACROSS the dry moat, the planks of the rolling drawbridge thundering beneath the hooves of the draft animals and the knights' horses. The little column swung to the right, heading north through the forested slopes of the Pennines. A pair of knights rode their horses at a walk a little way ahead. Hob followed with the lead rope to Milo the ox, who pulled the big wagon. Sir Balthasar kept to a slow pace beside the wagon's seat, where he could converse in low tones with Molly. The little wagon, driven by Nemain, and the midsized wagon, with Jack at the reins, followed, with four more knights bringing up the rear.

The road wound north through the forest. The

pass they sought, to descend from the Pennine heights, was to the northeast of Blanchefontaine. This was the way Sir Odinell had come, a way Molly's troupe had never taken. Usually they would descend from the highlands by passes to the southeast, making for Durham or York.

Hob was sharply aware of the varied scents that came to him down the forest aisles: the green world was awakening, and he felt himself to be part of this surging life. He was aware of the feel of his new body, his new strength, and he was these days always conscious of Nemain: where she was, what she was doing, how near or far from himself.

Molly had bade them wait till later in the year before they wed, citing signs observed in the curl of a raven's feather, the drift of clouds; and the clarity with which Molly read portent was not to be doubted.

Just before they came away, Hob and Nemain had snatched a moment for themselves, in a little-used upper corridor of Blanchefontaine, in a deeply recessed window seat, and there embraced and fondled each other, and murmured things, so close that the words were felt as well as heard, warm breath on the ear. When with others, the two lovers were almost secretive concerning their affection, but they fell into each other's arms whenever a private refuge offered itself. Now with the memory of Nemain's kisses on his lips and the beauty of the woodlands all about, Hob strode along, as near to perfect contentment as was possible on so doubtful a quest.

He felt on the verge of song. In sheer exuberance, he

turned half about, walking sideways for a few steps, the better to admire the new wheels on the wagons. Sir Jehan had insisted on having his wainwright fit Molly's caravan with lightweight spoked wheels, instead of the solid disks she had previously used. Molly insisted, however, on scuffing and distressing the wood, for appearances' sake, so to obviate unwanted curiosity, and to appear poor and unworthy of theft by bandits or suspicion by Sir Tarquin. But the new wheels turned more easily, rode over roots handily, and generally eased the work of both beast and driver.

The two knights ahead were deep in some discussion, swaying easily in the saddles. A tiny roe deer flashed across the trail ahead of them, obviously startled, and one of the knights' horses, trained to battle, snapped at it like a wolf, just missing it. After a bit of dancing about, the two horses settled down, and their progress resumed.

At length they came to a fork: a massive oak stood in the center of the way, dividing the road. The sinister branch continued the north–south trail they followed; the dexter branch was the charcoal-burners' road, running to the northeast, that would take them down through the forest, down the eastern slopes of the Pennines, and set them on their way to the sea.

The wagons rumbled to a halt, and Molly set the brake. This was where they had agreed to part. The knights backed their horses to the side of the trail. Sir Balthasar turned his horse, the tall heavy-boned animal coming around smooth and silent as a cat, docile as an old dog. Hob knew that in a battle this horse would strike forward with its war shoes, horseshoes with projecting spikes, and bite at the faces of opposing foot soldiers.

"I am uneasy, madam," said Sir Balthasar, "that you travel toward this evil, and ourselves staying behind."

"There's safety in ourselves being seen as harmless, poor travelers that we are," said Molly. And then, with a laugh, "And when was it that poor musicians were traveling with an escort, and that escort led by the dread Sir Balthasar of Blanchefontaine himself?"

The grim knight's mouth twitched up at the corners, and he made the grudging muffled sound that served him for a laugh. He turned his horse again, and rode up beside Hob. From the pouch fixed to the saddle he drew out a dagger in a scabbard. To Hob he said only, "Remember your lessons," and leaned down, handing the dagger to the lad. Then he backed to the side of the road again.

Hob began to stammer thanks, but the knight waved him to silence, and pointed down the trail. Behind Hob, Molly said, "Well, put it on, then, *a rún,* you'll be wanting it where you can get at it."

He quickly slipped off his belt, slid the scabbard onto it so that it rested on his right hip, and did up the buckle again. Then, bowing to Sir Balthasar as he had been taught to do at the castle, he caught up Milo's lead rope again and set off, grinning mightily, down the charcoal-burners' road.

After a short while, when they had left the knights behind, and were moving along a straight stretch of the path, he drew the knife from its scabbard to admire it. It was the same type as the wooden daggers that Sir Balthasar used when teaching him the art of combat with knives. Like Sir Balthasar's own dagger, it was heavy and functional, one of the newer double-edged daggers, with a heavy point for punching through mail, a leather-wrapped wooden hilt, and an unornamented iron ball for a pommel. He slid the gleaming blade back into its scabbard, made sure it was settled securely, and strode on, pleasantly aware of the weapon's weight at his hip.

THE ROAD PROCEEDED DOWNWARD, albeit at a gentle angle. Shafts of sunlight pierced through the ranks of tree trunks, the canopy of new leaves, to lie in broad bars of yellow warmth against the dark earth of the trail. The air was moist here under the green roof, and the fragrance of growing things was a constant pleasure. Hob began to enjoy the beauty all around him, the rhythm of the march, even the soothing presence of the ox, companionably pacing behind him: the coarse rope in Hob's hand tensing and releasing as he and Milo fell out of and back into step; the ox's homely familiar snorting and snuffling; the muted impact of the great hooves on the dirt.

Sir Odinell had assured them that the path would be

wide enough for the wagons, and so it proved. The charcoal-burners were men for whom felling trees was nothing; they were born to it, and they kept the road wide for their own purposes: for ease of dragging tree trunks to the fires, or to allow their wains to trundle down to the lowlands, filled with the product of their labors. Here and there the road narrowed a bit, or the wagon wheels would bang and bump over big roots not completely covered by the soil, but generally they made good progress.

The troupe had traveled much of the day without pause, always descending, for Molly had hoped to come into open land as soon as possible; in the forest lay too many dangers. But now, as the day waned, they became aware that the amber late-afternoon light striking down into the occasional clearing was filtered through a blue-gray haze, and the harsh perfume of woodsmoke bit at their nostrils. In some places the smoke grew so thick that the sunlight separated into shafts, dark gold against gray. A distant murmur, that Hob realized he had been hearing for a while, began to resolve into the various sounds of human activity: male voices, female voices; the hum of conversation and the odd shout; the thump of a mallet, the crunch of an ax into bark.

The smoke thickened until there was a distinct curtain of haze visible as Hob peered down the trail ahead, a channel that ran between walls of trees. As he looked, two men stepped into the way; lean men, but sinewy. They stood some little distance ahead and watched the troupe approach.

They bore long-handled axes, but placed them head-down in the dirt, their hands folded on the handle ends. The noise had quieted considerably; a child's voice was raised somewhere, then hushed abruptly.

Molly bade Hob stop a few paces shy of the men, who seemed wary, but not hostile. Their eyes flicked from Hob to the ox to the wagon, quickly settling on Molly. Hob glanced back at her. She wore that expression of authority and benevolence that made everyone trust her.

"God save all here," she said, as though she were the devoutest Christian.

"Amen," said the charcoal-burners together. They stepped around the ox and came up to the wagon seat. "Where be ye bound, Mistress?" said one.

"We're away to the coast," said Molly. "We're musicians, and we're just after playing at Castle Blanchefontaine. There were some knights there, up from the coast, Sir Odinell and others—do you know him? He with three blackbirds on his shield?—and they telling us of your good road through the forest here."

The axmen looked at one another and nodded. Sir Odinell had passed them and spoken to them on his way to and from Blanchefontaine. This reassured the burners, for though Molly and Hob seemed inoffensive enough, and the more formidable Jack was not easily visible back there in the last wagon, the wagons might be full of hidden thieves.

One of the burners was a bit older, streaks of gray beginning to show in his hair, an air of command, a decisive manner. "Do ye stop the night wi' us, Mistress," he said. "Thae woodlands are nowt to gang through i' t' darkness."

Molly beamed at him. "It's delighted we'd be to take some rest and no mistake, and what's better than a night among friends?"

The axmen turned and walked ahead. Milo had begun to investigate some grasses beside the trail, and Hob had to pull for several moments before the great head came around. The ox gave the obligatory snort of protest at being so put upon, and began to place one ponderous foot in front of the other. The little train of wagons went only a little way before Hob began to see children flitting in and out of the underbrush ahead of them, and then the charcoal-burners turned in at a break in the trackside trees. Hob followed them in, pulling Milo into the turn, and a cleared space opened up before his eyes.

One side of the clearing was given over to heavy wains, used to haul logs into the camp for burning. Beyond was another of the natural meadows: lightning and fire had downed several great trees some time ago, and grasses were abundant here. Here were tethered the black or brown fell ponies used to pull the burners' wains, strong sure-footed animals, with long drifting manes, some plaited; their sturdy legs bore long fine hair that formed a kind of veil about their hooves.

Hob looked about. Across the clearing, through the fine blue-gray haze from the burning that was more perceptible here in this open space, the other side of the camp backed up against a wall of trees. Here were pitched tents and lean-tos containing stacked wood, tools, bins to keep food from forest animals. There was a row of small cabins constructed of interwoven logs chinked with mud. In front of them, a group of women and near-naked children regarded Molly's troupe with shy wonder.

The men were more forward, gathering about, calling greetings, and minutely examining every aspect of the wagons' exteriors. Some, obviously come from the burn, had smoke-blackened faces and hands, and everyone's clothes were sooty and generally bore the odor of a cold fireplace, but those not on duty had conscientiously washed hands, faces, necks. What could not be cleaned, however, was the residue of charcoal that had, over the years, in some cases over the decades, worked its way into the tiny crevices and wrinkles about the knuckles and elbows, even of the children. Older men and women bore these marks wherever the skin had wrinkles.

"Bring yon o'er be t' cuddies," said the younger axman, nodding at the ox and walking away. Hob followed him and guided Milo over to the meadow side where the ponies, called cuddies in these mountains, were tethered. The wagons were pulled up in a line and chocked; Milo and the little ass Mavourneen and the mare were turned out into the grass, and the company went to sit about the communal cookfire. Their hosts brought up benches to sit on, and fetched bitter ale in wooden cups, carved in idle hours by those charcoal-burners who were skilled in this way.

In short order Molly, in many ways the mother of all the world, had acquired three children, two leaning at either side and a very small one on her lap. But she pointed to a fourth, in among the women, and beckoned.

The child came forward, part interested, part wary, cradling her left arm in her right hand. Molly had seen the burn from yards away, and now she took the girl's arm gently in her hand, and *tsk*ed over the red weeping flesh, and gave an upward nod to Nemain, who got briskly to her feet and trotted over to the small wagon. The child was clearly in some pain, and made halfhearted attempts to retrieve her arm; the men standing about the newcomers grew silent, and the girl's mother came right up to Molly, a tense watchfulness in every line of her stance.

Nemain returned with three jars and some strips of clean linen, and Molly, clucking and smiling at the child, and speaking soothing nonsense in that wonderful deep voice, honey with a faint rasp to it, contrived to clean and salve the wound and wrap it in linen. All at once the child broke into a great smile, a smile like a shaft of sunlight slanting through forest gloom, and reached back to tug urgently at her mother's skirt.

"What, hinny, what?" The woman bent down and the child said something very low in her mother's ear. Her mother slowly relaxed, straightened. She did not smile, but her expression softened; she looked around and said to the company, "T' wean's nae mair dole tae her arm!"

This prompted a general warming in the burners' attitude, hitherto somewhat shy, and a young man came forward, and it soon became apparent that burns and splinters formed a part of life in a charcoal camp. Molly turned her sleeves up, exposing her strong shapely forearms. Then she sighed, stood, and went around to the back step of the little wagon. Nemain went up the steps and began to pass down pots of this and jars of that, and more bandages, and large and small needles for splinters. Hob was pressed into service to hold various implements, and Molly spent some time tending to ailments—most of them small, but a few rather more serious.

All the while she drank the burners' beer, and even this carried an undertaste of smoke. Hob had his own wooden cup, which their hosts kept filled, and though he sipped where Molly drank heartily, he began to feel a bit dizzy: an empty stomach, a day's long march, were not the best preparations for all this generosity. Molly, of course, with her formidable constitution, seemed almost unaffected as she tended one person after another.

Finally, as Hob was watching her deftly tear off thinner strips from the linen she was using for bandages, creating ties to finish the dressing on a wrapped shin, he became aware of a crackling, spitting sound above the general murmur of conversation and comment, and a delightful aroma began to compete with the general smokiness. He looked over to the cookfire. Two men were turning a pig on a large spit there, and cauldrons suspended from tripods steamed and bubbled.

In a short while the company was summoned to dinner. The woodsmen had contrived a novel solution to the lack of a table: stumps of wood, most about a cubit across, served as small tables lined up in front of benches set next to the cookfire. Hob and Nemain sat near a young man named Henry, who seemed to have been delegated to serve them. He kept their trenchers heaped with pork, and portions of pigeon stew flavored with alleluia, the leaves imparting a tart undertone, the stew ladled direct from the cauldrons, and he saw to it that all had hunches of dark bread studded with garlic, and that their wooden cups were filled with beer. He urged them to have some *scranshums,* as he termed the crunchy pork skin bits served as a delicacy.

Molly was deep in conversation with Simon, the senior axman who had greeted them; he seemed to be a kind of patriarch of the group, and indeed many of them resembled him. Hob could just hear snatches of their conversation. She was questioning him closely about the road ahead—its safety, whether there were bandits or other dangers. In particular she was concerned about any sharp drops from one level to the next, where the wagons' brakes might not hold. He was reassuring about the physical qualities of the trail, but had heard rumor of outlaws in the forest to the east, and had doubled the size of his work parties, and always left sufficient men in the camp to defend it.

The troupe's arrival had occasioned a bigger meal, and a more communal meal, than was usual, and there came a period when everyone, except those on duty at the burn site some distance away, just sat and contemplated the meaning of contentment. Then Molly roused herself and sent Hob and Nemain for the instruments. There was a fair amount of room between the cookfire and the meadow where the dim shapes of the draft animals drowsed at the end of their tethers. This was augmented by moving all the benches and log-end tables to the other side of the fire, creating a passable dance floor.

Jack took the goatskin *bodhran* that Molly had taught him to play, a flat drum that he propped on his left leg; in his right hand he had a bone drumstick, with a knob at each end, that he could twirl, striking with each end to produce a rapid skipping beat. Molly and Nemain each took up a *cláirseach,* an Irish harp, and began the arduous task of tuning—they had not played for at least a week and the dampness, the changes in altitude, had affected the instruments, even in their leather cases. Hob himself struggled to get his symphonia ready: it had three pairs of strings, two of which were drones and one that played the melody. He tuned to cues from Nemain's harp. Then there was the wooden wheel which moved upon the strings, producing the sound—this wheel must be resined before he could play.

At last they were ready, and, following Molly's lead, they struck up a simple dance tune. Hob cranked the wheel with one hand and fingered the keys with the other, listening to the rapid tap-and-boom of Jack's drum on one side and the two harps, Nemain providing a harmony for Molly's main melody. The music filled the small camp, and one or two of the animals moved restlessly.

At first everyone was too entranced, too eager to drink in this sound, to get up and dance—when did they ever hear much music, away here in the depths of the forest, let alone music of such quality? After the troupe had played two or three tunes, though, people began to go out on the flat dirt clearing and form circles, the women inside, moving widdershins, the men outside, moving deasil, and the children generally underfoot.

They played for much of the evening, till the fires burned low. Men left and relieved those on duty at the working part of the camp, and others came in, ate, and joined the dancing. Those resting from dancing began to drink deeply, parched from the effort and the smoke haze that overhung everything.

Hob began to feel that a sort of enchantment was descending over the camp. Nemain had put down her harp, and had gone to sit by Jack, the better to do the intricate counterclapping at which she excelled. The music echoed from the forest around, and the firelight cast a golden flickering glow partway up the surrounding trees; above that the trunks vanished into the darkness. The very smokiness of the air diffused the light. The thud of the dancers' feet augmented the beat of Jack's drum and the rippling claps that Nemain produced, almost too fast to follow; arpeggios from Molly's *cláirseach* fell like jeweled rain around the somber moan of the symphonia. A breeze brought them the scent of the high-slope forest, and over everything the tang of burning, sometimes harsh, sometimes surprisingly fragrant.

After what seemed a great while weariness set in, for dancer and musician alike. The children had been sent to bed long before, and now the charcoal-burners drifted off, singly or in couples, to the cabins, and finally Molly quaffed off one last cup and led the troupe to the wagons. Molly and Nemain climbed into the large wagon to sleep, as was their custom except when Molly had summoned Jack to her bed. On those nights Nemain had the smallest wagon to herself.

Jack and Hob had beds in the midsized wagon, but tonight, although their reception had been hospitality itself, Jack was professional soldier enough to want some kind of watch set, and he undertook to sleep atop the wagon, on blankets spread there, on this April night that was warmer than usual. The wagon roof, though shaped like a half barrel, had a wide flat strip down the center that could be walked upon, and here would be Jack's bed. He retrieved his war hammer from the main wagon, two and a half feet of ponderous destruction: the steel head a hammer for crushing on one side, and a beak very like a crow's, for piercing, on the other. Blankets over his shoulder, he climbed the rope ladder one-handed, arranged his rough bed to his satisfaction, and lay down facing the camp, placing the hammer with a faint *clink* on the roof beside him. He settled himself, resting his right hand on the weapon's handle.

Hob was the last abed. He opened the shutter in the side of the wagon, and looked out on the clearing. The fire had sunk to ember, against which two or three of the burners, in silhouette, moved quietly about their final errands. He lay down and, after the long day and the beer, slid smoothly and happily down some sort of slope, at the bottom of which was sleep.

He woke once in the night, and listened to the sounds of the night forest—the *kew-wick* of a brown owl, and, very faintly, a hedgehog's snuffling; the occasional whicker of a cuddy at its tether in the meadow; nothing else. This began to rouse him—was something wrong? Then he realized that he missed Jack Brown's heroic snores, which sounded like a bear, nearby and very angry. But he knew Jack was a little wary tonight, and Jack, veteran of many campaigns, could when necessary keep himself to a light doze, and then he made little or no sound. Hob thought vaguely of stepping out of the wagon and checking to see that all was well with Jack and that the silence had no sinister explanation. Then he thought that he might wait a moment or two before getting up, and then he opened his eyes and found that it was morning.

CHAPTER 5

IN THE MORNING, MOLLY EXAM-
ined the sufferers who had come to
her the day before, changing bandages
where it was required, giving elixirs and powders
to alleviate pain or clean a wound, with instructions for the days ahead. Afterward the troupe sat to
breakfast, and there Simon tried to persuade Molly
to stay awhile at the camp. This was such a common
occurrence with Molly that she had become adept
at extricating the troupe without giving offense to
their hosts. Everyone hated to see her leave, with
her medicines, her music, her wisdom, and that
dim but bone-deep feeling of calm and safety that
surrounded her, that sense that she, or her man Jack

acting at her direction, or both, would keep from harm anyone who was near her.

Perhaps as a means of keeping them in camp longer, Simon offered to show them how they worked wood into charcoal, and Molly, insatiably curious about the workings of the wide world, could not resist. Opposite the entrance to the camp was a broad road that led deeper into the forest. Simon escorted Molly and her troupe, surrounded by a small group of the charcoal-burners, into this road, which proved to be a short alley between the camp and the clearing where burning was done. In a large circular space cleared by the axes of the burners, three mounds stood, and a fourth in the process of construction.

Hob and Nemain trailed along behind Molly, Jack, and Simon. After a bit Hob became aware that a lad, about his own age or a bit younger, was walking along beside them. The three young people came up to stand beside Simon, who was explaining to Molly the way they made the charcoal.

"Here ye see t' clamp as is bein' made, Mistress," he said, indicating a mound of precisely stacked wood. "Theer's a clear space i' t' center, that's where we set un alight." And indeed the lengths of wood all butted up to a hollow central shaft, into which a torch could be dropped to ignite the clamp.

He turned to one of the three earthen mounds. "Then 'tis covered wi' soil, sithee, wi' some openin' left at bottom, and set on fire down central hole, and when 'tis well alight, we cover up holes, and leave but a wee opening here and there, and she burns quiet-like one, two, mayhap three days, and then she's ready, and we cover her up and damp all fire down, and then we may open it. But she mun be watched, for if she breaks oot through t'dirt, she'll all burn up and turn to ash, or if she smothers, ye've got a lot of half-burned wood. So she mun be watched, weary work, and that's what Edulf, there, is aboot. Be it that he sees flame brast its way oot, he'll throw more dirt on't."

He indicated a young man sitting on a curious stool; a seat with one leg from the center. The young man sat so that the one leg of the stool and his own two legs formed a tripod that kept him balanced.

The young man who had walked in with them now explained to Hob and Nemain, "If Edulf falls asleep, yon stool will pitch him over and he'll wake soon enough." The youth was speaking as though from a desire to be helpful, but Hob had realized that he was stealing admiring glances at Nemain, and that he was speaking mostly to her. For some reason that he himself could not fathom, this attention to Nemain pleased and annoyed Hob at the same time. Nemain seemed unaware of the almost furtive way the lad looked at her, looked away, looked at her again.

Then Simon must show them the closely woven sacks that the charcoal was put into, and how they paid in kind to the lord whose woodlands these were—one of the Percys, with strongholds to the north and on the coast—and the uses of charcoal at the forge, and how it burned hotter than wood, until Hob thought they would never get away on the road again. Molly, of course, was interested and alert; she always wanted to add more knowledge to what Hob felt was an already immense store.

At last they returned to the wagons, and then there followed the inevitable greasing of axle shafts, hitching of the draft animals, accepting a "wee bit storkenin'"—baskets of food for the trail—from the burner women, extended leave-taking. Then Hob was leading Milo out onto the forest path again, moving northeast along the green corridor, the diminishing chorus of farewells fading into silence behind him.

He soon fell into his easy travel pace, breathing deeply: the haze from the charcoal-burners' camp was quickly left behind, and the air was much cleaner. The breeze was rich with the scent of spring, and the varied perfumes of flowers mixed with the salty smell of the ox's great body. Along the edges of the trail, silverweed formed an impromptu border; in under the trees were carpets of bluebells; ramsons with their clouds of delicate white stars put forth the scent of garlic. Where wildfire or storm had felled some of the huge grandfather trees, grasses sprang up, and slim young trees drank the sun and strove upward.

They walked till the sun began to slant past the zenith, when Molly called a halt. A brief pause for the midday meal, and they took to the trail again. For a time they proceeded without incident; then Hob became aware of some noise coming up behind them. He turned and walked backward for a few paces. Coming around the bend after them was a group of about eight—no, more, perhaps ten or twelve—men, roughly dressed, some with sacks such as the charcoal-burners used slung over their shoulders. There was some banter, and from a couple of the men at the back, snatches of song.

They were marching along at a good clip, and soon overtook the wagons. Their little column parted to either side; they wished Jack a good day—Jack, with his ruined voice, just nodding and smiling as he was wont to do—and as they moved past the wagons, touched their foreheads to Nemain up on the seat of the second wagon.

Hob kept turning round to see. Their faces, their hands were black and grimy with charcoal. To Molly, the leader, pulling at a greasy forelock, called out, "God save you, Mistress." Hob saw that the back of his hand was nearly black with charcoal, the little creases at wrist and knuckle showing white against the darkness.

Molly answered, "And yourself as well," but quietly, without her usual good cheer. The leader nodded to Hob, and gradually the men pulled ahead. Some way on, there was another bend, the road disappearing behind tree trunks, brush, outcroppings of rock. Hob slowed, paid out the lead rope, and walked back toward Molly.

Milo looked around for Hob, his steps slowing, and Hob slapped him lightly on the rump to indicate he was to keep going. The ox made one of his peculiar snorting sighs, which to Hob's ears always sounded mildly aggrieved, and resumed his pace.

Hob gestured, and Molly bent down to hear. Hob, with a glance at the bend ahead, said urgently, "Mistress, there is something amiss with yon charcoal-burners."

"It's a bad feeling they had to them, surely," said Molly.

He was almost whispering, though the men were plainly out of earshot. "Those we have met, the burners of charcoal, they were careful to wash hands and face when not at toil, though they yet had black lines where the . . . the black, the burnt wood had settled and they could not scrub it out."

He glanced again over his shoulder, walking backward, one hand to the wagon to steady himself. "But these men— their faces, their hands are as black as though they had just been working, as though to say: *Look what a charcoal-burner I am.* But, Mistress, the lines in that lead fellow's wrist and knuckles are white against the black, where they should be ground-in black."

She looked at him, shaking her head slowly, beginning to smile, and said, "My keen-eyed little hawk!" She pointed to his new dagger. "Loosen that *scian,*" she said. Then she took the lead rope from him and told him to relieve Nemain on the driver's seat and to send her forward to consult.

When Nemain came back she told him to do the same for Jack, and then Hob went forward again. Molly handed him back the lead rope, saying only, "Be ready."

The dagger that Sir Balthasar had given him was in a leather sheath waterproofed with beeswax and wool grease; within this sheath was a birchwood liner. Hob loosened the knife in its scabbard, working it up and down a few times inside the wood till he was sure it would draw quickly. He took a deep breath, aware of a tension in his chest, a tingling in his limbs, not entirely unpleasant.

Now they were nearing the curve in the road. Milo, who was of a contemplative rather than an observant nature, maintained his straight-ahead course, and was heading, perhaps disingenuously, for the grasses at the outer side of the bending track; Hob, accustomed to this, leaned his shoulder against the vast head, and so pushed the ox gently into the turn.

And there was the little party of men, off the trail, apparently at rest. The band lay in positions of ease on either side of the road. One, at the end farthest from the oncoming wagons, lay supine with his forearm over his eyes, while their chief knelt and examined his ankle. A sprain, then, or some other injury, and the group taking advantage of the pause to rest against the grassy slopes through which the road wound.

Now the leader stood up from his injured comrade, and stepped into the road, a hand raised to stop them, an easy smile on his face. From the other side of the road, another stood and stretched, as though preparing to resume his travels. Yet most reclined peacefully, obviously reluctant to rise.

The chief indicated the groaning man. "Mistress, young

Thomas here canna gang mair," he said in a deferential manner, ambling closer to the wagon seat.

"Hob, stop," said Molly, setting the brake. "Is it that he needs to ride?" she said to the leader, now almost at the wagon seat. On the right side the other man moved closer, as though interested in their conversation.

Molly's face grew apprehensive, and she seemed to shrink in on herself, and she grasped the hems of her shawl and drew it tightly about her, crossing her arms beneath her breasts as she did so. She looked nervously from one of the approaching men to the other, and her voice came again in such an old woman's quaver that Hob almost laughed aloud.

" 'Tis not a great deal of room we have," she said, and at once the men began to move quickly toward her, and then Hob was certain: *Outlaws, wolf's-heads!* They were big men but not fat, and they were swift men, agile men, and in a trice they each had a foot in a rope loop and a hand on the wagon, beginning a rapid climb. Their other hands reached for Molly; the men leaned, they stretched toward her.

At this moment Molly straightened in her seat, the fear running out of her face like water, leaving a lofty abstracted expression. Her hands flew out from her sides, the arc of her unfolding arms spreading the shawl like wings, the dagger thus revealed in each hand burying itself in a brigand's throat with a muted *chunk*.

Both bandits now froze, unable to believe this horrid turn their lives had taken. Molly rasped the daggers out again. The outlaws' lifeblood began to pump from their throats, and they slid away to either side, hands at their necks, desperate to stem the flow, but in vain, in vain.

The whole band now leaped howling to their feet, whipping weapons from beneath their clothes. Most of them rushed toward the wagons. Hob had his new dagger out and pivoted in place, striking backhand and taking one of the men in the side as he ran past; the man stumbled on a few steps and then went down.

Forewarned by Hob and by their own fey ability to sense evil, Molly and Nemain were ready for the furious burst of violence. Nemain was already up on the little wagon, bow in hand; she tossed Molly's bow and quiver to the roof of the first wagon. A moment later Molly had swarmed up the rope ladder and thrown herself onto the roof, rolling, snatching arrows from the quiver and seizing the bow as she rolled, coming to her feet and nocking an arrow even as she rose from her knees.

Two men had veered toward Hob, and now he flipped the dagger to a forward grip and backed away in the knife-fighter's crouch that Sir Balthasar had drilled into him, until he came up against Milo's shoulder. The bandits had knives, one of them very long, and they were grown men, and, tall and rangy a lad as Hob was, they had the reach that he did not, and the weight.

"If you cannot fight the man, fight some part of him," Sir Balthasar had said at one of Hob's private lessons in murder, held in an unused corner of Blanchefontaine's cloistered herb garden—grim afternoons amid the droning of bees and the drowsy scent of thyme. "Most men seek to deal a mortal blow, but you are young, and have not your full strength. Yet, being young, you are quick: dance away, run backward if you must, but keep from their reach, and the while you must make them bleed in those parts they are not protecting: the off hand, the shin, the forearm, whatever they neglect. The wounds will be of small account, but the pain and the blood will sow doubt in their hearts, and lessen their valor, and if you can keep alive the while, ten or fifteen small wounds will drain a man to weakness. Then you may come round behind him as he staggers, and hack head from body."

Now Hob watched the bandits' hands, and as they separated, intending to come at him from each side, he leaped at the one with the shorter knife, sliced at the back of his empty left hand, and leaped away, putting distance between himself and the other soldier, Master Longknife, as well.

Shortknife was no soldier: he immediately wasted time looking at his left hand, where two fingers had stopped working. Hob was aware that he himself had stayed too long in one spot: here loomed the other bandit with his cubit-long knife, poised for the downstroke. At that moment a hiss, a meaty thump, and Hob was looking at one of Molly's arrowheads, protruding three fingers' width from Longknife's neck: the shot had gone through from back to front, and he toppled forward, dead or dying.

Hob leaped at Master Shortknife again, cut his left shoulder, and danced away. The man shook himself awake and charged Hob, who jumped aside and cut him again, high on his left arm. None of these wounds was serious, but the man's arm was sheathed in blood, two fingers would not obey him, and his comrade was dead. A moment later, the panic of the untrained took him, and he ran off into the trackside brush, disappearing among the trees.

Hob whirled and looked back along the little caravan. Jack had come up at a fast limp with his crow-beaked war hammer in his right hand and a spiked targe on his left forearm, and he was battering at two opponents, as matter-of-fact as a carpenter nailing a piece of wood. Two others lay dead at the dark man's feet, heads—for none wore helmets—misshapen from the terrible blows Jack had given them. Here and there were bandit bodies, sprouting the long arrows, fletched with crow-feather, that Molly and Nemain used.

Even as he watched, Jack broke one man's arm with the hammer, sidestepped smartly, and blocked a knife thrust from the other bandit with the targe. Jack, off-balance from avoiding the blade, batted the second man in the side with the hammer, a weak and ineffectual blow that nonetheless served to make the bandit stagger a pace or two away—all the opportunity that Jack needed. The war hammer came up, crow-beak pointing forward, and fell like a tree. The arm the bandit flung up to stop it was battered aside and the beak, deflected from its capital target, plunged into the man's chest. He fell flat upon his back and lay there, wheezing pink foam. In very short order he became still. Jack looked around. The man with the broken arm had surrendered the field, disappearing into the trees.

Jack and Hob stood still a moment, breathing heavily, and looked about them. Up on the wagon roofs the women, with arrows nocked and bows half-drawn, turned in slow circles, searching for any threat, but all was quiet. Nine bodies lay scattered about; two more blood trails led into the forest, one so heavy that Hob doubted the bandit who had made it would survive.

Molly and Nemain slung their bows, still strung, to their shoulders, and climbed down the rope ladders to the wagon seats, and thence to the ground. The women were unscathed. Hob had a couple of bruises—he had no idea how he had acquired them—and Jack had two small cuts, both on the same shoulder. Nemain fetched some of Molly's remedies from the little wagon, and the women applied salves and linen bandages.

Jack wandered about, gathering up what arrows he could find, pulling them free from trees and corpses alike; they were not to be squandered, for there was no telling when there would be time and material to make more. He tied them into a bundle and put them in the middle wagon; when next they camped he would sharpen the points, repair or replace the damaged fletches—the feathers that guided the missile's flight—and redistribute the arrows to the women's quivers.

Jack and Hob checked the animals and the wagons for damage, but the attack had been too brief, the bandits too few, and no real harm had been done.

Hob went over to the man he had stabbed first, who had run on a few paces, and collapsed. He was not a small man, but in his dying he had curled up as a child curls up to sleep, and so he looked dangerous and vulnerable, both at once. Nemain came over and Hob said to her, "I killed this one. I wonder if he has a wife, or children, and they waiting for him to return." Hob had been in mortal struggles before, but this was the first man he had actually killed himself.

Nemain said, exasperated, "Must you always be thinking three times about everything? He's after trying to kill us, and he failed, and there's an end to it." She stooped and quickly went through his pouch, finding nothing of value or interest; examined the poorly made knife he carried, and tossed it away into the bushes; and stood up again. She set off briskly toward her wagon, slowed, then wheeled on one foot and ran back to Hob. She hugged him fiercely, kissed him on the lips, heedless of whether Jack or Molly watched, and said, "I'm just— I know 'tis that you're a good man, 'tis why you're thinking the while about everything, about what you're doing, and . . ." She paused, getting a bit tangled, and said, "And 'tis not that I'd have you different. 'Tis not." Then she kissed him again and spun around and marched back to her wagon.

Hob stood there, feeling, as so often happened in dealing with his mercurial betrothed, somewhat disoriented. Then, with a last look at the body, he went and took up Milo's rope, and awaited the command to move.

Molly gave one more look around, grimacing a little as she surveyed the corpses. She signed to Jack and Nemain to mount their wagons, made a hand-dusting gesture, and swung up onto the big wagon's seat. She leaned out to look back along the line.

"Away on!" she cried.

CHAPTER 6

EVENTUALLY THE TREES BEGAN to thin, and they received glimpses, here and there, of the green folds of the fells, marching away to the east like waves of the sea. The trail wound among these, and always descending, descending. A rock outcropping seemed to be squarely in the center of the way, but as they approached, a dip in the land was revealed, where the trail dropped twoscore feet on a sharp grade and then ran around the outcrop.

Once around the rock they came upon a little cold-water burn, chattering down over stones and pebbles, and the trail swung in beside it. The slope steepened again, and for a time there was much play with the brakes, and Hob had to haul back on the rope to slow Milo down.

At last they came around the end of a ridge thick with bell heather and matgrass. The down-trending road now leveled out, debouching into what the Scots called a *cleugh,* one of those narrow, protected upland valleys that invite the traveler to camp for the night. The burn they had been following in its descent here ran straight, clucking and gurgling between green braes. Fescue grass covered the slopes; rushes bordered the little brook. Molly had them pull the wagons around in a rough semicircle, with the open end facing the creek. The animals were picketed on moderately long ropes and left to graze, the ox Milo plainly eager for the new spring grass.

Nemain went and brushed Mavourneen; the little ass was her special pet, and now she examined her ears, removing a burr, and stroking her nose, and speaking a great deal of low-voiced nonsense to her, soothing and affectionate speech without much meaning.

Jack was inspecting the mare's hooves. Molly had taught Nemain to ride on the mare, using only a bridle and a saddle blanket, and recently Nemain had decided that the mare had been nameless long enough, and was to be *Tapaidh* henceforth, signifying in Irish *fast, speedy,* although it was unlikely Tapaidh would win any races.

There were enough stunted, wind-warped trees—two were dead—here and there in the little coomb to provide them with a good-sized fire. Jack laid a nest of small twigs for tinder, and atop that small branches, and atop them larger pieces of wood. Nemain brought him a box of very fine dried grasses, and a flint and steel. Jack struck the flint against the steel, and tiny sparks of burning steel flew into the dried grasses, which caught immediately, lighting the twigs.

As the twigs ignited the smaller branches, Jack set up a tripod and hung therefrom a cauldron. Hob drew water from the burn, secretly pleased with himself that he could now, half the way to his fifteenth birthday, carry two heavy buckets without staggering.

Molly and Nemain brought forth the salt cod, oats, and dried apples they had carried away with them from Blanche-fontaine, and the loaves of heavy bread from the castle's ovens. The two women made play with spices and pans, and soon produced a tasty loblolly, served on rounds of the dark onion-studded rye.

When they had eaten, they rested comfortably about the fire. Jack had dragged a couple of logs up to serve as seats for himself and the women, and now he worked quietly at mending a frayed strap for Tapaidh's harness. Hob had spread a blanket upon the ground, and he lay propped on one elbow, blinking into the fire, hearing behind him the ceaseless conversation of the brook.

After a while Molly roused herself, and had Hob get up, get out the symphonia, and sit to tune it. She began to teach

Nemain the harmony she wanted sung to a new ballad she had learned at Blanchefontaine. They worked it out as was their custom: Molly would sing a verse, Hob playing along, mostly the drone strings at first till he caught the melody. Then Molly would repeat the verse, and this time Nemain would sing with her, chiming with some notes and harmonizing with others.

"*So much I think upon thee that I grow all pale,*" sang Molly, and then sang it again, with Nemain's light high voice interlacing with her own deep alto, a plait of sound. "*Between Lincoln and Lindsey, Northampton and London*—softer, Hob, softer," Molly singing and listening to the other two at the same time, gesturing to show them what she wanted, whether strong or delicate, tapping her foot for the rhythm. "*I know no maiden so fair, as the one to whom I'm bounden.* Nay, child, up upon '*whom,*' up upon '*whom.*'"

This last was to Nemain, and Hob, his fingers now clever enough upon the symphonia's keys to allow his mind to roam a bit, reflected that anyone else who addressed Nemain, that youngest of women, as *child*, other than her grandmother—whom Nemain loved with a wolf-fierce devotion—would be in some peril.

They began the song again, and though things seemed to be going well, Molly broke off, sat a moment, and then said, "Leave off, leave off, my heart is not in it."

She gazed into the flames awhile, then stood and paced off along the brookside, into the shadows just beyond the firelight. Soon, though, she came back and sat on the log again. She looked around at the other three, a look of such intensity that Jack immediately put down his mending, and Hob ceased his practicing and laid his open palm upon the symphonia's strings to hush them. Nemain sat down next to Hob.

"I'm after taking a step on the wrong road," she said. "'Tis one thing to be fending off the evil that springs at you, another thing entirely to run toward it. This scourge that Sir Odinell's telling us of, 'tis no light matter, and you two"— here she nodded toward Hob and Nemain—"with your lives long in front of you, and espoused to each other at that. Nay, I'm needing Sir Odinell's support, that I might restore our clan, but—should this business go agley, and what business may not?—I'm thinking 'twere better that you two were safe in Blanchefontaine; so Nemain should be left to head the clan." She did not mention Jack. Jack would follow her into Hell any day without stopping to put his boots on, and all of them knew it.

Nemain slapped her hands down upon her thighs. "And I to head a clan, after hiding like a milkmaid behind a Norman's walls? I am a queen as you are a queen, *seanmháthair,* and not a little help to you either, and strong as you are, you will be the stronger for me at your right hand, nor do I see myself scuttling back to Blanchefontaine, and any road I'll not do it."

And before he knew what he was to say, Hob heard

himself saying in his new man's voice, which for once, praise God, did not have one boyish note in it, "And Nemain and I are promised, and I will not leave her side, not for any reason."

Molly looked from one rebellious young face to the other, and burst out laughing. "It's a pair of badgers I've with me and no mistake." She grew grave again. "Still—"

Nemain, seeing the wind change back against her, said hastily, "Cast a feather, then, and see what the Great Queen sends you."

Molly contemplated her granddaughter for a few moments, then: "You may have the right of it. Let us see what She sends me."

Without further ceremony she got up and went to the large wagon, reappearing a moment later with a shallow wide-lipped black-iron basin, a leather bag, and a raven's wing-feather. Nemain took the basin from her and went to the burn to fill it. Hob watched as Molly began to take handfuls of flat round stones from the bag, some gray, some white, with rough pictures scored in them, the grooves blackened with ink or painted red to make them stand out: a lamb, a fire, a sheaf of wheat, a butchered sheep—these were for the four great quarter-days of the year; three raven's heads, for the Mórrígan, Molly's patron, a triple goddess; the cauldron and club of the Dagda; and so forth.

Hob had seen the stones before, but rarely used; in any event their use was not explained to him, was indeed forbidden to him, a matter between grandmother and granddaughter, priestesses and adepts both.

Nemain set the basin, with a gallon or more of pure water in it, down with a thump on the far side of the big wagon, so that the basin was sheltered from the golden firelight; in this way it was lit only by the cool half-light of the moon. Molly beckoned to Hob.

"Hob, *a chuisle,* stand over there, and say nothing nor move at all till I'm giving you leave." Hob was utterly mystified. Jack, who had seen this before, crossed thick arms and leaned back against the chocked wagon, the wood creaking under his bulk.

Molly arranged the stones, perhaps thirty in all, around the wide rim. She drew a slightly curved, beeswax-coated piece of bark from the leather bag, and placed the raven's feather upon it. Nemain fetched a small cask of the *uisce beatha,* the strong Irish drink Molly distilled herself, and two silver cups, very old and battered, featureless. Nemain poured a half cup into each.

The two women sat on opposite logs; they began a ceremonial chant, wavering harmonies in a minor key, that ended abruptly. Without a word they each drained a cup, setting it down with a thump upon the log they sat on.

Hob watched all this with some misgiving: he had been taught that such practice was of Satan, and he felt sure that old Father Athelstan, who had raised him, an orphan, in the priest house, and who was as a father to him, would not approve. Yet he held Molly in higher esteem than anyone he had ever met, even Father Athelstan, and he knew her to be good to the bone, and Nemain herself was his bride-to-be, and— It was too much to think upon, and he settled for crossing himself quietly.

Jack Brown, placid Jack, less imaginative, more stoic, grinned at Hob's uneasiness; the grin faded after a bit, however, as he thought more on it, and he crossed himself as well, the experienced soldier taking his precautions against danger from whatever direction.

Molly put the leaf in the center of the water; each woman took an end, and they spun it sunwise. The quill upon the leaf revolved; the point indicated first this stone and then that; finally it came to rest pointing at nothing, at a blank spot. The women contemplated this, and a discussion broke out in Irish.

Nemain had been in England for a third of her short life, and was apt to switch between Irish and English more easily, less consciously, than Molly. Now she spoke in English to Molly: "Blood?"

Molly thought. "Blood," she said, and straightway both women drew knives, pricked thumbs, and let a few drops fall into the basin. A small breeze wandered into the campsite at that moment, and troubled the water, and the point of the raven's quill swung to point at a gray-brown stone, and there it stayed.

"*Och!*" said Molly, and snatched up the stone. She

looked pensive, and began to gather up the other stones. She noticed Hob looking intently at her, a question in his eyes. "That's done, then. You may speak, lad; what is it?"

"Does it say we may go on with you, Mistress?" asked Hob.

"'Tis more than 'may' that it says," Molly said. "'Tis a *command* that you should do so. As though Herself had some hand in this—we thinking that 'tis Sir Odinell we're helping, and now . . . it may be 'tis Her bidding that sent us here all along."

MOLLY WAS THOUGHTFUL AND QUIET for a while. Then she took a deep breath. "Well, 'twill be what it will. It's ready we must be, and our skills at their keenest. A few rounds of the knife game, and then it's to bed."

For the time Hob had traveled with them—now almost three years—Molly had taken Nemain off into the woods, away from Jack and Hob, and there taught her the physical skills that went with a battle queen's warcraft, much of which was secret. To some degree this was to avoid confusing Hob, at first just an orphan boy traveling with them. Jack of course was privy to Molly's real nature, but there was very little that could trouble the phlegmatic soldier.

As they became more close-knit a family, they began to practice more in front of Hob, and indeed Molly was beginning, as she had promised him, to show him tricks and sleights of the body, to make him more formidable in battle, as Sir Balthasar was training him in the Norman martial skills.

One exercise that Nemain was set to master, that Molly did not trust Hob with, was the knife game. One hand spread on a log, the other with a knife darted between each of the fingers, slowly at first, then faster and faster. After a while they would play with each other, the two women's left hands flat to the wood, their right hands with daggers, each stabbing between the other's fingers, singing a chant in Irish that went faster and faster, the blades flashing, the points going *thock* and *thock* and *thock,* till grandmother and granddaughter were both breathless and, at a signal Hob could not perceive, stopped abruptly. No one was ever hurt, but Hob's blood would turn cold as highland brookwater when he watched the blurred gleaming steel frolic about his betrothed's delicate fingers, and he disliked it intensely.

Hob wandered away from the camp now, so to avoid the sight of Nemain's fingers in this quick-stepping peril. He strolled over to the water's edge. Here the little burn, its rumpled-silk surface studded with stones of modest size, ran level for a space, mumbling and chuckling between the green banks. The ripples in the water caught the firelight, so that shifting veins of gold were at play in the dark stream. Just beyond the campsite, the burn resumed its downward journey, tripping over a low ledge of half-submerged whinstone and angling downslope, running to the east, the lowlands, the coast to which they were bound, away by the wide cold waters that the English called the German Sea and the Hollanders called the North Sea.

Hob walked to the beginning of the slope, and he followed the burn's course downstream with his eye as it ran ahead of them toward the future. Within a short distance, though, the brook was lost to sight, wandering away into the gloom.

Part II

THE BURNING DOLL

CHAPTER 7

A ROAD THAT AT TIMES SEEMED little more than a sheep trail wound down into the folds and creases of the Northumbrian fell country. It wandered beside the little burn, now growing larger with each mile, as tributaries converged and swelled its waters. Heather, not yet in bloom, and bilberry shrubs covered the rolling hillsides, rising to either hand; mosses covered the wetter ground, and as they dropped lower and lower toward the coast, the scattered gold of lesser celandine brightened the walk.

The ridgelines were haunted by the feral Northumbrian goats, appearing, disappearing; sometimes they seemed to be keeping pace with the little troupe. Hob would see their high back-curving

horns, their flowing black and white locks, the almost ac-
robatic agility of their progress as they skeltered from level
to level; then they would be gone, only to return a little
while later.

The stream became more and more swollen, and a
rumble began to assert itself. A little farther and the rumble
became a bellow, as the little river ran out over a threshold
of rock into thin air, to plunge threescore feet into a deep
chilly pool. The road had to veer away from the water and
return again in a switchback to accomplish the loss of height
that the water did in moments, falling sheer through the
empty air.

After that the land rapidly began to level out, and eventually the crude track over the fells broadened, and the
roadbed turned to plain dirt, with nothing growing in it, but
with some ruts from wagon wheels. Dense dog-rose hedges,
a month or two from flowering, sprang up on either side,
then gave way to wood-pole fencing; beyond were quilt-like
fields cultivated in square parcels known as furlongs or the
long narrow rectangles called selions, each one worked by a
different villager. This ensured that no one would have only
poor land: each had a share of the good fields; each had a
share of stony or less fertile soil. The strips had little borders
of uncultivated land, again increasing the resemblance to
a quilt.

By imperceptible degrees the road descended; the land
flattened; they moved through level fields. Here and there

were rhines, the drainage ditches that kept the land dry enough for tilling, and avoided floods.

The road ran in beside a field newly planted to flax, and alongside the field was a rhine. Slowly Milo plodded along beside the ditch, which was perhaps six feet below the grade of the road. Hob walked in a rhythm that matched Milo's pace. In his ears was the dull thud of Milo's hooves on the dirt path, the creaking of the wagons; the effect was hypnotic, and he was in a vague daydream wherein he had a steel-colored destrier like Sir Odinell's, when two partridges, made uneasy by the travelers, exploded from the field and raced away north. This drew his eye to the birds, to the field itself, and, idly, down to the rhine. In the rhine was a shallow band of moving water, and in the water was—

"Mistress!" cried Hob, coming to an abrupt halt, snubbing up Milo with the lead rope, pointing into the ditch. "Mistress, there's a, a—" He was pointing to a body, half-submerged, horribly wizened.

The corpse lolled in the rhine, wallowing in the sluggish current of outflowing water. Molly took her hazel stick and clambered down the steep little bank to the water's edge. Without hesitating she reached out and seized the corpse by the back of its smock, and, with a heave, dragged the loathsome thing up till it lay half on solid land, face up. The horrid countenance seemed to gaze into the sky. Its skin was brown and harsh as bark—even the water had not softened its appearance—and its eyes, sunken back into its head, seemed almost lidless; the teeth grinned from a near-lipless mouth. Deep grooves in its cheeks, the meat of its forearms, the backs of its hands, seemed not to have been made so much by exterior insult as by interior collapse along fault lines deep in the flesh.

Molly squatted there beside the body for a long time. She put her staff aside, went to hands and knees, and sniffed it from head to thighs like a dog; she took the hand in hers and sat awhile with eyes closed, as though visiting a sick friend; she leaned over the ghastly face, which Hob could scarce look upon, and she peered into its deep-sunk eyes. All the while the corpse's lower legs in tattered hose, its unshod feet, swayed this way and that in the rhine's slow stream.

Where Hob stood on the bank above, an eddy of the wind brought the odor of corruption up to him from the cadaver. He paled and stepped back a pace. Nemain put a hand over her mouth, but she stayed where she was. Jack, on his several campaigns as man-at-arms, mercenary, Crusader, had had occasion to loot the dead after a battle, as was common practice, sometimes as much as three or four days later, when the battlefield had become a buzzing world of flies. Now he merely moved aside a pace or two, squatted and pulled up a handful of grasses, crushed and rolled them between his hard palms, and breathed from his cupped hands, fragrant with the broken leaves.

Molly stood at last, went upcurrent from the body, and rinsed her hands. She retrieved her staff and dug it into the soft earth of the rhine bank, and so climbed once again to the road. She looked back at the pitiful thing below. She said to Nemain, "Whatever other fragrance there is to that body, 'tis thick with the scent of sorcery as well. I'm after feeling it—'tis like a great footprint on that poor wretch, not seen but sensed. Sure and there's a fell being that haunts this coast: something dire, something vast."

They set off east again. Soon, as expected, they struck the first north–south road. They did not see the village, though: these were Sir Odinell's lands, but his castle and the attendant village lay a bit to the north and closer to the coast, along the coast road. Molly had Hob turn to the right, or south, and after no great while they came to a crossroads, and, on the northeastern corner, Adelard's Inn.

Like many inns, it had begun as a house willing to feed and bed down the occasional traveler. Profiting from its location, the inn grew with the addition of a stable, an innyard, stouter doors, and the like. Beside the inn itself was a strong wall, perhaps ten feet high, enclosing the innyard and the stable buildings; in this wall were double doors, very wide.

Hob stopped before these doors, Molly set the brake, and behind them the other two wagons drew to a halt, Jack and Nemain kicking the brakes on, dismounting, stretching. The inn door opened and a skinny boy of about twelve, thin-limbed, narrow-waisted, with a mop of brown hair, ran out and up to them. After a quick stuttering glance between Hob and Molly, the latter still up on the wagon seat, he settled on Molly, and asked her if they were seeking accommodation at the inn.

"It's perhaps a sennight we'll be staying, and our beasts are hungry, and ourselves as well," said Molly.

"Gie us a bit moment, Mistress," said the boy, and ran back into the inn.

Almost immediately they heard bolts being drawn on the other side of the innyard doors, and the boy hauled back first one leaf, then the other. At the same time a man stepped out of the inn itself, wiping his hands on a cloth: this proved to be the innkeeper. He came up to them, tugged an imaginary forelock, a forelock that had departed his scalp some years before. He made a bob that might have been meant to suggest a bow.

The innkeeper was a balding, hollow-chested man; he might have appeared sickly but for his sinewy arms—long arms that seemed longer because of his stooped posture—and his vigorous manner. He was brisk, he was energetic, yet there was a shadow over him: in the midst of saying something he would look quickly down the road, or over the nearby fields; a look of fear would flicker over his features, and then he would resume his speech, with a hint of a little furtiveness, as though afraid he had been seen looking for danger.

"God be wi' ye, Mistress," he said to Molly. Nodding

toward the boy, he said, "Timothy—yon spelk is Timothy—says ye're tae stay a sennight, and welcome tae ye. He'll stable yer nout beast"—here he patted Milo's neck—"and t'others as weel; bring em wi'in." And between gestures of welcome and pattings of the air and pointing, he got Hob to bring Milo around and through the gates, where Timothy waited to show them where to place the wagons, helped them to unhitch the animals, and ushered them into a ramshackle stable that was yet surprisingly clean and comfortable within.

Hob, as always, saw to Milo's comfort. The ox had been his particular responsibility since he had joined Molly's little family, and a bond had grown between them: the great beast, gentle and even timid, had come, somewhat incongruously, to regard Hob as its protector, and Hob had responded with an affection almost paternal. Nemain and Jack tended to the ass and the mare, while Timothy bustled about, showing them where to find feed and water, and assigning appropriate stalls.

Afterward they tramped in a group across the innyard, an expanse of hard-packed dirt within the high walls, to the back door of the inn. Inside, Hob was blind for a moment, but as his eyes adjusted to the gloom after the yard's sunlight, he began to make out some detail. They had come in at the back of the long common room, beside the large stone hearth that took up most of the eastern wall, with its heavy cookpots hung to iron hooks. Here most of the cooking was done, the cauldrons swiveled on iron dogs over the fire to seethe the stews and pottages prepared in the kitchen. In the autumn there would be a pig, or perhaps a sheep, roasted on a sturdy spit. To Hob's left, along part of the south wall, was a counter used to set out food and drink. On pegs set in the wall behind this counter were mugs made of birch or cow horn or tar-jacked leather, for barley beer or honey beer or whatever the alewives of the neighborhood who sold to the inn had in season.

Beside the serving counter were two narrow doorways, one that opened onto the kitchen with its small side rooms that served as pantry and buttery, the other that led to a creaking stairway that went to the upper floor, where there were the sleeping accommodations. The common room was empty, and indeed there was an air of desertion about the inn: there was no bustle from outside or upstairs, no murmur of voices, as there would have been in an inn with guests.

Adelard showed them upstairs. Here a quarter of the space had been set off for the family's use, with an internal mud-and-wattle wall. The rest was divided into sleeping booths walled by hanging cloth. The cots were crude wood-and-leather strap affairs, the accommodations spare to the point of severity, but orderly and well-kept.

Molly looked around briefly, then said, "'Tis with you we'll be eating, friend Adelard, but 'tis our wagons we'll be sleeping in, and you having the more room for other guests."

The innkeeper sighed. "It's few enow the folk who stop here the noo."

"But it's that you were having more in days past?" asked Molly.

"Och, aye. We'd a fair bit from travelers tae Durham, them as didna tak' the coast road, but nae sae mickle any mair." He looked as though he would say more, but then turned suddenly and led the way back down. They trooped down behind him, the stairs protesting a bit as Molly passed and groaning alarmingly under Jack's weight.

Here they met Adelard's wife and daughter, just come in from the kitchen; Timothy had been telling them of the new guests. Joan was a stout woman with a face that might have been formed in a flowing stream, all angles smoothed and blunted by the rushing water: a short wide nose, rounded at the tip, full cheeks, a soft round chin. Yet it was a pleasant face, if not bonny, framed in brown hair shot with gray, beneath a linen veil. Her habitual good-natured expression, welcoming to the tired traveler, yet had a hint of vexing worry, expressed in the way her brows tilted up in the middle, even when she smiled, and the vertical lines that persisted between those brows.

Her daughter, Hawis, was a young woman of perhaps sixteen years, hanging back shyly behind her mother. She had a certain plainness of feature that was redeemed by large hazel eyes, full lips, and the appeal of healthy youth. However, she seemed unaware that she might be attractive: she was diffident, almost timid, and completely without any hint of affectation, much less flirtatiousness. The sleeves of her kirtle were pushed back to her elbows, and she was wiping her hands with a cloth; evidently she and her mother had been in the midst of cooking when Timothy had run in. They gave a little half curtsey to Molly, whose large stature, heavy silver mane barely concealed beneath her veil, and regal bearing projected an imposing, if kindly, nobility. Molly greeted them with her usual casual warm courtesy, and Hob, standing some paces behind with Nemain and the ever-silent Jack, thought to see the wariness drain from the two women.

There were tables and benches through the room. Closest to the fire was a sort of approximation of a lord's high table: a larger table set crosswise, with crude chairs instead of benches. Adelard gestured toward the chairs at the table, an invitation to sit, and himself sat down at one side of the table. Molly sat nearest to him, with the others taking chairs down the other side.

"Daughter," said Adelard, "bring us honey beer, and a bit scran as weel, fer Ah'm sure thae guid folk are yawp, what wi' not eatin' a' the day."

Hawis turned without a word and quickly disappeared into the kitchen.

"Yon's a guid lassie," Adelard said, looking at no one in particular. His fingers drummed a bit on the table, and Hob thought he looked ill at ease, as one who gnaws at some inner trouble while speaking of other things.

Molly undid a soft leather pouch from her belt, and spilled out a number of coins onto the tabletop—the short-cross silver pennies still being minted with the legend *Henricus Rex,* for long-dead King Henry, and a few of the larger silver coins from Florence known as *grossi.* She selected two of the smaller pennies and pushed them over to Adelard, and swept the others back into her pouch, thus establishing her credit in the innkeeper's eyes while paying for stabling and board at the same time.

"I'm after being directed to your inn by a godbrother of my cousin," said Molly, lying blithely. "He's a cook up to the grand castle they're calling Chantemerle, and hasn't he got the ear of the seneschal, and he telling him of our skill at the harp, and the symphonia, and we've hope of being invited to the castle, there to play, and perhaps to acquire a patron the while. It's here we'll stay for a sennight or so, in hope that the castle will pay us heed. We'll be playing for your custom the while, and perhaps that custom will be increasing, what with ourselves playing so gaily here, and then it is you'll be seeing whether we owe you more, or less: 'twill be your decision and none else's."

The innkeeper was not a stupid man, but things go slowly in the countryside, and he sat and looked from the coins to Molly's face, as one who is thinking and thinking. He was also an honest man, and finally he sighed and said, "Mistress, Ah mun tell ee summat. Theer's been a mort of unco trouble o' late, and folk that used tae meet and craic here stay at yem the night, be theer fireside. An thae what come tae this inn are hard men, bound tae the south tae—"

"Whisht," said his wife, hovering by the counter. Now she came and sat down next to her husband. "Dinna mention—"

"Ah mun tell her a bit mair," he said to her. The innkeeper looked about as though there were spies in every corner, and dropped his voice till, between his hushed tone and his thick dialect, Hob could hardly understand him. "Theer's anither castle tae the sooth o' Chantemerle, a few miles tae t' sooth, sithee, an there's talk, terrible talk, of thae folk in't, and thae hard men comin' sooth and gaein' north frae Duncarlin, that's t' castle, an' some unco new folk in't. Theer's been quarrelin' and fightin' and siccerlike, even a man kilt ootside yon threshold"—here he nodded toward the inn's front door. "T' villagers are afeared an' sae are we afeared. Sithee, Ah tell ee this sae theer's nae talk that Ah didna warn ee."

Then Molly did an odd thing: she put a hand on his wrist, and squeezed it a bit, and patted his forearm as one might pat a dog, looking into his face the while, and then said, "Let us but stay a sennight, and see what may be. 'Tis often that your cloudy morning brings in a sunny day."

The innkeeper sat back and sighed; he looked both uncertain and happy, as though he were happy, but unsure *why* he was happy. Hob thought: *He can tell. She is here now, come to help him, and he feels safer; everyone feels it from her, that they are safe now. Dogs, horses, people. Myself.*

Hawis came from the kitchen with a large bowl of

cruppy-dows, cakes made of oatmeal and fish, and trenchers on which to serve them. She disappeared and reappeared with a big pitcher of honey beer, and began to place birch-wood mugs before the company. Her mother served out the cruppy-dows, which Hob ate with relish. Of course, since he had entered manhood, beginning to grow precipitously, everything tasted good to him, a source of some humor to Nemain.

There was a silence while the troupe ate and drank, but soon Molly spoke again, her tone carefully neutral. "We're after hearing of folk being killed, there by the castles of the coast road, Chantemerle and Duncarlin, and their bodies found, and they strange to look upon. Is it this that's keeping your custom away?"

"Weel, Ah dinna ken, Mistress. 'Tis two or mair miles awa', ye ken"—this said as though it were on the moon—"but rumors come tae us, sithee, an' make t' folk hereabout afeared, as Ah hae told ye. But we've mair fear o' t' hard men that gang aboot, passin' through tae and fro yon castle."

"If 'tis only men we've to deal with," said Molly, "we'll not be fretting overmuch. I'll set my granddaughter on them," and she nodded at Nemain.

The innkeeper smiled a small sad smile, as at a poor joke, and said nothing. Hob himself wondered at it, and only later understood.

CHAPTER 8

THE SUN SLANTED TOWARD AFTER-
noon, and two men from the tiny
village of Oldham, just to the west,
on the way home from their fields, had stopped in
to drink ale, and bide a moment before continuing to their cottages. A country inn is a center of
the surrounding community; the innkeeper knows
more than anyone what transpires in the scattered
dwellings, and despite the anxious times, or perhaps
because of them, these two were eager for any word
of doings among their neighbors.

Molly and her family were sitting at a table in the
corner by the back door to the innyard. When she
saw the farmers come in she had Jack and Hob fetch
the musical instruments: Molly's *cláirseach* and the

somewhat smaller one that Nemain used; the goatskin drum; the symphonia.

"For 'tis time to let them know we're here," as she put it in a low voice, nodding toward the pair of drinkers but meaning the country folk in general. The men, lanky, tow-headed—they might have been brothers, or cousins—and more than a little smirched from a day working the soil, had already been eyeing the newcomers: this was a change from dull routine, this was fascinating! When the musical instruments were brought in, their interest doubled, and they took their ale to a table.

Hob took his place by Molly and Nemain, and Jack sat to the other side. Hob kept as quiet as possible while the women, each with a *cláirseach* set upon a knee and leaned upon a shoulder, tuned the willow-wood harps. The harps were decorated with endless-knot ribbonwork, ending in hounds' heads; the gold wires and silver wires with which they were strung were fastened to brass pegs.

Then Hob put the symphonia on his lap and tuned to Nemain's harp, the two young people trading notes back and forth. The three pairs of strings sang under the resined wooden wheel that Hob cranked, while his other hand danced over the keys. The strings stretched a bit and he retuned.

Soon the troupe began a lively reel, Hob for once providing the main melody, the two harps accompanying him, and Jack, deftly wielding his knuckle-bone striker, keeping time with a rattling, bouncing succession of raps on the drum frame, and booming blows on the goatskin. The two peasants looked at each other; one pounded his mate on the back a few times in celebration of their good fortune. They clapped along; they had more ale; they shouted encouragement. Beneath the table their feet were tapping to Jack's rhythm, and for a moment Hob thought they would spring to their feet and dance. The reel came to its abrupt end, and Molly signaled to Jack and Hob to be silent.

Molly and Nemain next played together, the harps interweaving in a complex counterpoint. Echoes woke in the corners of the near-empty space; the showers of tinkling notes filled the long room. This was music of a quality never heard in a little backcountry inn. Folk made their own dance music, and sang old traditional songs, keeping more or less to the melody, singing more or less well. To the few listeners here in the inn's common room—the two farmers, the innkeeper and his wife—Molly and Nemain's playing seemed the work of angels.

The shutters were all open. The sun was near the horizon, and the honey light, pouring low across the fields outside, striking in through the two windows in the western wall, gilded the battered tables and benches. The shadows along the walls and in the corners were the deeper by contrast. The music, the light, combined in some way, and the shabby room put beauty on like a garment; the farmers had grown solemn, and gazed on Molly and Nemain almost as though in prayer.

Hawis came slowly and silently in from the kitchen, and at that point the two women began to sing, the words in Irish, the melody a twining of Molly's deep womanly voice with Nemain's high sweet girlish tones, chiming together, moving apart, so that Hob, who had heard it all before, yet breathed shallowly lest he miss the slightest note. He looked over. Hawis stood with her fist pressed to her mouth, and tears ran silently down her cheeks. After a moment she buried her face in her apron, and did not raise her head till the song was done; yet she did not move away either.

At last the song ended, and the harps came down from the women's shoulders, and still no one moved. After a short while the innkeeper came over to the table and placed a mug of beer before each woman, an action curiously like someone placing an offering at an altar.

MOLLY AND NEMAIN put their harps aside. After a bit Hawis turned and went quietly back to the kitchen. The afternoon began to slide toward evening, and the two villagers left for their homes. With little to do, Molly's small band sat around a table, down the room a little for privacy, and spoke very quietly, nursing mugs of barley beer.

"Be said by me," said Molly, "those two will be telling all they meet what they've heard this day, and it's half the house will be full tomorrow, and no room at all the night after that. 'Tis a narrow path we're on: we must be noticed enough by the folk hereabout, so that Sir Odinell can be inviting us to his castle without remark, and it seeming natural, what with our good repute here among these country folk and my—what is it I'm after telling this Adelard, my cousin's godbrother?—my cousin's godbrother up to the castle; and for this we must have folk to play to, and for that we need those two yellow-haired farmers to be talking to their kin and neighbors, and Adelard himself speaking of us as well.

"But 'tis true that sheep draw wolves, and so these hard men from Sir Tarquin's castle may be coming here as well, and we must be showing Adelard and the other folk that they are safe here with us, but not making Sir Tarquin suspicious of us. And that's the narrow path we're on, nor can we be veering too much to the one side nor the other.

"If it should be that any of these spalpeens are coming in with an eye to mischief, 'tis in my mind to set Nemain on them first, and they being pulled to heel by a wee lass, 'twill be a lesson to them and another thing to make folk want to come see what's toward at Adelard's Inn."

Hob scowled; he drew breath to speak, to object, to volunteer: at any rate, something to remove his betrothed from danger. Just then Molly pointed a minatory finger directly at him: "And I'm not to be having a word from you, young man. 'Tis soon enough you'll be having your chance to fight, and if 'tis a wife you wanted, and her to be a slight flower, and you to be protecting her at all times, 'tis that sweet helpless thing in yon kitchen you should have asked, and not a battle queen out of Erin, and her with her young hands dripping blood."

Hob closed his mouth—no one, least of all Hob, argued with Molly—and threw his hands in the air, a gesture of exasperated surrender. Nemain, who had indeed killed men, now extended her hands toward Hob, hanging limp from her wrists as if dripping blood. She shook them a little. From Jack's broken throat there came the rhythmic wheezing that indicated laughter, and in a moment Hob grinned, and then began to laugh. Laughter became general, and Molly patted his arm. "It's fine she'll be, lad, and ourselves poised near, and myself to have my own dagger out the while."

Hob had seen Molly make a fifteen-yard cast into the dead center of a target while hardly seeming to look, and knew that she could stop anyone in a heartbeat with that thrown dagger. And to himself Hob had to admit that, despite his lessons from Sir Balthasar and his increasing size and his increasing strength and Molly's second-sighted predictions of his future prowess as a great warrior in Ireland, at this moment Nemain was easily the more dangerous of the two of them.

They had a light meal, waited on by Hawis, who gazed at Molly and Nemain as one who looks on beings from Heaven, and then repaired to the wagons, for it had been a long day, and in any event they must await the next day to see the yield of the nets Molly had cast into the waters.

CHAPTER 9

THE NEXT AFTERNOON AND EVENING the country folk drifted in, drank, ate, haggled with Adelard over payment in kind or with the occasional coin, and fell silent when Molly and Nemain played and sang. Later, with sufficient ale inside them, the villagers danced to the rhythm of Jack's drum and the droning of Hob's symphonia.

Adelard's custom increased by bounds; suddenly he had patrons as soon as the sun began to decline, and farmers left the fields. Folk arrived from the nearby hamlets, the men carrying pitch-smeared torches, which were doused and left by the door, to be rekindled for the dark journey home. All went well for two days; on the third day the wolves appeared, following the sheep.

Molly sat at one side of the large table by the fire—the north side, by the door to the innyard, where the wagons stood against the protective wall. This side of the table had become the unofficial station for the musicians: they kept out of the patrons' way; they had access to the instruments in the wagons; and Adelard still had room to seat others around the large table, so convenient to the kitchen.

Toward evening on the third day, the inn was half-full with patrons, mostly drinking; Adelard was at the next table, brushing orts into a basket, when he looked down the room.

"Oh Mary Mother," he said in an undertone.

He saw three men-at-arms, who seemed like men who had done some campaigning, although they looked past their first youth, beginning to decline physically as a result of constant dissipation, and in fact not sober this night. Hawis was placing jacks of ale in front of them.

"Is it that they're known to you, the ill-looking *meirligh*?" asked Molly.

"Och aye, Mistress," said Adelard. "Thae carls is troublin' when sober an' more when wet."

"Be at ease, friend Adelard," said Molly. "We'll be speaking to them if necessary." She and Nemain went back to tuning their harps to each other, a task necessitated by each change in the weather, or the dampness, or proximity to the fireplace. Hob and Jack sat nearby; the symphonia and drum were propped by their feet. Soon the troupe, indeed, the whole room, became aware of a growing disturbance.

Hawis had been sent to require payment from the three men-at-arms. Loud drunken laughter came from two of the men; another was rapidly slipping into a rage, shouting at the young woman, who backed away, already in tears. Heads were turning; two of the village women slipped out the door, unwilling to be present for whatever was to ensue.

"Away wi' ye, ye fucking giglet. Be it that I tell ye tae trust me for payment, ye'll trust me, or I'll cut ee i' t' face, an'"—this delivered in a crazed bellow down the room, toward the front, where Adelard stood, frozen for the moment—"cut tha feyther's throat in tha sight, aye, an' tha fucking mither as well."

"Nemain," said Molly, putting down her harp.

Nemain, her ring-pommel dagger slung to her green leather zone, now quickly produced a second dagger, in a scabbard, from somewhere within her skirts, and slipped it into her zone where it cinched her gown at the small of her back. A moment later she was away and down the room. The angry brute was on his feet, and one of his comrades now rose to stand beside him, and the other to stand just behind these two. The bellowing soldier's comrades had hard grins on their faces, as if anticipating a pleasant one-sided brawl with the landlord, or the farmers drinking at the inn. Nemain strode up and stood before the shouter.

This fellow, pleased at such a vision of young beauty

before him, with her pale skin and emerald eyes and flame hair, was still angry enough that he must insult her too.

"What do ye want, coney?" he said. "If ye want some fucking gelt as weel"—here he patted himself—"Ah hae coin enow i' ma braies fer ee."

Nemain said nothing, but her hand swept up and across her body, snatching the dagger from its sheath in a reverse grip, the pommel up by her thumb and the blade below her fist. She punched the pommel into his stomach, just below the ribs, something he would never have foreseen from this young, this very young, woman. In a reflex he bent, not double, but far enough over to allow Nemain, still with the dagger in a reverse grip, to slice his scalp backhand, three times in an eyeblink.

A scalp wound is painful, and it bleeds profusely, out of all proportion to its negligible danger, and in a moment the bravo was blind with blood and convinced he was dying, and in that moment Nemain, with a small swift twirl, switched her hand to a forward grip on the hilt. Quick as a cat she had the point of her dagger at the throat of the second man, pricking him lightly just beneath the jaw where it runs into the neck, letting him know that she had but to push gently, easily, to wound him in a way that could not be remedied.

So little time had elapsed that the third man, behind the other two, was just beginning to stir, reaching for his own dagger, when Nemain, her right hand still as a stone saint's at the second bravo's neck, reached behind her with her left hand, pulled the second dagger from its nest at her back, brought it around in front of her and tossed it straight up, head high, and caught it by the blade, and held it ready to throw at the third man. He ceased all motion, his eyes fixed on that small white hand, the dagger held high with naught but three feet of air between him and it, the other keeping his comrade from moving.

"And it's now that you'll be taking your friend and washing him in the trough by the stables, and then away on, or myself will be killing the three of you, right here before everyone, it's not that I'm caring who sees, and then won't the inn be cutting you in small pieces, back there in the kitchen, on the stone table, the bones to the dogs, and our Hawis serving your lungs and livers in a pie tomorrow night, and you never seen above the ground again, nor your comrades hearing word of you under the sun."

The three were old soldiers, and might have delayed, and moved apart, and reattacked, were they faced with a man, but this small beauty, who seemed to have sprung from the floorboards and rendered them all helpless in two or three heartbeats, speaking calmly but earnestly of eating human flesh as though she meant it literally, filled them with superstitious dread, and what with the blood and pain of their comrade, a sort of collapse set in, and they wished only to retreat, and to make sense of what had just occurred, in a place of safety.

The first man was sitting, head in hands, moaning. The

man in back held up both palms, bent and seized his comrade's arm, hauled him to his feet. The second bravo took a cautious step back from the knife, but Nemain suddenly stabbed at his midsection, and he gave a sharp cry of alarm and a convulsive backward movement, and then the coin-laden pouch that Nemain had just cut free of his belt hit the floor with a clinking *thud*.

"And it's now you've paid your score as well," she said.

He gave one glance at the pouch, which contained far more than adequate payment for the ale. He drew breath as though to speak; he looked at Nemain; he closed his mouth. He began to help the other two, and so they all shuffled backward, turned, and were out the door.

Hob, looking on, tense, anxious, saw the steadiness of Nemain's hands, and then she moved so he could see her face, the two red patches burning over her cheekbones, and the glitter of her green eyes, and he thought: *She delights in this!* And then he thought: *My little demoness, my battle queen.* He felt that he should be dismayed at his betrothed, her un-Christian savagery, but instead there was a sort of pride at this ferocious little person, and she sworn to be his bride, and no other's.

A DAY OR TWO WENT BY, business prospered, the inn was full by the evening; the troupe played each night, sprightly or somberly. Folk also began to seek Molly's advice on healing as they became aware of her skills, and before the sennight she had allotted as their time at the inn was up, she had folk coming to ask for aid with this or that bodily woe: she dispensed herb Robert for toothache and angelica for digestive troubles and her own mysterious remedies for the cramps that assail women, often laced with the *uisce beatha*. She expected that, any day now, the messenger would come from Chantemerle with Sir Odinell's summons.

Before that, though, there were the Scots.

CHAPTER 10

O N THE SIXTH DAY AFTER THEY arrived, the inn was deserted and the afternoon dimming to evening, when four men-at-arms slouched in and took a seat near where Molly and Nemain sat with Jack and Hob at their evening meal. By their accents, their size, their sandy hair and light eyes, they stood out as men from north of the Tweed. They looked at Molly's group, but saw nothing to interest them. Hawis came out and went pale at the sight of them, a fact not unremarked at Molly's table. They told her to bring ale, and she brought it swiftly and left as swiftly, nor did she ask for payment.

Molly leaned over and spoke to Hob very low, sending him into the kitchen to ask about the quartet of roughnecks. Hob quietly got up and went in to find Hawis wringing her hands, and Joan stroking her hair, and Adelard looking troubled.

"My mistress asks if there is anything amiss with those men out there," said Hob.

Adelard said, "Theer's many a Scot being taken intae service by—" Here he would not say the name, but inclined his head in the general direction of the coast. "—and thae men are of them. They'm come in afore, and Ah'm feared 'tis ower t' ruction t' other night."

"For revenge? For what Nemain did to those three?" asked Hob.

"Summat like," said Adelard, his voice wavering a little. "Summat like."

"I'm sure you will be safe, with Mistress Molly here," said Hob.

"Thae be serious men," said Adelard. "Men o' their hands; serious men."

Hob went back as quietly as he had come, and reported to Molly. She nodded; she grew thoughtful, but said nothing. Hob pretended to resume eating, but he studied the men, drinking deeply from their mugs, refilling them from the beaker of ale Hawis had set in the center of the table. They were a different type from the three soldiers Nemain had faced down. These were hard men in excellent condition, malignant as the Northumbrian adders Hob had marked sunning themselves on logs and rocks along the trail.

The Scots took to muttering together in their own language, the Scottish Gaelic that was so close to Molly's Irish. They looked over at Molly's table, but plainly did not realize that they were understood.

After a bit, Molly and Nemain became very still, looking at each other, listening without seeming to listen.

Hob leaned close to Nemain. "What is amiss?" he said.

"They are just after making their plans to have their way with yon lassie when she next goes outside, in the dark, to the well—'tis behind the stable, and out of sight, that well—and then to throw her body down the throat of it, and that to be a lesson to the folk hereabout."

Molly put her hand flat to the plank table, dark with the oils and liquids of countless bygone spills. There was a dreadful finality about the gesture. "Jack," she said in low tones, "would you ever stretch us the length of these *bithiúnaigh* on the floor? And nor are they to arise again."

Jack, as unruffled as though she had asked him to fetch a spoon from the kitchen, stood quietly and walked to the fireplace. From the bin beside it he selected a piece of wood the length of his arm, and walked unhurriedly back toward their table. His manner was so matter-of-fact that everyone ignored him. As he passed the Scots' table he pivoted and swung the wood at the Scottish leader, catching him in the back of the neck. The Scot went down like a poleaxed steer, and Jack swung backhanded at the man beside him. The blow took the mercenary in the temple and swept him sideways, bench and man crashing over together on their sides.

The two Scots on the other side of the table leaped to their feet, one drawing a heavy double-edged dagger, but by then Jack was round the table and he thrust his impromptu bludgeon into the Scot's middle, folding him over, destroying his breath. With the impersonal ruthlessness of the professional soldier, Jack stepped back for a better swing and clubbed down viciously on the third man's head, producing a singularly unpleasant hollow thump, and the wretch went down at his feet.

The last mercenary snatched up a small bench and held it by a leg, using it as a shield; in his right hand was a dirk. He sprang over his fallen comrade and paced toward Jack, the point of the dirk weaving like the head of a snake, seeking a way past the bar of wood, which Jack now held two-handed as a horizontal shield, moving it to block the questing blade. Suddenly Jack stepped back two paces, raised the wood one-handed, and with all the strength of his right arm hurled it, spinning, at the Scot's face.

The Scot adroitly blocked the cast with his improvised shield, but he was distracted for an eyeblink, and quick as a snapping dog Jack's big hand closed on his knife wrist. Jack pulled the soldier past him and kicked the hinge of his knee, which buckled the Scot to a kneeling position. In the process Jack let go his wrist, letting him retain the knife, but to no avail: in a moment, Jack had seized his head, pulled under his jaw to bring his head back, and whipped it round to the right. There was a muffled *crack* as the neck snapped, and the soldier was dead on his knees, and the knife clattered to the bare wood floor.

The suddenness of the attack, Jack's skill, and especially his extraordinary strength, had produced four dead in eight breaths. Molly sat unmoving, completely at rest, a queen at the execution she had ordered.

"Christ-money!" cried the innkeeper, swearing by the thirty pieces of silver. He stood in the kitchen doorway. "What's toward?"

"We will need one of your wagons, friend Adelard," said Molly calmly.

He came into the room, looking at the carnage. "Did thae men fight amang theirsels?" Behind him, Timothy crept near, wide-eyed, and Joan and Hawis crowded in the kitchen doorway.

Molly explained what had happened. Adelard, though terrified at first, thinking of reprisals, grew enraged when Molly explained the cause of the mayhem.

"Christ save us! How can such men be?" said the innkeeper, hoarse with fear and disgust, and spat toward the corpses. He looked around; he beckoned to Timothy.

"Our Tim," he croaked, "hitch up t' team tae t' wain and bring un tae t' back door."

Jack squatted, got one of the Scots under the arms, and dragged him toward the back door of the inn, which opened onto the closed innyard, safe from prying eyes. Adelard, seeing what was to be done, beckoned to Hob.

"Gie us a hand, young maister," he said, bending and taking hold as Jack had under the man's arms. Hob went over and gripped the Scot by the ankles, and between them they managed to drag the second body up the room to the hearth. Jack was already picking up another corpse, and all four were by the back door when Timothy came in to tell them the wagon was just outside.

Adelard and Hob dragged the dead men outside, while Jack heaved them up into the wagon bed, the bodies sprawling awkwardly this way and that. When all four were up, Jack jumped up on the wagon, straightened limbs, and covered the corpses with horse blankets Timothy produced from the stable. Molly mounted the seat and Jack moved up beside her.

She called to Timothy, "Open the gate, lad." To Hob and Nemain she said, "We will return shortly; see that Adelard and the rest say nothing to anyone else about this."

THEY RETURNED not long afterward. When Hob finally got a chance to ask, Molly told him that they had driven the wain some little way into the woods, and there in the dark, Jack Brown had thrown body after body to the side of the road, then dismounted and dragged them in—"not far, not far atall"—to the woods, where it was unlikely anyone would find them for a while. "And then who's to say what came to pass, and they with hardly a mark upon them?"

Hob had no compunction about the killing of such vile men, but he was subdued for the rest of the evening: it had been made plain to him how swiftly four men could be removed from this life, and from the part they had played in it, and with none ever to know what had befallen them.

THE NEXT DAY WAS QUIET, although Joan and Hawis were noticeably anxious, and Adelard was tense and withdrawn. The day after that he was sitting down with Molly at the big table by the hearth, when Timothy came in from the roadside door and began making his way toward them with a well-dressed stranger.

"God's hooks!" said Adelard. "What new trouble's this?"

The stranger was a tall lean man, dressed simply in a dark-blue tunic and hose with a dark-green surcoat: the effect was of somber simplicity. Timothy brought him up to Molly.

"Mistress, here's Daniel, says he's fra Chantemerle—'tis a castle not far fra here—wi' a message."

Daniel bowed politely. Hob had an impression of restless intelligence held in check under a sober manner. Keen dark eyes under black brows, a long narrow face, a closed expression undermined somewhat by a humorous set to the eyebrows.

"Madam," he said to Molly, "my master, Sir Odinell, has heard of your virtue as musicians; he requests that you come to Castle Chantemerle, there to play before himself and his guests. You will be well provided while there—perhaps a day or two—and Sir Odinell is quite openhanded to his musicians."

"'Tis a welcome invitation, and we pleased to accept it, poor as we are," said Molly, who was nothing of the sort. She was playing her part. "We will be there on the morrow."

"I will so . . ." At this point Hawis came from the kitchen, and stopped just inside the common room. A south-facing window poured sunlight through the kitchen archway, and cast a nimbus about the girl's graceful figure, and struck highlights from her hair where it escaped from the simple linen coif she wore. She looked at Daniel—dark-clad Daniel, elegant Daniel—and stood very still.

For his part, Daniel became aware of her, glanced past Molly, past Adelard and Timothy, and fell silent. He seemed as one turned to a pillar of salt for a long moment; then he started, and returned his attention to Molly. He had gone very pale. "I will so inform Sir Odinell. If it please you, I must return at once." He gave simple directions to the castle, but in any event Adelard had been to Chantemerle, and could advise Molly further.

Daniel cast another glance past the hearth, to where Hawis stood just inside the room, absently kneading a kitchen cloth in her hands, gazing on Daniel with an abstracted air. Adelard looked quickly back and forth between them. Innkeepers tend to be close students of human nature, and Adelard was no exception. He let Daniel get a few paces toward the door, and then he called, "Coom tae see us again, guid sir, duties permittin', and try our fare. Our Hawis, there, is a great one for making your cruppy-dows, and t' ale is of t' finest."

Daniel stopped; he turned partway around; he addressed Adelard, though his eyes flickered once to Hawis, still standing as a statue stands, away by the kitchen.

"Yes," he said. "I—yes, I shall." And with that, he was out the door.

CHAPTER 11

THE NEXT DAY FOUND THEM TRAVeling east from the inn. Molly had roused them all before dawn, prepared the wagons, assured Adelard that they would return within a sennight, for so she planned to do, to avoid attracting unwanted notice by dwelling at the castle overlong. Timothy had thrown open the gates as the sky paled, and the three wagons rolled out of the innyard, turned south a few paces to the crossroads, and east again onto the transverse road. After some traveling, long enough for the sun to clear the horizon, the east-trending road ended at a north–south way, broad enough to indicate that it was heavily traveled. Hob led the ox in a wide leftward turn and they headed north up the coast.

The road here was still somewhat inland. Hob could smell the tang of the unseen sea, bracing, salty, a scent that aroused an obscure exhilaration in his heart. It was as though he remembered it from somewhere, but he could not imagine where, and as though it meant to tell him something, but he could not imagine what.

As they moved along, the coast road gradually trended eastward, closer and closer to the sea, so that he heard a rhythmic grumble, as of a giant in his sleep. They trundled along for a while with a long low outcrop on their right, shielding the view to the east from sight. Abruptly this outcrop slanted down, down, and disappeared, and the road ran into the clear, and revealed the sea.

Just beside the road the land now slanted down in a steep slope to the low humped shapes of rolling sand dunes, crowned with coarse marram grass; the dunes bordered a wide semicircular bay of dark wet sand, studded with flat upthrusting stones. Beyond stretched the leaden sheet of the German Sea, endlessly assailing the shore in waves of no great height. Hob, enthralled by the salt smell, the crash and hiss of the waves on sand and gravel, slowed to a halt, and Milo, after a few steps, stopped also, puzzled.

The rocks embedded in the sand trapped pools of water when the tides went out. Hob could see purple sandpipers, birds of modest size, plump bodies, narrow bills, teetering about the pools on thin legs, industriously foraging. In among them were sturdy little birds, turnstones, tipping small rocks to find their prey beneath; their rapid sharp *tuck-tuck-tuck* came clearly to Hob over the swash of the retreating tide.

Molly set the brake and called, "Well, look a bit, *a chuisle,* 'tis not every day one sees such a sight."

Hob leaned his folded arms on Milo's broad back and gazed across the ox at the water, running unobstructed to the end of sight, and breathed deeply: the chill damp air was like cold water on a thirsty day, and he felt he could never get enough of it. There were some islands, not very far offshore, but beyond that the water looked as though it might reach to the edge of the world.

"Is it pleasing to you, *a rún*?" asked Molly.

"Oh, yes, Mistress; it's . . . it's . . .'"

"Wait till we're in Erin, and you seeing the Western Ocean from the great cliffs. It's then you'll be thinking that what you saw this day was a puddle."

Hob set off again, tugging at the ox's rope; Molly kicked loose the brake, and the little caravan of wagons creaked into motion. Slowly the crescent bay was put behind them, Hob enjoying the constant breezes, the hypnotic pleasure of watching the waves break and break again on the sands until the bay gave way to a stony promontory, waves dashing spume up the face of the rock. Past this: another scoop of bay, and then another headland, but on this one crouched the great bulk of Sir Odinell's castle, Chantemerle.

The road split, the main branch continuing north to

Sandham Bycastle, the little village that served the castle's needs. The smaller branch turned seaward and mounted a natural ramp of stone outcropping, clothed in grassy soil. Hob swung onto the upward way, leaning a little against the slope. Behind him the ox began to snort as it took up the strain of hauling Molly's main wagon up the grade. The road gradually leveled off. There was a bare patch, and then the massive gatehouse of the castle's outer wall. The gates were closed, but figures watched them from the wall-walks, and even as they approached the gate the heavy valves began to swing inward.

There was a deep dry moat, filled with living thorn hedge, over which a drawbridge gave access to the gate-house. The wagons rumbled over the planks and into the dim-lit tunnel, laden with traps and slow-downs, that pierced the gatehouse, and so out into daylight once more.

They rolled into the outer ward, and here came Daniel Clerk, who bowed gracefully, and introduced a page, Guis-card, who was to be their guide. Daniel, attentive, polite, cast a quick burning glance down the little line of wagons; an expression of disappointment flickered across his face; then, once more the suave castle functionary, he bowed again to Molly, and excused himself, citing his duties.

Guiscard was about Hob's age, perhaps a bit younger, well turned out with his new hose of scarlet and his gilt buckles; he was polite, bowing first to Molly and then taking the lead rope from Hob with a murmured "If it please you, allow me to . . . ," his voice trailing off as though hesitant to be too obvious. But he was friendly as well: he grinned conspiratorially at Hob and said, as he led the ox—and so the caravan—around in a turn to the right, heading toward the wide stone stables set against the south wall, "We'll put the wagons on the lower level, and lead the beasts to the upper floor. Have you seen such a stable? There's a ramp!"

Hob admitted that he had not, smiling back—the page's enthusiasm was infectious. Through the broad doorway with the two doors, closed in inclement weather, but today opened flat to the outside stable wall, and immediately they were in an echoing dimness, in which was a bustle of grooms and water boys and muckers. They were enveloped in the perfume of hay, the sharp ammoniacal tang of urine, and the rich pungent smell of animal bodies; from the upper level, there was the *clop* and *boom* of hooves on the broad planks of the floor. Men descended upon them, and there was a flurry of activity as the ox, the ass, and the mare were unhitched and the wagons were muscled into place against the walls.

Everything that Molly owned was in the three wagons, including some hidden caches of coins she'd acquired: English silver pennies, and gold coins brought by Crusaders from the Holy Land. She had keys that hung from her girdle, the belt on which her pouch and her dagger were slung; now she caught Nemain's eye, and tapped the keys at her waist, and pointed to the wagons. Nemain disappeared into the large wagon and reappeared with a small sturdy sack.

From this she drew one of the iron barrel locks that Molly possessed, a mark of Molly's wealth, and secured the back door of the wagon with it, turning the disk-handled key in the lock, and replacing the key in the sack. She went on to place locks on all the back doors, the front hatches, and the side shutters of the three wagons, and when all were secure, to string all the keys on a thong and fasten that to her own girdle. The sack she tucked up on the wagon seat.

Jack and Hob now went with Guiscard and two of the grooms to stable the three beasts. The stables were so long that the ramp, which began at one end of the building, had a gentle grade for the animals to walk up. Hob brought Milo around to the beginning of the ramp, and Milo decided that it was too dangerous, and that he would much rather go back over by the wagons, and there were a few moments spent in earnest discussion.

Finally Jack handed the mare's reins to one of the grooms, came up and leaned against Milo's neck, turning his head around toward the slope. Hob pulled again, speaking soothing words about how comfortable it was up there, and how he could rest and eat to his heart's content, and finally Milo put a hoof to the ramp, and then all at once the ox went up, the wood rumbling under his weight, at what was for Milo a rapid pace.

All the shutters on the upper level were open to the warm weather. The space was airy and clean; the stalls were ample; troughs held water and feed. Hob and Jack satisfied themselves as to the three animals' safety and comfort, and went with Guiscard to rejoin Molly and Nemain. There was a bit of delay at the top of the ramp as two muckers wheeled barrows full of manure onto the ramp and down, destined for the castle gardens, then Guiscard led the way as they half walked, half trotted down the long slope.

Guiscard led the party through the expansive outer ward, where sheep moved placidly about, heads down, cropping the new grass, to another gatehouse set in the inner wall. This was reached across a moat, dry but very deep, the bridge across it set on a pivot, so that it could be turned sideways, thus removing access. The gatehouse, a square building flanked by two hexagonal towers in the French style, had an archway that ran right through to the inner ward, and the archway had a yett, an iron latticework gate, at either end. Both these yetts stood open, and parties of guards, five or six at a gate, stood at deceptive ease—all were well armed.

They passed through the cool stone archway, smelling faintly of horse and of horse urine, walking to one side as six mounted men-at-arms clattered through from the inner ward, off on some patrol or other errand. Hob looked after them. They rode in two neat columns, and seemed alert; there was no jesting, no chatter. He thought that Sir Odinell must be a bit of a stern master, maintaining a high standard of order among his men.

Hob looked up at about the midpoint of this short tunnel, to see several of the holes that they called *meurtrières,* murderesses. Through these holes, from an upper storey in this gatehouse, stones, arrows, hot oil, could be dropped down upon attackers who had breached the outer yett, but not the inner one, and who for the moment were trapped in the gatehouse.

Into the sunlight again, across the inner bailey with its smithy and other wooden outbuildings leaning against the curtain wall, and then they were at the keep with its attached halls and chapel. Hob looked up. The central tower of the keep soared up and up, the battlements studded with machicolations, outcroppings projecting from the walls, with openings here and there near the bottom, again so that hot oil and other unwelcoming stuff might be dropped on attackers. Set in the center of this tower was yet another gatehouse, and with it of course more guards, who—recognizing Guiscard and having been told to expect entertainers—passed them through swiftly.

They followed their guide up a dogleg staircase and at last were in Chantemerle's great hall. This was quite a bit larger than Sir Jehan's hall, as Chantemerle itself was much larger than Blanchefontaine, and there seemed to be tables set up even though it was between meals, and the hall relatively empty. The castle folk had two rows of trestle tables, running lengthwise down the hall, and at the far end of the long room was a dais, with a table set crosswise, and two smaller tables to right and left, just off the dais.

There were three fireplaces: the larger one was to the

left of the main table; two others were spaced along the lower reaches of the hall. As at Blanchefontaine, the walls were covered with tapestries and collections of weapons, among which was a particularly fine row of battle-axes, including Danish and sparth axes, and another of pole arms—voulges, fauchards, glaives—used by Sir Odinell's ancestors, or looted from their victims. Behind the dais was a bloodstained banner with the three blackbirds of Chantemerle, borne to the Holy Land by an ancestor of Sir Odinell, one Sir Fulk; the blood was that knight's own.

Sir Odinell awaited them in an alcove; with him was Daniel, hovering discreetly to one side.

"Thank you, Guiscard, that will be all," said Sir Odinell. "Do you wait upon Lady Maysaunt."

"My lord."

When the page had gone the knight turned to Daniel. "Wait outside; see that no one comes near enough to overhear."

"My lord," said Daniel, stepping out and drawing a heavy tapestry across the opening to the hall; this would at least muffle some of what was said.

"He is clever and he is closemouthed, our Daniel Clerk," said Sir Odinell. "He has trained for the priesthood, but— Well. 'Twas not something that suited him, but he can read and write, and even do sums, and has proved an able administrator. He will be my seneschal someday. You may trust him; he is privy to all my affairs. I have told everyone else that you are musicians, excellent musicians, but no more than that. We will seat you to one side of the dais, that you may observe Sir Tarquin the more closely.

"I sent this same Daniel to Sir Tarquin, to renew his invitation to a banquet, and with instructions to mention you—mention you by description: most excellent musicians, and so forth—and Daniel has reported to me that he felt that his offer was not proceeding well, till you were described to Sir Tarquin.

"Daniel is a very keen fellow, and it is why I sent him to Duncarlin—he has gone before, and hates the errand, for the castle and its inhabitants oppress him, and he feels unclean when he has been there. But he is, as I say, keen, and he did not overlook a glance that ran between Sir Tarquin and Lady Rohese when your troupe was described, and Sir Tarquin then accepted at once. I believe you must be doubly on your guard when he is here, for I fear your desire to be overlooked as beneath his notice may be offset by rumor that has reached his ear."

Molly looked thoughtful. "Sure and he may have heard some tale of our doings at the inn; indeed, I mistrust that our last encounter might have been with agents"—here she told him of what befell the Scots—"sent to probe what was toward at the inn, and to instill fear in the country folk."

"He is to come within the sennight," said Sir Odinell, "and will dine with us, but says he may not stay the night— may not stay long at all, he does not say why—and so will return to Duncarlin. He is no great distance from us, perhaps a dozen miles down the coast, but I think there is some other reason for his departure, for they are very . . . very . . . well, you will see, and tell me your mind on this matter when he has gone."

With that, he called Daniel in and had him take the party to a solar, a set of three rooms that they might have to themselves. This was unusually good treatment for traveling musicians, even excellent musicians, but Sir Odinell could not bring himself to establish two queens—however reduced their circumstances—in a common sleeping room, and in any event he did not want anything of Molly's private conversation to be overheard, for fear of gossip, if not spies.

So it was that Hob and Jack had a room to themselves, and Hob had a bed to himself that night, a real bed, and he stretched out in comparative luxury, goose-down pillows with smooth headcloths on them, and warm coverlets, for even in late spring the castle, high on its promontory, was cooled by the sea wind, and April nights could be chill. As he drifted to sleep he became aware of a scratching noise, and a rustling down in the rushes that covered the floorboards. He looked over the edge of the bed, but it was too dark to make anything out, even by the glow of embers in the small fireplace.

He lay back down again, not overly concerned: all castles had mice, and rats, and cats and terriers to hunt them. The scratching came again, and he turned on his side, facing away from the fire. By chance he opened his eyes as he lay there. The glow from the hearth was caught and reflected by something in the far corner, something faint, something blue. Through the low-lidded eye of incipient sleep he watched this tiny point, or points—was there more than one? Were there two? A bit of enamel that had fallen from a piece of jewelry, echoing the firelight? As his body drifted into ease, he almost thought to see the bits of color move, and then vanish, but his eyelids closed, and by the morning, the scent of the sea in his nostrils and Jack bustling about, he had forgotten everything.

CHAPTER 12

THE SHUTTERS IN THE GREAT HALL, though fastened, were flexing against their latches, producing a muffled banging that underlay the howl of the wind and the crash of the surf outside. Hob had awakened to a mild breeze outside his window. By the time the troupe had assembled and descended to the hall, a stiff wind blew from the German Sea.

Sir Odinell had established their status as that of visiting troubadours, although Molly composed neither song nor poem. He wished to avoid comment on the fairly good treatment a band of musicians was being granted. Accordingly they were given their own table, just off the north side of the dais, opposite the little table reserved for Sir

Odinell's daughter, Mistress Eloise, a girl of about eleven years, and her nurse.

After a perfunctory breaking of their fast—a cup of ale, toasted bread—Molly and Nemain went off to the solar, citing preparations having to do with their Art that required an absence of males in the immediate vicinity, and leaving Hob and Jack to lounge about the hall.

For the rest of the morning Sir Odinell held halmote court in the hall, adjudicating matters involving the tenants of his manor. Normally such estate business would be done outside—there was an oak under which it was traditional to conduct this business—but the steadily deteriorating weather necessitated that transactions should be conducted inside.

The usual stream of tenants waited at the lower end of the hall, and were conducted to the dais by the sergeant-at-arms. A pig had strayed from the yard of one villein, and destroyed part of the vegetable garden of another; the necessary settlement was established. Another of Sir Odinell's tenants had, by dint of clearing and planting, turned hitherto unused ground into farmland, and now the rent for the new patch of ground had to be agreed upon. A complaint was brought by a Mark Petty that another tenant of Sir Odinell was persisting in an affair with Mark's wife. The Sieur de Chantemerle fined the adulterer a small amount, but warned him in the severest tones that the next penalty would not be so light.

Hob found the proceedings of great interest: the workings of manorial life displayed before his eyes. He had seen something similar at Blanchefontaine, but Sir Odinell's manor was much more extensive, encompassing farm and forest and fishing village, and the problems were accordingly more varied.

Jack had managed, by sign and a painful word or two and Hob's interpretation, to obtain a flagon of ale, and sat happily drinking—with his size and robust constitution, it had little adverse effect—and watching the parade of witnesses, the arguments and counterarguments, the decisions by Sir Odinell and his advisors.

So the morning slid by, and as the court concluded, the wind outside, consistently loud, began to rise to the occasional shriek. Through this din Hob now heard the golden notes of a trumpet, a series of four notes repeated three times, a signal of some sort. Sir Odinell rose with his senior staff, including Daniel Clerk, and made for an archway. As he passed Hob and Jack he said, "Come, then, my friends, and you'll see a sight—a ship in this gale. This alarm signifies pirates, for who else comes to landfall here? Yet it may be only a merchantman driven close in by this storm."

Into a turret stairwell they trooped, Sir Odinell and his staff, followed by Hob and Jack. They went up and up, passing several levels, the stair winding to the right. They emerged on the roof of one of the two most seaward towers, and immediately had to squint against the force of the wind.

The gale drove rain almost sideways, a moderate rain interspersed with drenching squalls.

They gathered at the seaward parapet. Far out, a ship was barely discernible through the battering rain and spray. Closer in, its companion, clearly not a pirate ship but a heavy, flat-bottomed cog from one of the German trading cities—Hamburg, perhaps, or even Lübeck. This ship was obviously in trouble, driven by high wind far too close to a lee shore, with many of its sheets loose, writhing like snakes in the gale, and the big square sail beginning to tatter. Tiny figures of sailors, their canvas smocks whipping about their bodies in the terrible winds, could be seen struggling desperately to turn the yard enough to go about on the other tack. They had just cleared the headland on which Chantemerle stood, but the scoop of the bay to the south was far too close for safety, and the next headland loomed before them.

Hob found himself clenching his fists. The ship wallowed, it bucked and plunged, its head came around, and it just scraped past the next outjut of rock, and on south. For a moment it was still in sight, and as Hob watched there was an enormous *crack,* and the sail split up the middle. A heartbeat or two later, and the ship was obscured by the intervening promontory. Its sister ship, unable to help, could be seen for a while longer, then it too vanished to the south.

Sir Odinell turned away—he had been prepared to issue orders to resist a landing by pirates—and led them below. As they trudged down and around the stairwell, Hob could hear him giving orders for a Mass to be said for the sailors, that they might be safe, or if not, for their souls.

THAT EVENING, Dame Maysaunt presided over dinner. A brisk, cheerful woman younger than her husband, she kept the conversation flowing, was conversant with doings in London and on the continent, asked riddles, proposed songs in between courses, and generally filled in the gaps in Sir Odinell's conversation—the latter was inclined to dignified silences, well enough on campaign, but disconcerting at the dinner table.

The troupe played some lively music, though there was no dancing, and Molly, fortified with wine, waited for a relative moment of quiet in the great hall, raised her harp, and executed a breathtakingly complex and rapid piece, the notes falling like a heavy rain, so quickly did her fingers pluck the strings, a waterfall of sparks, a torrent of beauty, echoing through the hall, till even those farthest from the dais were completely silent.

Hob himself had never heard Molly play such a dense and swift piece, and found himself with mouth slightly open at its end. There ensued the usual moment of stunned silence, and then the loud and enthusiastic tributes.

After that, Sir Odinell considered that the troupe had established themselves as special guests, if of no great social standing, that might be housed and treated with some consideration, even respect, and he demanded no great amount of music from them that night, but let them play when the mood would take them and, in between, encouraged them to partake of the dishes enjoyed at the high table.

Soon enough they were abed again, and Hob, now remembering vaguely the scratching, the faint blue glimmers, of the other night, looked into the shadows for vermin, but there was nothing, and soon he drifted off to sleep.

In the morning the wind had abated, the sun shone in the bluest of skies, clouds like piles of bleached wool drifted lazily along the horizon, and monstrous corpses began to wash up on the sandy shore beside the castle.

CHAPTER 13

THE MORNING HAD HARDLY BEGUN when a page sent by the tower sentries gave Sir Odinell notice that bodies had begun to wash up, in horrid condition, on the strand to the south of the castle. The Sieur de Chantemerle and a council of his senior knights hastily assembled and prepared to investigate. Molly was sent for and soon the four members of the troupe were tramping after Sir Odinell and his advisors.

No need to saddle mounts: the monstrosities were within walking distance. Out the inner gate and across the outer ward, Sir Odinell striding a bit ahead, uttering curses under his breath. The outer gates were being pulled open as he came up and he led the way out and down the long slope to the coast road, then back past the walls and down to the strand.

A knot of men-at-arms awaited them. Three of the corpses had been dragged up above the high-water mark. They were in the same hideous state as the body Molly had half pulled from the rhine. The group stood upwind from the bodies. Molly and her family stood a little away from Sir Odinell and his council, for the knight was making arrangements for disposal of the wretches, but Molly was more interested in how they came to be here.

As they watched, every ten waves or so a dead man, deeply wrinkled, presenting the aspect of a man long deceased, was cast up on the sand, as though in some ghastly parade from the sea. As each came drifting ashore, floating in with the last dying force of a wave and snagging enough on the wet sand to remain on land, Sir Odinell's soldiers, every line of their bodies expressing not only distaste but fear of the uncanny, dragged them up above the borderline between wet and dry sand.

For a time there was nothing from Sir Odinell and his knights but a kind of stunned contemplation of the frightful scene: bodies could be seen near in to land, farther out, and yet farther out, one following the other, the only sound the rush of the sea wind, the muted crash of the waves, and the abrasive rasp as each corpse was pushed up onto the damp sand.

The bodies showed every evidence of long corruption,

and there was a darkening, almost an under-skin browning, as though they had been burnt, or bathed in tanner's acid.

After a time the dreadful procession slowed, and the bodies came more slowly, and finally the last one, or at least the last that could be discerned, approached closer and closer, and drifted into the shallows, and was nudged up onto the strand by the modest waves.

Molly went closer as she had with the body in the rhine, and called to Sir Odinell. She pointed out to the knight the dead men's canvas smocks, most split up the back for some reason, their earrings, their pigtails held together with tar.

"It's the sailors you're after watching yesterday," she said, "but it's a trouble to me to think how come they here, and in this state."

"I can tell you the way of it, madam," said Sir Odinell. "We have observed over the years that there is a current, at least in this part of the year's course, that comes up from down the coast, and eddies in here round yonder rock"—here he pointed to the promontory to the south of Chantemerle that formed the southern bound of this bay or inlet—"and casts up its burden here, on these sands. This comes from Duncarlin, from Sir Tarquin's stronghold. Let us saddle horses and ride south awhile."

She put a hand to his arm. "Nay, 'tis a great evil and a powerful sorcery there is to this, and 'tis I must be warning you not to force a contest between yourself and this Sir Tarquin. If 'tis he who is doing this, he'll be destroying you, and you lacking my help, and perhaps destroying you even with my help. I'm not to be seeing which way this will end, but there's no settling it at the end of a lance: not at this time, perhaps not ever."

"You mistake me, madam," he said. "I had no intention of setting foot outside my own lands. But I want to see if there is any sign of what occurred, without alerting him to my actions."

"So be it, then," said Molly.

"Let us mount, and ride south along the beach, and see what may be discovered. Do you ride?" he asked.

"I do, as do my people here."

Molly and Nemain were from Ireland, and had learned to ride as children; Hob had been taught by Sir Balthasar; Jack could ride if need be, but had always been a foot soldier, and would never be happy on horseback.

A SHORT WHILE LATER the Sieur de Chantemerle, his inner circle of senior knights, Molly's troupe, and a half-dozen mounted men-at-arms were clattering over the stones of the outer gatehouse, down the ramplike approach to Chantemerle and south on the coast road. Sir Odinell hastened past the crescent of sand beside Chantemerle— nothing of the ship had drifted in with the sailors, which was odd in itself. When he had passed the rocky headland to the south of the castle, he set a slower pace, scanning the shoreline for planks, rope, cloth, cargo—any evidence of what had happened to the ship. But there was nothing here either.

"If they went down with the ship, madam," he said to Molly, who rode knee to knee with him, "then some small part of the ship, if not more, should have drifted in with them, borne by the same currents. And they have not drowned as one might expect, but have died as others here have died."

"'Tis not the sea they're dying from, you have the right of that," Molly said. "'Tis some form of sorcery, and haven't I seen it before, and that in your own lands, and we on our way to Adelard's Inn."

"You have seen it yourself?" the knight asked.

"'Twas in a rhine, and the poor thing wizened and decayed, and it appearing just as you described to us, back at Blanchefontaine."

They had reached the point at which the coast road wandered inland behind a screen of rock, on its way to meeting the road that led west past Adelard's Inn. Sir Odinell turned his horse toward the shore. The riders plunged down the short slope to the beach, their horses' front legs rigid as they braced themselves against the grade, kicking up sprays of sand and torn-loose clumps of marram grass. They trotted over to the hard-packed surface of wet sand, and turned south again.

Sir Odinell turned in his saddle. "Thibault!"

One of the knight's men spurred up to the head of the column.

"My lord?" he said.

"Scout for us," said Sir Odinell, gesturing ahead. "We seek anything to do with those sailors."

Thibault, a younger man, of some repute for his tracking skills and excellent sight, took station a little way ahead of the group, and rode leaning over, watching the ground for tracks, or for wreckage, however slight.

. The rhythm of the coastline here was rocky headland, followed by scooped-in sandy bay, followed by another headland. Another such promontory loomed ahead, and Thibault, coming to the rocky wall that was the root of the headland, turned his horse inland and urged it upward. The horse scrambled up the bank and Thibault turned it south again.

Sir Odinell drew rein and the scouting party bunched up around him. They stood there for some moments, waiting for Thibault's report. The horses snorted and shifted about on the wet sand; the waves crashed in, hissed over the sand, pulled back again. The damp breeze from the sea imparted a sheen to the leather of the saddles and the reins grew slick with moisture.

Then there was a hail from above. "My lord! The ship's all agley out on the bar!" Thibault was pointing south to the next bay.

Sir Odinell leaned forward in his saddle and set his

mount at the slope; the horse made a swift, half-jumping ascent, and everyone followed. When they had reached the upper bank, Thibault led them south to the next bay, and here was an extraordinary sight.

The cog had been pushed by the gale toward the land, and had run aground on a sandbar, perhaps two hundred yards from shore. It lay on its side, rigging trailing in the water like seaweed, the split sail and the mast overboard, the yardarm dug into the sandy bottom and serving as a sort of anchor. The sea was pounding the ship's hindquarters, and the vessel was slowly breaking to bits. The forecastle, a crenellated wooden tower, was intact, but the aft castle was half-destroyed by the battering of the waves.

Already the shore was littered with wreckage: pieces of strake; the odd length of rope; barrels intact and barrels staved in, littering the sand with honey, with flax, with resin from the Baltic; bolts of fine cloth, sodden and twisted. Amid all this a large longboat was drawn neatly up on the sand.

Thibault drew their attention to the number of footprints near the longboat—prints of bare feet, the mark of sailors. The sand here yesterday had been damp with the surge of water pushed ashore by the storm wind, but the next high tide had not come so far up the beach. In this way the footprints had not been erased by the subsequent high tide. There was a confused jumble of prints around the boat, and then the tracks set off to the south.

"To the south is Sir Tarquin's stronghold?" asked Molly.

"Aye; there is little else for a league," said Sir Odinell. "But this is my land, this bay. Let us follow these prints and see where they sought refuge."

"Nay," said Molly, "it's only alerting him to what we're knowing. If they're walking south, where else would they be heading? They were in good health when they were walking here, and then they're turning up as we're after seeing them this morning. 'Twas not the sea that did this to them. Let us return to the castle, and let me view this Sir Tarquin, and learn what I may learn."

Sir Odinell turned his horse's head, and the mount walked around in a circle till they were facing north again. He looked out to the bar, where pieces of the ship were coming loose at irregular intervals.

"William!" he cried.

A young man rode up to him. "My lord?"

"Ride with all haste to Chantemerle; find Daniel Clerk; have him tell off a work party, with three wains, and send them here—this is my salvage, and I am losing it by the moment. They can use this longboat. Thibault will await them on the road, and guide them to the wreck. Come, madam, we will have a feast, and you will see this strange knight for yourself, and then you will give us your rede."

CHAPTER 14

THE HALL WAS BRIGHT WITH torches, loud with the hubbub of the evening meal, the castle's folk filling the lower tables. And at the high table, Sir Odinell and his wife, Lady Maysaunt, sat with some ten or eleven household knights and, in many cases, their wives as well. Some of the younger knights were bachelors, but most were married, and men and women alternated in the seating. Molly's people had eaten a bit earlier, that they might be ready to play. They were seated at their own small table again, opposite little Mistress Eloise's table.

Sir Odinell had presented Eloise with the two Irish wolfhound pups that Sir Jehan had given him, and she had promptly named them Erec and Enide, after her favorite romance, one that she never lost a chance to hear recited. The demoiselle was entranced with her two puppies, and was always with one or the other, chattering to her charge, instructing it in serious tones, and leading it about by a thin silver chain; one end was fastened to the dog's collar and the other terminated in a leather strip, which the girl wound about her delicate fist. Today it was Erec who was her escort, Erec and a large woman named Brangwayn, a nurse or handmaid of some sort.

Now Eloise came in and sat with Brangwayn at her side table, snubbing Erec's chain about one of the heavy table legs. A serving-woman brought her a small silver goblet, and another woman set before the little maid a tureen of herbed goose in a sauce of pear and grapes and garlic. Immediately she plucked forth a morsel of goose and held it beneath the table, where Erec made it vanish.

The main table awaited Sir Tarquin. Molly and her little troupe played a succession of quiet tunes; the knights and ladies drank wine and sampled small pastries; the time drew on. At last the Sieur de Duncarlin and his wife, Lady Rohese, were announced, as were five of his household knights. Sir Odinell started a bit to hear Sir Gilles announced, one of the knights who had left his service for that of Sir Tarquin, but he said nothing.

The music ceased for a moment, and Hob sat, symphonia on his lap, head turned, afire with curiosity. Down the central aisle came Sir Tarquin, and by his side, holding her right hand supported on his left hand's upturned palm, Lady Rohese. Hob saw a tall, broad-shouldered man, stern-featured, with a certain pallid smoothness to his skin. Against this complexion his burning black eyes stood out. They were set somewhat close together, but not so much that it was unpleasant; his hair was a sleek dark pelt worn in the Norman style.

Sir Tarquin strode up the aisle, exuding a certain—not *joie de vivre,* perhaps, but—power, vigor, a gliding athletic gait. This last reminded Hob of . . . what was it? Yes, yes, he had it: when a small boy, he had once seen, in Father Athelstan's tiny larder, a snake, perhaps hunting mice, sliding in slow curves among the jars and sacks, silent, muscular, smooth as oil. Plainly Sir Tarquin walked, though he made less sound than might be expected, yet there was something of that serpent's glide about his movements.

Beside him: Lady Rohese, a woman of smoldering beauty, a woman neither young nor much past youth, dark-haired, dark-eyed. Hob had just begun to think how beautiful she was when she looked at Molly's table, and he thought to see an expression of the sourest evil, covered over with an attempt at neutral cordiality—an effect as of powdered sugar on a dish of spoiled meat. The sight was profoundly disorienting, a sensation of being pulled in two directions at once, and he began to understand Sir Odinell's odd reaction to her, and to understand as well the knight's difficulty in expressing it.

The knights followed, pacing slowly, almost somberly.

Hob thought them formidable men at first glance; but then he saw that they moved as men wading through thigh-deep water, slowly, ponderously. Their expressions were inward, as though in deep thought, or in waking dream.

As Sir Tarquin and his wife mounted the dais, the young dog Erec emerged from beneath the table, his long flexible tongue swiping goose grease from his nose. This would have been a droll sight but for the dog's aspect: his eyes were fixed upon Sir Tarquin, his lips drew back from what were still mostly puppy teeth, his ears flattened, and a low rumbling groan came from deep in his chest. He stalked stiff-legged to the end of his chain, and followed the Sieur de Duncarlin's every movement, his stance expressive of the greatest hostility.

Brangwayn said something to her young charge, and Mistress Eloise pulled Erec to her side, and pushed his hindquarters down till he sat, and offered him a bit of goose, but the dog for once was not interested, and when she held the meat beneath his nose, he averted his muzzle, and looked off to the side, indicating refusal.

Pages swarmed about the newcomers, seating them in order of precedence, Sir Tarquin at Sir Odinell's right hand, Lady Rohese at Lady Maysaunt's left; the pages dispersed the five knights who had come with Sir Tarquin throughout the rest of the company at table. Hob was keenly interested in these men, for he too had recognized Sir Gilles's name, and knew him for one of the two knights that Sir Odinell had dismissed. And it was immediately apparent that there was something very disconcerting about them. They were grave but vacant; they nodded slowly and responded slowly when spoken to, and while they evidently could speak—Hob could not hear the conversation from where they sat—it was also evident that their seatmates were struggling to make conversation.

It was not so with Sir Tarquin. His voice was rich and strong, a mellow supple baritone, and it rose above the hum of conversation. Indeed he dominated the table, commenting, discussing—at one point it seemed to Hob that the talk was of wine, at another point it was Chrétien de Troyes, perhaps in regard to Erec and Enide, words coming to Hob's ears in gusts and then sinking into the general sound, for there were many at the high table and many more in the hall. The Sieur de Duncarlin had a hearty laugh, and essayed some humor of his own, for at two or three points several of Chantemerle's knights and dames laughed at things he said, but Sir Odinell had throughout the evening a guarded expression, and as time went on it seemed that Sir Tarquin made people more and more uncomfortable.

While they waited to play, Nemain drew a handkerchief from her sleeve, wiped her brow daintily with it, and then contrived to drop it. Hob bent to retrieve it, one hand on the symphonia to steady it. Nemain bent to take the handkerchief from him, and while they were leaning toward each other, she said, barely moving her lips, "Watch him eat."

There was a great deal of natural noise—so many people talking, eating, serving, moving about, laughing—yet as low as Nemain had spoken, Lady Rohese suddenly looked over at their table, and Hob felt immediately that Nemain had been heard, although that seemed impossible. After a long moment, the woman looked away, but she had made Hob very uneasy.

He watched Sir Tarquin closely for a while, flicking glances at Lady Rohese from time to time to make sure she was not observing *him*. Sir Tarquin was animated, forceful, witty, and talking, talking constantly. But he was not eating very much. It was not that he ate nothing: Hob saw him put food in his mouth, chew, swallow; but there was very little being consumed. He moved his food on his trencher; he cut meat; he signaled that he was through with this or that dish, most often when he was making some emphatic point—a hand outstretched, a finger raised in the air, and the like. The page would come and remove the dish while everyone paid attention to Sir Tarquin's latest quip or statement.

Lady Rohese said almost nothing, but she observed everyone in turn, almost to the point of rudeness; she ate more than her husband, but not a great deal more; and whenever he reached one of his crescendos, that was when she would signal for a dish to be taken away.

As Sir Tarquin spoke, and gestured, and continued with a kind of sham dining, Hob noticed that there was a sinuous ease to the knight's movements that at first seemed graceful, but soon became disquieting, in ways that would be hard to articulate, but that he felt deep in his flesh. The knight's arm, when he reached for the goblet of wine that he touched to his lips—but did he swallow?—had an anguine curve that for a moment did not seem to match the underlying structures of human bone.

Sir Odinell also reached for his wine cup, and often, and there was no doubt that *he* swallowed, his throat working strongly: he seemed very ill at ease, and at last he remembered Molly, and asked that they play for the company. As they had at the inn, they struck up a pair of lively dance tunes, and then Hob and Jack stilled the symphonia and the drum, and the two women addressed their harps. Hob placed the symphonia gently on the rushes beside him, and when he straightened he found Lady Rohese's eyes, magnificent and horrid, fixed upon him. He felt the flesh of his face go stiff and cold; the look in those eyes was so hostile that it was like being bathed in venom. What did she know about them, or was this just the face she presented to all the world? He could not think where to look, but at that moment the women began to play, and he fixed his eyes on Nemain's fingers.

As was so often the case, when the harps began to play, the hall grew more quiet, and when the women began to sing, the hall became silent. Hob let the song, with its complex two-harp underpinnings and the Irish knotwork of Molly's alto, Nemain's soprano, speak to him of the beauty that is in the world, the good that runs like a half-hidden seam of gold through the ore of existence. He took a deep breath.

Then he dared a glance at the high table. He did not notice whether Lady Rohese was staring or not, because he encountered the gaze of Sir Tarquin, which rendered the hostility of his wife's glare almost bland by comparison. He kept his face neutral, but his black eyes held an ophidian glitter, and they were fixed on Molly with a bitter malevolent rapacity. Hob glanced at Molly to see what Sir Tarquin saw. Just then Molly raised her head; she turned her large and comely eyes, blue as the sky echoed in lakewater, to the Sieur de Duncarlin's face and looked at him with the utmost calm, still singing, as though she were gazing at a quiet garden on a summer afternoon: an astonishing display of self-control in the face of thrice-distilled malice.

Then she bent again, unhurriedly, to her harp, and she and Nemain finished the song, the harps ending on a minor chord, the notes lingering for an instant, returned to the ear by the plaster walls. There was a moment while everyone sat quietly, attention turned inward. Then there was acclamation, from high table and low. Even Sir Tarquin feigned enthusiasm. Only Lady Rohese and the five spectral knights of Duncarlin sat silent, she gnawing very slightly at her lower lip, and they gazing distractedly out over the lower hall.

Sir Odinell made a signal to Molly, and she led the group in quiet unobtrusive music thereafter. They had been shown to Sir Tarquin and, more important, had seen the Sieur de

Duncarlin and his wife, and so the troupe's pretext for being there had been established, and the less attention paid to them from now on, the better.

And indeed it was not long before Sir Tarquin, with suave politeness and self-deprecating humor, indicated that they would have to return to his stronghold. After the necessary pro forma protests from Sir Odinell—they had not yet come to the sweets, and the bakers had prepared swans and ships of hardened sugar, and so forth—there was acceptance, with apparent reluctance, from the Sieur de Chantemerle, and Sir Tarquin said his farewells in his musical baritone, and Lady Rohese nodded a curt, indeed barely civil, agreement.

Sir Tarquin stood, giving his hand to his wife; she took it and got up, and his knights rose in a cloud about them. Sir Tarquin now made his way slowly along the long table, so to round the end. As he went he had a word or a jest for each knight or dame that he passed; as he walked he took his riding gauntlets from his belt, and drew them on.

The knights drifted after Lady Rohese. Not a word had Sir Gilles said to Sir Odinell or any of his former comrades. Five strongly made men, moving with sureness and purpose, and yet they made Hob think of a mist, a fog—something vague-bordered and insubstantial. He wondered at it: they seemed solid enough, but their expressions, their gestures, were such that it seemed they were in a dream, and he peering in at them from outside that dream.

Sir Tarquin stepped from the dais and began to walk down the aisle. Erec, who had been lying flat but tense, his hindquarters bunched beneath him on the floor, his eyes and ears fixed on Sir Tarquin, suddenly exploded into motion with a roar, teeth flashing, lunging to the limit of his chain, which was snubbed about the heavy table leg. Mistress Eloise cried out to him in a shocked voice.

Sir Tarquin, agile and sinuous as a serpent, swerved just out of the young dog's reach, the sudden movement toward Hob's side of the room necessitating a supple sidestep against a tall-backed bench that stood nearby, a gauntleted hand thrown out to preserve his balance. There was a small silver disk on the gauntlet's cuff, there to fasten a wrist thong against the winter winds; Hob just caught the flicker of the button, scraped off against the bench-back's edge, as it tumbled winking down among the rushes on the floor.

Hob had had a moment when the sudden eruption of sound disoriented him; he had caught a whiff of vile corruption, and now he looked to the floor—had the dog scrabbled up a dead mouse from the rushes as he launched himself at the Sieur de Duncarlin? But there was nothing—where the rushes had been disturbed by the dog's claws, the floor seemed clean and dry—and now Mistress Eloise was reeling the dog back by his chain.

Sir Tarquin recovered his balance smoothly and stood, nodded to Sir Odinell and Lady Maysaunt again, and stalked out. Erec never took his eyes from Sir Tarquin's back, while

Mistress Eloise, her arms about the dog's neck, spoke in his ear: soothing, meaningless phrases.

Lady Rohese followed her husband, smiled at Mistress Eloise, and, without pausing, stooped as she passed Erec, spat in the dog's face, and continued down the hall, trailed by the five odd knights. The young dog sneezed.

Sir Odinell looked at Molly with an expression that said plainly: *You see how strange they are.* Molly said nothing; her manner was thoughtful. She kept watch on the departing group as they made their way toward the archway that led out to the stairwell. Mistress Eloise had quieted the dog, except for an occasional sneeze. When the party had left the hall, and they could hear them on the stair, Molly turned back to the knight.

"Be said by me," she began, and then there was a racking, rasping cough, and a loud wheezing breath: Erec was standing square on his feet, looking at nothing, his eyes wide and his breathing choking off to silence as they watched. The dog took a step and collapsed onto his side, his legs twitching.

"*Father!*" cried Mistress Eloise in a horrified urgent voice, and Sir Odinell rose, uncertain.

"Nay," said Molly, "I'm not having it! I'm not having it!" and she sprang from her chair and knelt by Erec's side. Nemain came around the table in a flash, rooting frantically in a pair of pouches at her side. Molly picked up the wolfish head and, closing the mouth, blew strongly into the dog's nostrils. Nemain gave her a little vial, and Molly pulled the stopper with her teeth, put a thumb to the dog's lip and pulled it away, and poured a small line of golden-brown powder in the lip's inner crease, then closed the animal's mouth. She spat out the stopper and Nemain deftly snatched it from the air. Molly handed the vial to Nemain, and began to blow into the dog's nostrils again. In between she muttered a rhythmic phrase in Irish, to which Nemain gave a repeated antiphon; all the while Molly massaged Erec's lower jaw while keeping his mouth closed.

The women's call-and-response murmurs were barely audible to Hob where he, with others, bent over the small group on the floor. The dog gave a great snort and shuddered; in a moment he began to breathe on his own, with a deal of difficulty at first, but with increasing ease. His tongue explored his mouth, and he smacked his lips, and gulped, again and again: gradually he swallowed all Molly's powder.

Mistress Eloise, crying quietly but furiously, stroked Erec's side, and after a fair amount of time, Erec's tail began to thump sideways upon the rushes. Folk stood up, exhaled, stretched. Molly sat back on her haunches.

"That vile *cailleach*," she said in a low voice.

Hob, watching with the others, was standing just behind Sir Odinell and Lady Maysaunt. She was gripping his arm with both hands, still caught up in the shock of the event. Sir Odinell bent his head toward his wife and said, just loud enough for Hob to hear, "I see . . . I begin to see it, now; Jehan has not failed me. Strange fevers require strange physic."

Suddenly Hob remembered the button, flashing silver as it fell to the rush-strewn floor. Folk were dispersing; Sir Odinell was telling off two servants to help Mistress Eloise with the dog, now scrambling to his feet, a bit dazed, but with wagging tail. Hob turned about. He had been sitting . . . there. And when Sir Tarquin was leaving, he struck against the bench over there. . . . Hob quietly walked over, held to the bench-back with one hand, and moved the rushes aside with his foot.

There was nothing to be seen but the wide bare planks of the hall floor. Discreetly he began a search, probing with the toe of his shoe, moving small patches of rush stalks and the dried wildflowers sprent in with them. Hob saw tansy, lavender, lady-of-the-meadow, and what might be cowslips—all these were to control vermin and to impart a pleasant scent. He uncovered a bone from a chicken or other bird, some cat droppings—the floor had not been swept and fresh rushes laid in a fortnight or more. Hob considered, with perhaps some partisan feeling, how much more efficiently Sir Jehan's hall was maintained.

He looked about; no one was paying attention. He began to widen his search, a hand's-breadth to this side, a hand's-breadth to that, and yet there was noth— There! Brightness was just perceptible beneath some of the long tubular stems of the rushes. He crouched swiftly, and, still crouching, retrieved the button, brushed it off, and dropped it into his pouch. He put a hand to the bench-back, about to stand up, and froze.

The table's far side was almost against the wall and, hunkered down as he was, he could see beneath the table and the benches on that side to the wall beyond. He was looking at a large rat. Rats were not uncommon in castles—the cats and terriers allowed to roam the keep held them at bay and kept them from becoming a nuisance, but they would get in occasionally. What was unusual about this rat was its size, and its imperturbability. It regarded Hob with a steady, unfriendly gaze, and by some trick of the shadow beneath the table, its eyeballs seemed to have a bluish luster. A cat was nearby, but it was flat to the floor, its ears back.

After a long moment when Hob and the odd creature stared at each other, the rat calmly turned, walked a short distance, hugging the wall, and paused. It looked at Hob one more time, as if memorizing his features, and then squeezed into a small opening at the base of the wall. The cat's ears came up; it backed away a few steps, and then turned and ran. Hob stood up, wondering at the uncanny encounter, and the unpleasant impression it had left on him.

CHAPTER 15

LATER THAT EVENING, IN THE solar Sir Odinell had assigned to Molly's party, Hob seized the first opportunity to speak with her privately, and to give her the button.

"Mistress," said Hob, "that knight—Sir Tarquin—he dropped this, and I thought . . ."

Molly's eyes lit up, and she reached for the silver disk. Hob dropped it into her palm.

"*Sah!*" Molly cried, a meaningless exclamation of shock, and dropped the button as though it were white-hot. She drew a little ivory box from her pouch. Hob could just see that the box's surface was carved with a decorative knotwork pattern. Molly slid the cover off partway with her thumb, then bent down and gingerly retrieved the button; quickly she dropped it into the box.

"It's a grand evil he has to him," she said. "I'm just after feeling it in that button, that was on his person, and it stinging me like a wasp, the wide deep evil of it."

Hob looked at the box in wonder. "I felt nothing, Mistress."

She patted his shoulder. "A blind man is spared horrific sights, a deaf man hideous noises. It's a man of your hands that you are, and not a man of the Art. You to learn your weapons, and Nemain to protect you from all else, those things that come from the shadows; you'll raise up a clan of little ones, great as the Uí Néill, and they safe between the two of you."

Hob felt himself, all unwillingly, beginning to blush.

He said, partly to change the subject, "I saw Lady Rohese looking at us, Mistress. It was not a pleasant look, and I saw Sir Tarquin looking at you, and it was worse."

"It's an ill look to her, and no mistake," said Molly. "As for himself, he is evil to his bones, and they are partners in evil. But this," she said, hefting the box, "it's a weapon against him, and you've done well this night."

She said this with such heartfelt sentiment that Hob looked down in embarrassment. For a moment he was looking at the rushes, and this brought back the memory of his search for the button, and this led to—

"Mistress," he said. "I saw something else: when I stooped to take the button, I saw a rat beneath the table."

"A castle like this—" began Molly.

"I beg your pardon, Mistress," said Hob, "it was not that it was a rat, but a strange rat, very large, that looked at me with a . . . look."

"Looked at you with a look . . . ?"

Hob grimaced in frustration. "It looked at me as, as though it were a person, as if it could *see* me, if you understand. As if it *understood* matters, and, and—the cat was afraid of it, and it had blue eyes. Not blue eyes, Mistress, such as your own, but a bit of a blue shine to them. I can't say it properly. But the cat was afraid of it, and it did not act as such vermin act, and it—it was strange."

But Molly was paying attention to him now, and her face grew more and more grave, and finally she sighed.

"'Tis clear enough you are, lad; I'm thinking that I know what you've seen, and 'tis some sort of familiar, and who would it belong to if not that evil *gesadóir,* that enchanter. 'Tis some kind of watcher he's left here; it may have come in with his party, and 'tis our tongues we'll need to watch. This matter we're about, 'tis more fey and more dangerous the more we see of it."

She put the box carefully into her pouch; she put her arm

around his shoulder. "On the day after the morrow we're away, and 'tis easier we'll breathe outside these walls, and they haunted by who knows what creatures."

IN THE MORNING Molly and her troupe met with Sir Odinell.

"Take care in what you say," said Molly, "for this *do-dhuine* and his wife may have left spies behind."

"Spies? But where would spies hide?" asked Sir Odinell, confident in his defenses, his well-trained knights and guards.

Molly told him about the rat; with some difficulty he accepted it, although with some bemusement.

"Speak out of doors, or on the battlements—where it is open, and speech difficult to overhear. We'll be going through your castle, and mayhap we can find some of these vermin, and remove them, for they're a great danger to you. Even if we miss some, I will rid you of Sir Tarquin, and then this creature will have no power, but for now, guard every word."

She thought a moment. "Give us your best ratter for today, and we'll be using it to flush out our rat spies before we leave."

"A ratter," said Sir Odinell, in the distracted voice of one in a small boat on a downrushing stream, seeing the rocks slip swiftly past, and uncertain what might lie around the next bend. He raised his voice. "Jacques!"

The door opened and a man-at-arms appeared. "My lord?"

"Send for the groom Herluin and have him bring us a good ratter. Quickly, now!"

"My lord." Jacques bowed himself out, and they heard him clattering on the stair.

CHAPTER 16

A SHORT WHILE LATER, THERE was a knock on the door of the solar.

"Enter," said Sir Odinell.

The groom Herluin entered, a small fell-terrier bitch under one arm. She was about fifteen pounds, stiff-haired, otter-faced. Her bottom left fang had grown askew, coming up outside her upper lip, which gave her a wild-boar expression of ferocity, somewhat at odds with her diminutive size.

He touched his forehead to the Sieur de Chantemerle. "My lord."

"This is our best ratter?" asked Sir Odinell.

"But yes, my lord. Sweetlove lives to find and kill

rats. She's a mort of trouble, but well worth it. Is it that you wish us to hunt these rooms?"

Sir Odinell looked a question at Molly.

"We will take her with us, and scour the castle from the deep cellars to the parapets," said Molly.

At this the groom looked unhappy, and shuffled his feet.

"What is troubling you, man?" said Sir Odinell.

"If it please you, my lord, our Sweetlove can be a bit . . . difficult. She's small, but sometimes I believe her to be part wolf. Even Luc and I—and we her keepers since she was born—have been bitten. We named her before she was a day on live, and did not know how she would grow. Were she not such a nonpareil at ratting, Luc says, he would have had her drowned long since."

"Let her down, lad," said Molly pleasantly to Herluin, who was thirty if he was a day.

Herluin looked at Sir Odinell, who nodded.

Herluin did not shrug, but his shoulders twitched, and he bent and let the little dog slip from his opened hands, somehow managing thereby to convey a Pilate-like hand-washing.

In the moment it took her to fall the few inches from his grasp to the rush-strewn floor, Sweetlove twisted in midair with a yelp and snapped at Herluin's hands.

The groom snatched his hands high, muttering a barely audible "Fuck!" under his breath, slowly straightening.

"Sit down," said Molly quietly, looking the dog in the

face. After a moment's hesitation, the terrier folded her hind legs and sat down, stiffly. She looked up at Molly expectantly, but after a moment, became restless, and began to look past Molly. She squirmed, and whined a bit.

"What ails her, man?" demanded the Sieur de Chantemerle of his groom.

Herluin shrugged. "Nay, my lord, I know not. She is an odd one, and has always been headstrong; sometimes defiant."

Molly put her hand down toward the dog, palm up. Sweetlove came to her feet and approached in a crouch, tail wagging, ears down. She gave Molly's hand a lick, then darted around Molly and leaped into Jack's lap, where she settled with a sigh.

"Christ sitting above us," muttered Herluin.

Jack placed a large hand on Sweetlove's back, almost covering the little dog. She wriggled with pleasure, then stretched out along his thigh like a marten along a tree limb, and sighed ostentatiously.

"Sure, and it's a new friend you've found," said Molly, grinning. "If Master Herluin will be our guide, we'll start low and work up through Chantemerle."

"As you will," said Sir Odinell. "Herluin . . ."

"My lord," said the groom, and held the door for Molly and the others. Jack scooped the terrier up with one hand, and the company made for the turret stairs.

They descended first to the deep cellars, below the

blind first floor. Entrance to the keep was at second-storey level, and below that was a windowless first floor, a storehouse. Below that were cellar rooms where were kept the rolls, the rolled-up parchments that recorded the legal records of the castle, the tax records of its tenants, and other documents of importance. Other rooms held items not needed every day: spare lumber, iron ingots for the forge, and so forth.

Molly and her troupe, Jack with the dog under one arm, followed Herluin and the page Guiscard down a steep crude wooden stair. Herluin held a cudgel, Guiscard a torch. The page had been supplied with keys to various doors normally kept locked, and now they proceeded along dank stone walls to a stout oaken door. The passage ran away into shadow before them. Guiscard bent to the lock, handing the torch to Herluin, who angled it to illumine the work. After two false starts, Guiscard found the correct key; the lock clanked open; the door opened with a groan.

They stepped into a wide shallow room lined with cases and cases filled with pigeonholes; from almost all protruded rolls of parchment. A table with an inkpot and a sheaf of quills stood along one wall. Guiscard retrieved his torch, and went about the walls lighting oil lamps, and soon the room was much brighter, although darkness lingered in the corners.

Jack put Sweetlove down—she did not snap at him as she had at Herluin—and the little dog immediately made a circuit of the room, nose to the ground. She stopped now and then, looking at what to Hob appeared to be blank wall, her ears erect and one forepaw lifted, listening, listening.

Suddenly she darted at the wall, scrabbling at it with her forepaws, the claws scraping against the stonework. There was a scuttling behind the nearest manuscript case and Sweetlove immediately abandoned the wall and galloped down the front of the case, skidding into a turn, darting into the space between this case and the next, all the way back to the base of the wall. There was a small shriek, and she backed out with a rat in her jaws, shaking it furiously. A moment later the rat was dead, its spine snapped, and she dropped it at Jack's feet and looked up, wagging.

Herluin shook out a coarse-woven sack, and clucked his tongue at the little dog. "Bring it here, Sweetlove," he said. The terrier looked at him a moment as though trying to recall him, her tail drooping, then looked back to Jack; she began to wag again. Jack held out his hand for the sack, and the groom deposited it in his grasp. Jack bent, seized the rat's tail, and dropped it into the bag.

Sweetlove turned at once and paced around the room, nose to ground, stopping to listen. Snuffling at crevices and gaps in the cases, and in one instance peering into one of the lower pigeonholes, she started two more rats; one she ran down, seizing it by the neck, shaking it till it went limp. The other ran by Herluin, who swung his cudgel once, and then again, clubbing it to death.

Sweetlove trotted around the room a few times, then sat down in the middle and looked at Jack expectantly. "There's no more in this room," said Herluin. "That's her signal that she's done here."

Out into the passageway again, Guiscard locking up behind them, and into a storeroom of some sort. Here were sawn planks, sacks of lime, a pyramid of stacked iron bars for the castle smithy, and piles of stones for ammunition—small ones for throwing, large ones for the catapults. All these irregular stores afforded many bolt-holes and secluded spaces for a mother rat's nest.

Jack set Sweetlove down in the middle of the room. The terrier's ears went up at once, and she dashed into a murky corner. A squeak, and she backed out with another corpse; Herluin darted forward and struck into the shadows with his cudgel, producing another victim. This went on until Jack had another eight or nine dead in his sack.

Sweetlove worked her way between two stacks of planks. A moment later she backed out rapidly. She was snarling, but her ears were down and her tail partly tucked; her head was lowered and her back hunched. From the narrow alley between the two stacks of wood, two rats, very large, prowled forth slowly, with an unratlike air of physical menace, pacing like hunting wolves.

"Mistress!" cried Hob. "Their eyes! It's what I saw!"

And indeed their eyes, dark as any ordinary rat's, would, as they turned their heads this way and that as though questing, catch the light and show a bluish sheen, almost a glow. Sweetlove retreated as they advanced, matching step for step. Suddenly she whirled and ran behind Jack's legs, whence she peered out at the sinister rodents.

"Now she's turned white-liver!" said Herluin, exasperated. He paced toward the rats, cudgel held high.

The rats, so far from fleeing, separated and circled his legs. One sprang at his right calf, drawing blood from the muscle, and the other curled around his left foot and bit neatly through the tendon that ran up from his heel. Herluin bellowed with pain; his left foot was no longer willing to support him, and he went down like a sapling gnawed through by beavers, and crashed to the stone floor. The rats ran up his chest toward his throat. A moment later two silvery wheels spun through the air: Molly and Nemain had each thrown a dagger, and each found its mark. The rats were knocked off Herluin, dead or dying, impaled. A moment later they were still, and the women retrieved their daggers and wiped them clean.

Molly knelt by Herluin, who was groaning in agony, and tore a strip from her hem to bind his ankle. She took the torch from Guiscard and sent him for men to carry Herluin to safety.

Then she put a hand to each of the dead rats. She looked up at Nemain. "There's still a wee tingle of that *gesadóir*'s spell to them. There is to them the same . . . *flavor* . . . of evil as there is in that button Hob's after finding. Feel."

Nemain put her hand to a rat's side, and her face took on the blind look of someone listening intently. After a moment she nodded. "I have it," she said.

Four sturdy men-at-arms clattered down the wooden stairs; a moment later they entered the storeroom. Herluin was gathered up, groaning softly, and borne up the stairs again.

The troupe followed Herluin and his bearers up the second flight to the great hall, and thence to a niche in the wall where a cot awaited. Curtains were drawn across the opening, and Molly sent Nemain for herbs and powders and linen bandages from the wagons. Soon Herluin was treated and bandaged, and given a half cup of one of Molly's sleep-inducing and pain-quelling potions.

Molly was rinsing her hands in a bowl held by the page Guiscard when Sir Odinell came in. After a brief inspection of Herluin, the Sieur de Chantemerle drew Molly outside for a report.

"'Tis worse each time I peer at it," said Molly. "I'll be needing some archers from you, and we'll have to be scouring the castle and that swiftly, swiftly, for these watchers that Sir Tarquin has set on you will be reporting to him what you know of them, and so will he be forewarned."

Sir Odinell stood a moment, his mouth tight with disappointment; then he turned and began bawling orders. In short order a squad of six archers had appeared, leather handguards in place and quivers slung to their backs, carrying their unstrung lug bows. Their leader was a fellow named Godfrey, a lean gray-eyed man with lank blond hair.

Down the steep wooden stairway—almost a broad-tread ladder—they trooped again, Guiscard with the torch, Jack with the terrier under his left arm and poor Herluin's cudgel in his brawny right hand. They swept through the rolls room again, just in case one of the rat spies had returned there, then on to the storeroom where the battle had taken place.

Molly and Nemain circled the room, and so did Sweet-love. The women and the dog could detect no evidence of rats, haunted or otherwise. Guiscard led them out again, locked the storeroom, and took them to another, larger room that occupied the whole back half of the keep. Hob held the torch while Guiscard struggled again with the lock, and then they were in the large, echoing space, where tools of various types were stored, including a wall against which a score or so of spare wagon wheels leaned. Sweetlove began to growl the moment her feet touched the floor, and she faced the northeast corner, where shadows were deepest. Hob employed himself in lighting some of the oil lamps in brackets around the walls. Molly arranged the archers in a slant line facing the corner, so that no one was in their line of fire. The men bent the six-foot Welsh longbows against the stone floor, leaning on them and pulling the bowstrings taut to the upper limbs so to nock them securely. Each archer drew an arrow from his quiver and fitted it to the string. They set their feet and looked to Molly for orders.

Molly and Nemain walked close to the corner; they half closed their eyes and became still. Then they looked at each other and shook their heads: Nothing, or at least nothing redolent of witchcraft.

The terrier charged into the corner, and there was squeaking and the occasional shriek, and scuffling that went on for a long time, and then she came out with a corpse in her mouth, that of a quite ordinary rat, and dropped it at Jack's feet, and went back into darkness and came out with another rat, and so on, like a mother cat transporting kittens. She brought out six killed rats, and then sat on her haunches, looking quite pleased with herself.

The women had completed a circuit of the walls, and detected nothing, and Sweetlove herself lay down at Jack's feet and seemed about to doze off.

"Away on," said Molly, and they trooped out again and upstairs to the first level.

Here were the more readily accessed storerooms: grains, dried apples, and the like. Molly immediately turned toward the south wall—the usual sacks and boxes cast shadows against the plaster, and the spaces between them were like small dark alleys.

Sweetlove approached one of these alleys. On one side was a barrel, as high as Jack's head. On the other were three wooden boxes, stacked atop one another. The little terrier growled into the shadows, but would not enter the alley. She sat down and looked around at Jack.

"Jack," said Molly, "would you ever clear us a space to see?"

The silent man handed his cudgel to Hob and stepped forward, careful not to come between the archers and the dark cleft between the boxes and the barrel. He seized the bottom box, and with a powerful wrench pulled it away from the barrel. Deep in the gloom near the wall, Hob could see faint blue gleams, perhaps twelve or fourteen. Hard to tell: the rats were shifting about restlessly.

Suddenly a wave of the very big rats, with glaucous eyes and lips drawn back from shining ridges of teeth, came boiling out of the darkness. One turned left and leaped, knee-high, at Jack. An eyeblink later Molly's dagger pinned it against the side of the box her man stood near. The rest fanned out. There was an almost simultaneous humming snap of a half-dozen bowstrings. Four of the rats were impaled by arrows and another by Nemain's hurled dagger. Two arrows thudded uselessly into the barrel, and the fastest archer managed to nock another arrow and kill yet another rat.

The remaining one came straight at Hob. Its speed was disconcerting, and it jinked and feinted at the last moment, for all the world as though it had planned the maneuver—another sign of more intelligence than was natural in such a rodent. Even as the lad swung at it, it curved toward his ankle and he was forced to skip aside; the white fangs flashed and closed with a tiny but perceptible *click*. Hob swung, but he had been thrown off balance enough that his cudgel dealt only a glancing blow. The rodent skidded a foot or two, but was stunned enough by the stroke that Hob was able to leap forward and strike again, and then once more, and then the rat lay still.

Hob looked at the corpse. There was something, even in death, disturbing about its appearance—its size, certainly, but also something about the set of its features suggested a *face*, with its final expression one of anger or hostility, rather than the simple blank beast visage of the rats Sweetlove had killed. The thought of being bitten by this malignant little demon sent a shiver of repugnance through him.

Suddenly both Molly and Nemain whirled toward the door. Molly's hand shot out, pointing, and she cried, "Archers! Out there, now!" Godfrey cried, "With me!" and ran toward the corridor. The archers were a picked group, and spun without hesitation and ran after their squad leader to the doorway, hands plucking arrows from their back-slung quivers even as they went. They were scarcely outside the storeroom when cries of discovery went up. Hob, running full tilt toward the door, could see them already loosing arrows in the direction of the stairs. When he skidded into the corridor, he could see one of the large rats dead near the foot of the stairs and another actually pinned to a riser.

Molly and the rest came out, and Godfrey said, touching his forehead, "There's one on 'em as made it up yon stairs, Mistress. Maybe two."

"Up you go after them, lad," said Molly. "We're right behind you." She turned to Nemain. "Go with them, *a rún,* and help them find those vile things. Hob, Jack, stay with me a bit."

Nemain set off, and Molly quickly swept through the rest of the first level, the terrier questing into corners and Molly turning slowly in the center of each room, seeking the traces of Sir Tarquin's sorcery. As she tried to explain to Hob later, "'Tis like the scent one of these high-born ladies, that perfume themselves, leaves behind when she goes out of a room: 'tis faint, but 'tis there, and it's telling you who was in that room."

Sweetlove started and killed two more rats, but that was all, and Molly led them all up swiftly to the second floor, where was the great hall. Here Nemain had completed a sweep of the walls, and was walking up and down the center of the room. She looked at Molly and shook her head.

Molly in turn walked about the large room, but could detect no trace of the "scent" of Sir Tarquin's wizardry. Jack put Sweetlove down, and the little dog ran about the walls, eventually flushing out a pair of very ordinary rats, both of which she killed.

So it went through the rest of the very large keep, a search that consumed most of the day. At last they were on a landing at the top of winding stairs, the archers, bows slung to their backs, strung out on the first dozen steps below them. A heavy oaken door, banded with iron hinges, led to one of the tower rooftops, but this was bolted shut, and they were about to descend again, when Hob said, "Mistress!"

He pointed to the lower corner of the door, where a small bit of daylight showed. He stooped and looked closer. The corner had been gnawed just enough to allow a rodent in or out. Godfrey threw the bolts and they trooped out onto the roof of the tower. There was nothing: a flagpole from which Sir Odinell's banner flew when he was in residence; tar-covered wooden bins with spare arrows and bowstrings; jars of oil to be heated and poured on attackers; stones, large and small, to be hurled or dropped. Otherwise, the space was bare. They were about to reenter the tower doorway when Molly stopped, cocked her head as though listening, and then turned to Nemain with a questioning look. Nemain said, "No." Then, a moment later, "It may be. I cannot tell." Molly said to the small party of men, Hob and Jack included, "I'm feeling a sense of those cursed rats. They're not here, but they *were* here, or so it feels to me."

Godfrey told off men to search the bins, but in vain. He himself stood in the middle of the tower rooftop and turned slowly in place. All at once he ran to the parapet on the outer side of the tower and sprang up into the crenel, the space between two merlons. He put a hand on each merlon and leaned perilously over. He turned and called, "Dickon! Steady me by my belt!" even as he slipped the strung bow from his back and reached for an arrow.

Dickon was the burliest of the archers, and ran to seize

the back of Godfrey's belt. He braced a foot against the inner edge of the crenel, while Godfrey leaned out, holding his bow horizontally across his thighs, and from this awkward position nocked an arrow to the string and drew it back up toward his face.

Hob stepped into the next crenel and, holding fast to the adjacent merlon, leaned out cautiously, and looked down the dizzying expanse of rough stone wall, to the rock of the headland Castle Chantemerle stood on. Halfway down the tower, two rats, head down, were creeping groundward, claws gripping irregularities in the surface of the stone blocks that composed the tower wall.

Godfrey loosed an arrow at the rats. It struck near them—the steel arrowhead sparked against the rough rock surface—and skittered away earthward. The head archer drew and loosed again. This time he pierced one of his targets; the rat was plucked off the tower and fell, missing the edge of the headland and tumbling, tumbling all the way to the sea that surged about the feet of Chantemerle.

Godfrey sped three more shafts downward with astonishing rapidity, but the final rat had reached the bottom of the castle wall, scampered to the headland's edge, and disappeared over it. A few breaths later, Hob thought he saw movement at the water's edge, a dark form scuttling up the sandy foreshore and vanishing into a clump of marram grass, heading southward. South, where lay Sir Tarquin's castle.

"Sure, and he'll be reporting to that wretched *draíodóir*," Molly said. She clapped Godfrey on the shoulder. "Well done, though, lad," she said. "It's a fine day's work you've done." She stepped down from the crenel. "Well, it's time to tell Sir Odinell that he'll be the talk of Sir Tarquin's supper table tonight."

CHAPTER 17

THE SHUTTERS WERE LATCHED back in this tower room, and the warm breeze brought with it the salt scent of the German Sea, the iodine scent of the seaweed drying on the sandy beaches north and south of the headland on which stood Castle Chantemerle. Hob could just hear the swash of the breakers far below, the mewing of the cloud of gulls that haunted the castle middens.

Molly and her family sat at a table with Sir Odinell and Daniel Clerk. Molly was reporting on the state of Sir Tarquin's spies. "'Tis fairly certain I am that there are no more of these unnatural things within these walls, and your little friend there"—she gestured toward Sweetlove, now asleep in a curl between Jack's feet—"has cleansed a mort of ordinary vermin as well from your rooms. But there's one that has escaped us, and that one last seen heading south, and it's sure to be reporting on us in some way."

"Christ save us," muttered Sir Odinell.

"'Tis of no great moment," said Molly. "It's yourself who was telling us that 'twas not till Daniel mentioned that we were to play within your hall that Sir Tarquin accepted your invitation. I'm fearing that I had aroused his suspicion before ever he came, and it's a look of hatred and loathing he gave me, the while I was playing, and my lad here"—she indicated Hob—"telling me that his hag-wife looked on me and on himself the very same way. They're coming here to make sure of us, and, being sure of us as enemies, they're sure of *you* as an enemy, no matter how blithely himself jested at table. And to poison the lassie's dog, and that in front of us all—'twas an act of sudden spite on her part, but also that she felt it time to drop all pretense. 'Tis war between your houses—you cannot avoid it now, nor delay it. 'Tis no longer a matter of should you move against him, or should you wait. He will come for you, and that when you're not expecting him."

"Should I prepare the castle for siege?" asked the knight.

She thought a moment. "Be said by me: you must send for Sir Jehan and Sir Balthasar, and what knights and men-at-arms they can spare, without delay. There is no telling how or when Sir Tarquin will move against us, but 'twill be soon; 'twill be soon enough. It's back to the inn for ourselves:

it may delay the attack if we are seen to leave Chantemerle, and we play now for time, till Sir Jehan and Sir Balthasar can come to us—Balthasar alone is more demon than man, and a great comfort it is to have him fighting on your behalf.

"But the very moment Blanchefontaine arrives, send us Daniel with word of it and we will come to you. As for that *buidseach* and his wife, it's a closer look I'm to have at them, and I cannot do that within the walls of this castle. Nor must you ask me how, but only trust me."

The knight looked at her for a moment, and then said, "I trust you utterly, madam. Between the word of Jehan, and what I saw last night with my daughter's dog, I trust you utterly, nor will I question you in anything you seek to do. I place myself and my people in your hands."

"It's four horses, and they with saddles, that we'll be needing from you, that we may move the more freely, and we may come up to his castle, not to be noticed the while we're having our closer look. I'll be putting watchers on him as well."

"Watchers? Who will you—" He broke off as she put a hand on his arm.

"Is it questions you're asking, and you just after promising the reverse?" she said, but she was smiling. "And if that *gesadóir* has rats to do his bidding, do you think I am friendless among the creatures of the earth?"

"Your pardon, madam, I withdraw all questions," he said, shaking his head at what sounded too near to witchcraft for his liking. But Molly was hard to refuse, or to take offense at, when she smiled.

"Four horses," she said again.

And so it was that when the wagons rolled out through the gatehouse of Chantemerle there were four mounts tied behind, their tack stowed inside the main wagon. Two were fastened to the rear of the large wagon and two behind the small one, with Jack in the midsized wagon coming last and making sure no horse broke loose. Beside Jack on the wagon seat, nose lifted to the new scents outside the castle walls, was Sweetlove. The dog had been haunting Jack's side since the rat hunt, sleeping at the foot of his cot in the solar, and following him downstairs to the hall, and up again to the solar, trotting behind him when Jack's duties took him across the inner ward and out to the wagons for something Molly wanted.

The little dog would have nothing to do with Herluin, hobbling about with his rat-bitten heel tendon bandaged and a yew crutch under one arm, nor with his fellow dog-groom, Luc.

At last Sir Odinell had asked Molly if she would like to take the terrier with her. She looked at Jack, with the dog curled up on the bench next to him. The silent man, seeing her looking, put a very large hand on the dozing terrier. Molly sighed.

"It's after being decided for us, I'm thinking," she said. Jack broke into a grin.

Now the troupe came down the slope from the castle, the brakes being plied constantly, on and off again, and swung in a wide curve to the left, heading south along the coast road. Behind them Chantemerle, with its thicknesses of stone, its complex defenses, its armed men, its safety, dwindled into the distance, and was gone.

CHAPTER 18

SOME MILES BEFORE THEY CAME to the inn Molly had them pull off the road, down into a gentle swale. They proceeded for a short while, then swung around behind a heavy stand of beech trees, the lower branches trailing to the ground, making a kind of veil. Purple heart's-ease, blue forget-me-nots, dotted the grass; dog-rose shrubs climbed outcroppings of rock; and a deep stream ran chuckling through the dip between two hillsides. Here they were in an open space, but protected from sight on three sides by trees and on the fourth by the rise of the land to their west.

They drew the wagons up into a crude semi-circle. The three draft animals and Sir Odinell's four horses were picketed on long tethers where they had access to the brook, and good grazing as well. Jack and Hob went about gathering firewood, and soon they had a rough camp set up. They made a simple meal from cheese and bread packed for them at the castle, and cool water from the stream, Jack feeding Sweetlove—sitting as she always did now, close beside him—morsels of cheese and bread as he ate. After a bit Molly sighed, clapped her hands together once, and came to her feet.

"Let's be about it," she said. "We peering at this vile *do-dhuine,* 'tis like playing in filth, or playing in fire, easy to be smirched or burnt, and the sooner we're at it the sooner we're done."

Jack scooped the terrier up under one arm, opened the back door to the midsized wagon, and deposited her within. She was a well-behaved little dog: when the door shut on her she gave a little whine of protest, but then she could be heard settling with a *thump* against the door, and she was silent thereafter.

Once again the women placed the large black-iron basin in the shadow of the large wagon, on the far side from the fire. The moon lit everything with a deceptive light: things could be seen, but dimly, so one saw while yet struggling to see.

This time the preparations were far simpler, yet the mood was far more grim: Nemain filled the basin at the brook and returned in silence, while Molly went about assembling a few things—a stone, some wool thread, the little ivory box with Sir Tarquin's button inside, and the like— that would be needed for the planned ceremony. She placed them on one side of the iron vessel. When they were ready, she turned to Hob.

"Hob, *a chuisle,* you are to stand near, and gaze into this water, and see what you may see, as Jack and Nemain and I will strain to see what we may. The more there are to see, the more that will be seen. But 'tis a dangerous, dangerous man we're to spy upon: you must say naught"—here she took him by the shoulders, and rocked him back and forth a little for emphasis—"not a word, *nor yet make any sound at all,* no matter what meets your eye. 'Tis death to do so."

He nodded, his eyes wide.

"Say you understand me," she insisted.

"Death if I make a sound," he said, very low.

"Death, and worse," said Molly, and turned away.

She placed Jack to the north of the basin, and Hob to the south. She stood to the west, and Nemain stood to the east, and for a long time the women stood and said nothing, Molly with her eyes closed, Nemain watching Molly's closed eyes.

Molly began a low chant in Irish, and her eyes opened, and Nemain began a counterchant, in some way that Hob could not quite grasp interleaving with Molly's voice, and this went on for what seemed a long time, and then ceased abruptly. Molly stooped and picked up a small skein of pure white lamb's-wool thread and a small flat gray stone with a raven's image scored in its surface. She tied the thread about the stone and carefully placed the stone beside the basin, and paying out more thread around the perimeter, reached across the water to hand the skein to Nemain, who paid it out around the other side of the basin and gave it back to Molly. The older woman bent down and fastened the rest of the thread to the stone.

Now the basin was encircled with an unbroken boundary of white lamb's wool. Hob, to whom Molly's rituals and practices were mysterious, and uncomfortably reminiscent of old Father Athelstan's warnings against impious practices, tended to avoid thinking as much as possible of this aspect of his adopted family. But suddenly he saw this thin thread, this fragile boundary, as protection against what might be seen in the dark ironbound water: white lamb's wool, a protection with the strength of innocence. Though he knew this was no Christian ritual, he knew Molly was good to her depths, and the lamb's wool made him think of Christ, whom the old priest called the *Lamb of God*, and he crossed himself, and felt inexplicably reassured.

Yet Molly and Nemain were obviously tense. They resumed a chant, and in the intervals drank from a cup of *uisce beatha* that they passed between them, and then they poured some from the little cask directly into the basin, and then they each bled a small amount into the water, and then there was a pause. Molly looked into Nemain's eyes; some understanding, some agreement that all was ready passed between them. Molly bent swiftly, picked up the little ivory box and slid the cover partway off, and turned it upside down over the basin.

Sir Tarquin's silver button tumbled with a glint of reflected moonlight into the dark bloodstained water. There was the faintest of hissing sounds, as of iron being quenched at a smithy some way in the distance, and a little swirl of vapor blew this way and that on the water's surface; a vein of milky whiteness mottled the darkness in the iron basin, as though the moon were dissolving in the vessel's depths. Gray mist or smoke began to rise from the water's surface, but remained within the basin, so that the water was covered with what looked for all the world like a miniature fogbank, on a miniature lake.

Hob stared in fascination. Was there movement at the center? The mist began to revolve, the gray mass moving in a circle, but so gradually that Hob was not sure at first that it was moving at all. Striations appeared in the fabric of the vapor, and soon the swirling cloud circled the basin more and more quickly. An aperture opened in the dead center of the bowl, widened, and widened further. Eventually there was a ring of fog running round and round the inner rim of the basin. It thinned; it thinned; it vanished. The surface of the water was now opaque, black as a bat wing, and then a glow in the depths appeared, wavering as torchlight wavers.

Hob bit at his lip in order not to cry out. "Death, and worse," Molly had said, but his astonishment had nearly betrayed him. He looked at the image of a torch, centered in the water, and then it was as though he were moving away from it. The torch became smaller, and he saw it was in a bracket on a stone wall, and that in a dim-lit room. Back and back he seemed to move, till he could see more of the room: walls of dressed stone, one wall deep in shadow.

Along that wall was a bench, and on the bench sat six knights. Some had been with Sir Tarquin when he visited Castle Chantemerle; others Hob had not seen before, but in some ways they were all alike as brothers. They sat motionless, their faces composed to the point of blankness, their hands on their knees, and they stared before them. As they sat, just apparent in the deep shadow that lay over them, Hob could see a faint blue sheen to their eyeballs, and—somehow even more unpleasant—to their fingernails.

Along the base of the stone wall, where it met the stone floor, eight or nine rats sat on a long low white pillow, unnaturally still, back on their haunches with front feet placed together, like dogs awaiting a command, and all facing outward. Hob thought there was a sense of awareness in the narrow faces, more intelligence than the animals' ordinary cunning; in any case their behavior was as odd in its quiet attentiveness as was the knights' somnolent passivity. He strained to see. Their eyes, so small, were harder to perceive, yet seemed to have something of the eerie blue luster of the knights' eyes.

A rat at one end shifted position a little. Past its hindquarters two fingertips came into view, and Hob squinted at the pillow on which the row of vermin perched. It was a woman's arm, from fingers to elbow, and ended in a bloody stump. Hob felt burning liquid rise in his throat, and he checked it with a furious effort of will, desperate not to cough or retch. "Death, and worse," Molly had said, and now he began to feel, however indistinctly, the weight of those words.

Molly, Nemain, Jack made no sound, and Hob could not tear his gaze from the water-mirror to see, but he felt their fixed attention on the scene before them, which now showed him a clearer view. Now he saw that the walls were dripping with moisture, and he saw that there was a heavy oaken door set in the wall to his left, and he saw a stone in the floor to his right that had a great iron ring set in it, and finally he saw that the knights were not alone in the room.

Somewhat to the left of Hob's view, a broad shoulder became visible, and the room moved farther from Hob, or he from it, and he was looking at the back of a knight clad in a ring-mail hauberk, and he knew even from this angle that it was Sir Tarquin.

A screech of unoiled hinges, and the door in the left-hand wall opened, and two more of the eldritch knights came in, holding by the arms between them, his legs all but useless with terror, a man about forty, by his dress a peasant. His shirt was torn open at the back, his hair was in wild disarray, his eyes showed white all around the irises, and where he was not held in the knights' iron grip, he trembled as with fever from the severity of his fear. Yet he did not seem to have been harmed.

When he caught sight of Sir Tarquin, he said only "*ahhh,*" in a whispery moan; "*ahhh,*" as though he would have screamed it had he been able to draw breath into his lungs. The knights released him and he fell to hands and knees, his gaze fixed on Sir Tarquin's face, which was turned away from Hob, and he began to crawl, a movement of blind hopeless instinct, for he was in a cell, and there was nowhere to go. The two knights blocked the door, the row of knights sat against the far wall, and against what must be the near wall sat Sir Tarquin.

And so the peasant crawled ahead, toward the ring in the floor, toward the wall away from the only door, a distance of perhaps twenty feet, for the room was much longer than it was wide, and all at once Sir Tarquin stood up and turned to the right, to follow the wretch's progress, and Hob could at last see his face.

Despite everything, Hob almost cried aloud. Sir Tarquin's strong pale face was a mask of malignant hunger. Hob had seen a hawk standing with taloned foot on a mouse and tearing it with its hook-knife bill, and it was a model of sweetness beside this face, this expression, that might have been the portrait of Satan in a rage.

Sir Tarquin's lips pulled back in a rictus, and Hob rather expected to see fangs, but it was the knight's incisors that seemed overlarge, not huge, but crossing that border into the eerie that caused the hair on the lad's neck to prickle. He covered his mouth with his hand; he could hardly bear to look at the Sieur de Duncarlin, but he could never have looked away, either.

The peasant had almost reached the far wall when Sir Tarquin took a step toward him, and another step, and then sprang, a tigerish leaping dive that Hob would not have believed a man could make, covering the distance in one bound and landing atop his victim's back.

The peasant shrieked once with surprise and terror. Sir Tarquin gripped him by the shoulders; Hob could not see clearly, with the speed at which events were unfolding, but it seemed to him that the knight's fingers ended in nails that seemed longer, that seemed more pointed, than a true man's should be, and where he gripped the unfortunate's flesh, little wells of blood sprang up around Sir Tarquin's fingers, and ten blots of red stained the fabric of the peasant's shirt.

And now the lord of Duncarlin bent his sleek dark head, and sank those ghastly front teeth into the peasant's spine, between two knobs of his backbone, and there was a flash of blue light and a muffled *bang*, and both knight and peasant became immobile, and flickers of blue played about the knight's mouth, and after a long moment the peasant's eyes rolled up in his head, and he settled to the floor, his death rattle wheezing from his compressing lungs.

Sir Tarquin rode him down, and stayed motionless for another long moment, resting on the corpse. Then, with a fluid powerful grace he sprang to his feet, looked about the room, and stretched his arms toward the ceiling, a long luxurious stretch of satisfaction. The knights looked on in stolid fashion, unperturbed, uninterested almost, their faraway expressions hardly registering the murder of the peasant.

Hob looked at the victim, and his blood seemed to freeze. The peasant was shriveling before his eyes: slowly, slowly, his skin was wrinkling; his eyes began to sink back into his skull; a brownish undertone to his flesh was setting in. Sir Tarquin motioned to the silent row of men along the wall. Three knights came forward, seized the ring set in the stone, and heaved. The paving stone, some four feet by three, swiveled on an unseen pivot and stood upright. Hob could hear what sounded like the faint swash of sea-water echoing up through the opening thus revealed. With no ceremony the knights seized two arms and a leg, and dropped the body through the trap. A moment later there came a splash, and two of the knights pushed at the stone. It leaned, tilted past the point of no return, and crashed back into place.

Sir Tarquin, his step that of a vigorous young man setting out for an evening of courting, started toward the door. Suddenly he stopped in his tracks; he stood as though listening; and slowly he turned his head and looked straight up through the surface of the water, right into Hob's eyes.

Hob managed not to cry out, though he took a silent step backward. He could not believe he was unseen: Sir Tarquin appeared to be looking right at him, and the malevolence of his gaze felt to the lad as though it drew the strength from his bones, the heat from his blood.

Molly's hand flicked over the basin, and a fine gray-gold powder flew out and settled on the surface of the water, and Sir Tarquin's image, the stone-walled room, the knights, vanished instantly, and there was just a basin of bloodstained water with a scum of what appeared to be dust or pollen or both on the water's surface.

Molly and Nemain stepped back a pace each, then Molly sat down on the earth, right where she was. Nemain came around the basin and scooped up the cup and the little cask, handed Molly the cup, and stood and poured it full of the *uisce beatha*. Molly drank off half of the fiery stuff without stopping, and handed the cup to Nemain, who took a sip, then another. She sat down next to Molly and began sipping steadily from the cup, coughing a little.

Hob looked at the iron basin, an inert and harmless thing, and the arrangements around it; then he bent and looked more closely. The white lamb's-wool thread was now of two colors: the original white, and an inner border that had been charred black and brown. Molly's voice came from behind him:

"Aye," she said, "that's where he tried to see through, to see who spied upon him, or even—he being so strong, so very strong—even to come through and to come at us, and it's we who were fortunate that this little thread held fast, and we safe outside its circle."

Hob turned and regarded her. She was as one who has run a long race, breathing heavily; Nemain was not much better, although so much younger.

Molly sighed. Exhaustion hung on her; her handsome face was slack with fatigue and the *uisce beatha* was now taking hold a bit. "He is a magus of the first rank; I have never felt such a will thrust against mine, and myself and Nemain pushing with all our might to hold him in, and the little lamb's-wool thread our bulwark against this horrid *buidseach*, this . . ." She put her palms to her eyes. "It's a great weariness there is to me. Nemain, child, what is *buidseach* in English?"

"A wizard, *seanmháthair*."

"So it is, so it is—this horrid wizard, then, and he nearly breaking through to us, and we not ready for him. He will be hard to kill."

"Can you kill him, then, Mistress?" asked Hob.

"Anyone can be killed, lad, unless—" Molly scowled; her eyes narrowed; then she shook her head. "It's something that's whispering to me, far back in my thoughts, and 'twas at the castle, something about this *drochdhuine,* and I marking it at the time, but what . . ." She passed a hand down her face. "Nay, I am destroyed with weariness. Jack, *mo chroí,* settle the campfire; Nemain, Hob, to bed—this night is done."

CHAPTER 19

OLLY AND NEMAIN SLEPT through much of the next day. Jack and Hob went with hooks and lines along the stream, Sweetlove nearly treading on Jack's heels, down to pools where trout hunted the caddis flies. There they caught three fish for breakfast. Jack was expert at whirling the hooks, weighted with little stones, with feathers for bait, about his head and casting them so they lingered for a moment just above the water's surface, the fish erupting from below to seize the hook.

After a while Hob just lay back on the stream bank, propped himself up, and watched Jack hurling his weighted hooks into the river. Sweetlove sat by Hob and did not let Jack out of her sight, but she would take little excursions up and down the riverbank, never out of view. By Hob's elbow were burrow entrances: the holts of otters, asleep during the day; Sweetlove went to investigate them, walking on Hob's legs in the process. She thrust a muzzle into the opening and snuffled deeply. Soon she wearied of this and came back, placed an extremely cold and wet nose against Hob's eyelid by way of greeting, and lay down beside him, contemplating Jack and his fishing out in midstream. Hob himself was weary from the night before; soon he sank back and turned his face up to the sun.

After some time spent in drowsy sunlight, the chill water chuckling and running between green banks, Jack shook Hob, who had begun to drift to sleep, and patted Sweetlove, who was snoring in a reedy tenor. Jack and Hob returned to the campsite, cleaned the fish, and had them ready for whenever the women arose.

At last Molly and Nemain joined them, and Jack cooked the fish on spits. The company prepared to eat, sitting here and there on cloths spread on the grass. All at once Hob arose, lifted the cloth he had sat on, and scuffed at the grass with the toe of his shoe. There was a dead field mouse there, partially decomposed. Hob kicked it away, followed it along, and kicked it twice more, till it was far enough that the odor would not spoil their breakfast.

He came back and sat down again. "It's as bad here as at the castle," he said, laughing. "There was a dead mouse or rat or something among the rushes there, though I could not find it. It was the night we played for Sir Tarquin, when they rose to leave, and that pup went at him. I think that the dog was pulling to get away from the leash, and its paws were digging up the rushes the while, and disturbing what lay beneath. It was strong for a moment, and then . . ."

"I'm noticing it that night as well," said Nemain idly. She was shaving slices from a hunk of hard cheese and placing them on rounds of bread. "It—*seanmháthair*?"

Molly had risen abruptly, and taken several strides this way, and then back; turned, and walked away, and then back, as though too agitated to sit still.

"'Tis worse, and yet worse," she said. She sat down heavily. "Let us eat, and drink, and then it's a council we must have, to speak of what we know, and of what we must do."

They breakfasted on trout and bread and cheese, washed down with clear brookwater. After they had finished, Molly filled their mugs half-full of *uisce beatha*, diluting Hob's and Nemain's with water. Then she called a council of war to order.

"It's not a thing I'm to be telling those knights, not even Sir Balthasar, and nor am I speaking of it outside this family, and nor must you," she began. "Nemain's already knowing this: In my dreams, at whiles, a raven is coming to me, and sitting on a stump or, it may be, at my bedhead, and it speaking."

She paused and took a sip of the strong drink. "This raven, there is Irish at it."

Seeing a look of utter bewilderment on Hob's face, she paused and, realizing her error, translated the sentence again, for often she thought in Irish at moments of stress, and then translated it to English speech, sometimes too literally. Now she corrected herself. "The raven is knowing Irish; any road, it's seeming like Irish that it's speaking to me, and it's telling me . . . things. I believe it to be Herself, the Great Queen, the Mórrígan."

Hob stopped himself from making the sign of the cross, feeling obscurely that it would be insulting to Molly, although also feeling that it might be advisable.

"I'm just thinking on my dream of last night—'twas Hob brought it to mind, and he in my dream as well. There was a live rat, and it was very old, and its mate was a dead rat, and it lying at Hob's feet, and he pointing to it. Then there was only the one rat, the dead rat, and Hob still pointing to it, and the raven, wasn't it saying that I must use my two spears of the moon to trap this rat, and to destroy it."

"But—" Hob stopped, unwilling to interrupt.

Molly was subdued, and did not seem upset with Hob. "But what, lad?"

"But the rat was already dead," Hob said.

"'Twas. And this morning, I waking up and thinking on this dream, I'm not understanding it, and let it be, that I might be pondering it later, and Hob's now showing me . . .

"The raven's after telling me it's a *geis* upon me—an obligation from Herself, do you see?—that I trap this rat, and it dead all the while. I'm to be holding it immobile from midnight to dawn, and then destroying it utterly. And it's only now I understand what the rat is."

"*Och,* it's—" said Nemain, eyes wide. Then: "And he's—"

"He is," said Molly.

Hob looked at Jack, who shrugged massive shoulders, and drank more of the *uisce beatha,* licking a corner of his mouth, rather enjoying himself despite the dire circumstances. Jack had been on many campaigns, and was used to waiting for orders from superior officers, and was more patient than Milo the ox, and especially with strong drink in front of him. He would wait for Molly to tell him what to do, and then he would do it.

"'Twill be difficult, but I will explain," said Molly, speaking mostly to Hob, but also to Jack. "You're smelling something dead in the rushes, and Nemain, and myself—'twas that which I was trying to remember last night, and you asking me could I kill that *buidseach,* and myself about to say anyone may be killed save that he's dead already. For didn't I notice that breath of carrion myself, that night at Chantemerle, and then didn't I forget it with all the ruction round saving that poor pup. 'Twas almost in my grasp last night, but my grasp was weak, weary as I was.

"The rat of my dream is Sir Tarquin himself. We have

seen his rat familiars sitting in a row; you have seen one of his rats, and it more knowing than a rat should be, acting the spy. He has bound these vermin to himself in some way, and so Herself is using such an animal, in that way of dreams, to signify Sir Tarquin.

"It is he, as you saw, who's killing these people, and worse, he's drawing the life from them for his own purpose, and that is to give him a kind of life, for he has none of his own. 'Twas his own scent that you noticed, and you thinking it must be something in the rushes. His body is dead, and he alive. It has been dead a long time, I'm thinking, and he maintaining it by taking the *beatha*, the life force, from others. I'm thinking he's made a bargain with some Power, and there's no telling how long agone that bargain."

"A bargain, Mistress? With Satan?" asked Hob, now in a daze of horror.

"With Someone," said Molly. "There are many Powers, and some are vile indeed. 'Tis not a simple thing to say Whom he has persuaded, or—mighty mage that he is— forced, to help him."

"Ochone!" said Nemain, an exclamation of woe. And then, echoing Molly, "Worse, and yet worse!"

"'Tis," said Molly.

The terrier, sensing the tone of extreme dismay in the women's voices, crowded next to Jack, leaning into the great body for warmth and reassurance.

"But how— He is alive and his body is dead?" asked Hob. "How does it aid him to kill these people?"

"What is the difference between a living person and a dead person?" asked Molly.

"The difference," said Hob, "is, well, is that the soul has fled the dead person."

Molly sighed. "A dog, then, one that's died in its sleep, very old, with no violence—does a dog have a soul, then, to your priests?"

Hob thought that Father Athelstan had been fairly clear that animals had no souls, though Hob himself had his doubts, thinking, for example, of Milo, who seemed to him like a very young, albeit very large, child, who looked for Hob to be a friend, or even a parent.

"Nay, Mistress, it has no soul."

"Then what's gone from it, and gone for aye?" asked Molly. "'Tis the *beatha,* the force of life itself, and it's that force that Sir Tarquin must have from others, his body having none of its own."

Hob, always trying to think his way through things, was quiet for a long moment. Then: "Mistress, you said at Blanchefontaine that the, the dried-up . . . wrinkled bodies, they were a new thing to you; how come you to know these things?"

Molly said, "'Twas yourself put me on the track, reminding me of that scent at the castle. That young dog's after startling Sir Tarquin, and his concentration, that maintains his body and its appearance, wasn't it slipping with the great surprise, and for a moment his body declared itself. And I'm thinking of that which I saw in the water-mirror, and my dream, and what I know—and 'tis not a small amount—of these matters, and all at once I had it, had it in my palm, had it as though himself had told me."

Another pause and then, suddenly, Hob asked, "But who is the old rat, the one that was alive, and that—what? Went away?"

"I believe that is Lady Rohese, the mate, and she very old—not as old as he, perhaps, for he may be ancient, to have heaped up so much power, and who knows when he made his bargain, and who knows when his body died—but she is very old natheless."

"But she is not—"

"She does not seem old, but they are like two spiders in one web, and if he kills to maintain his life in his dead body, and to preserve that dead body, she may do the same to stay alive—for she *is* alive—and to stay young, or seem young. He may lend her his power, for aught I know. I do not fear her, but I fear him; she may be killed, he may not."

"Then, then, you *cannot* kill him, Mistress?" Hob said, groping his way through this thicket of nightmare. "Then what is to happen?"

"Wait, lad. Nemain, come with me."

The two women went to the wagons. Molly cleared a space in the dirt with her foot, and the two queens squatted down while Molly drew symbols in the dust with her fore-finger, looking up from time to time to see if Nemain under-stood, while her granddaughter nodded, and nodded again. At one point Nemain stood up and walked a few paces away, her hands to her hips, her face distressed; then she came back, and squatted again, and nodded again.

Molly, who had watched her keenly, now resumed. After a time, Hob and Jack looking on from ten or twelve paces away, unable to see what was drawn there on the earth, the two women finished; Molly thoroughly erased whatever was there, and they went into the large wagon.

They emerged a few moments later, Nemain carrying what looked like two golden sickles. Molly went to the side of the wagon, worked a cunning latch, and from a compartment beneath the overhang of the wagon roof that Hob had never suspected was there drew two spear shafts.

The women came back, and fitted the sockets of the sicklelike blades to the shafts, working a hidden lock—Hob heard a distinct *click* as each blade was made fast. Molly let him look on them, but told him to avoid touching the weapons. Grooves had been cut lengthwise in the ashwood shafts, and the grooves filled with the same golden metal as the curved spearheads. From the top of the crescent shape, which strongly suggested the sickle moon, proceeded a leaf-shaped spearhead, so that the weapons might be used for thrusting, or as scythe-like cutters, or—as Molly now explained—in concert, one locking with the other about an enemy's neck. Molly could wield both herself at the same time, but not against so mighty a foe.

"And what locks them about the foeman's neck, Mistress?"

"My will, and Nemain's will."

She held one so that Hob could examine the curved head. It was decorated with engraved knotwork along both sides of the outer, blunt edge of the blade, while on one side, at the widest part, was a simple picture of what looked like a woman washing clothes by a stream, this last represented by several wavy lines.

"Is this gold? And what is this picture, Mistress?"

"'Tis steel that has been prayed over, and coated with gold, and infused with power, and that by Art. That picture shows us the Washer at the Ford," said Molly, "one of the masks of the Great Queen."

"If you meet her before a battle," said Nemain, "it's your bloody clothes she's washing, and won't you be dying in the battle, and no escaping it!" She seemed rather enthusiastic about this dismal prospect.

"Attend me," said Molly, speaking to Hob and Jack. "I'm explaining this to you, and you only: I'm not to be speaking of this with those outside this family, and I'm just after showing Nemain what is to be done, drawing in the dirt over there. From my dream, from what I know of these things, I am to understand that this loathsome *gesadóir* is not to be slain with the weapons that I have, but they're burning him, oh, they're burning him, and Nemain and I holding him still all the hours of darkness, if we can, until I'm able to be accomplishing his destruction. He's not to be escaping the collar of blades we're putting on him, and he's not to be able to hold to the shaft of our weapons, because of the strips of holy metal."

She paused a bit, perhaps wondering how much detail she should burden Hob and Jack with. She reached for her mug.

"*Is túisce deoch ná scéal,*" she said, half to herself. Then, seeing Hob frowning, she translated: "First the drink, then the story." She took a swallow, then another.

"I'm having a visit from that raven, or Herself in the form of a raven, 'tis many years agone; and she's telling me what I must do, and I'm waking and it still night, and at the foot of my bed a lump of metal, gold it was, and the size of it!" She shook her head, remembering. "I'm bringing it to one the raven told me of, a woman who made weapons. These were weapons of power, weapons that this spell-woman, this smith, blessed the metal of, blessed it by the name of the Phantom Queen. And she's making them, shaft and head alike, and spellcraft woven into them, and prayers said over them, and holy symbols—the Washer as you see—graven onto them. And they are potent."

Hob was turning all this knowledge this way and that. "But, Mistress, why can you not thrust this metal, this metal that will burn Sir Tarquin, through his heart, and so slay him?"

Molly had another drink of the *uisce beatha*. She sighed. "'Tis that you're not listening: *his body is dead*. His heart is not beating, and 'tis by witchcraft he's sustaining himself, and by the life force of others, and by the power of his will, and that will being immense. There is no vital spot in his body—'tis all dead, or all alive: dead but suffused through-out with the force of his sorcery, and so a thrust is paining him, but 'tis doing no lasting harm. He'll be pulling himself from the blade, and attacking and killing us before we're making the next thrust. Nay, we can but hold him till his destruction arrives."

"And what is this destruction, Mistress?"

"Nay, I'm not to be speaking of that, even to you and Jack, for fear that the small breeze will be bearing my words to his ears. Nemain is knowing, for I'm after telling her by signs in the dust; and she being experienced, young as she is. But to say more of my plan, it's risking a defense against it by this terrible magus. I'm not to know what he knows, and nor what he's able to find out. Rat spies, indeed! What if it's one that's lurking in yon bush?"

Hob, startled, looked around quickly.

"Nay, I'm sensing nothing. But it's only this that I'll be telling you: We will have one chance, and I staking every-thing on one roll of this game of knucklebones that we're playing with him. If it's going with me, it's Sir Tarquin who'll be destroyed utterly, and if it's going against me, we're all to die, and his power beginning to stretch out over the land. 'Tis not that I'm doing this for Sir Odinell anymore; Herself is after giving me this command to expunge this evil, evil that's now so mighty, it must not be allowed to flourish more, that it not overwhelm the world."

CHAPTER 20

OLLY AND NEMAIN MADE
preparations for war. They had
Hob and Jack stay by the wag-
ons, under strict instruction to be silent, and they
went several yards off, just into the woods. There
was a little clearing there. The trees screened it, but
only somewhat; the women could be seen but not
heard. Jack lounged in the grass, up on one elbow,
stolid as usual, waiting while the women did their
incomprehensible rituals. There was no need to
restrain Sweetlove—she could not be persuaded to
go any real distance from Jack, as though there were
an invisible tether between them; indeed she became
agitated and snappish on the one occasion when Hob
had tried to pick her up to pet her, and had made the

mistake of taking her just the few steps to the opposite side of the fire from the dark man.

Hob was always interested in learning what skills his unusual family practiced, and now he sat up on the seat of the main wagon, sitting sideways with chin in hand, watching Molly and Nemain in fascination.

The women built a little fire; they had the iron basin filled with water again, and various stones and feathers, and the crescent-headed spears, and a ball of green ribbon. There was chanting in Irish, which just reached Hob's ears, and casting of powders into the fire, which made the colors of the flames change, and then more chanting. The spear-heads were passed repeatedly over the fire, and plunged into the basin, although they had not really been heated: it was a symbolic, rather than actual, tempering of the blades.

More powder was tossed into the fire, and now billows of smoke issued from the heart of the flames. Nemain passed green ribbon through the smoke, to the accompaniment of repeated forceful commands by Molly, while Nemain was silent. Nemain brought forth a silver box, and Molly carefully deposited the ball of green ribbon there, and fastened the box, and put it aside. The wind shifted, and the smoke reached Hob, a surprisingly pleasant aroma; Father Athelstan had taken Hob to hear Mass at Easter in the nearby market town, and there had been incense like this: a scent as of mingled spices.

The time was now near dusk: the women had been at

it all afternoon. It was the hour when the birds of the day began to call to each other, preparing to retire; in a little while the bats would appear, wheeling this way and that to follow the clouds of insects, to whom they are as dragons; and then the birds of the night would awaken and shake out their feathers. Molly crouched down and spread a cloth on the ground on this side of the fire. She scattered bright bits of metal across the cloth, a double handful. Hob could not see just what they were from where he perched on the wagon seat, but some seemed bright as silver, and some were a leaden gray. Molly called up into the trees, almost casually, and down came three crows and two ravens, and landed on the cloth, and inspected the metal bits, their heads cocked to one side, moving up and down to provide focus. The birds walked about on the blanket, looking at each trinket, for all the world like purchasers at a fair, which would have been comical had it not been so uncanny.

Molly spoke to them the while; the occasional word that came to Hob was in Irish. The birds were silent; they seemed to be listening, glancing back at her while walking amid the metal. At last the crows gave a caw or two, the ravens croaked, and they sprang up into the trees. After a bit, one by one, they flew off.

Bats now ruled the air. Nemain built up the fire, and Molly threw something in it, producing more colored flames, more perfumed smoke. Full dark crept in, and again Molly called out, and now four brown owls floated down from the trees, utterly silent, to land upon the cloth. They walked stiff-legged among the bits of metal, and Molly addressed them, and after this had gone on for a while, they leaped up and flew into the branches, where Hob lost sight of them.

The women doused the fire, packed things up, and came back to the wagons. "That's done, then," said Molly. She hefted the cloth, now tied as a sack, and a muted *clink* came from within. "We'll be going on the morrow, late in the day, when 'tis neither bright day that we may be seen nor full night when that evil *buidseach* may be at the height of his powers, and it's these metal amulets we'll be leaving, and don't they have symbols of power grooved into each, and we placing them as guides for our watchers—crows and ravens by day, owls by night."

The next day, late in the afternoon, Sweetlove locked in the middle wagon and the draft animals grazing on tethers, they set off, riding the four horses that Sir Odinell had provided. They took the coast road south, perhaps ten miles; they arrived near Duncarlin at sunset, as Molly had planned. When the castle appeared in the hazed distance, Molly turned her horse's head and led them into the trees. They proceeded along parallel to the coast road, the strand just visible now and then through the gaps in the pillars of the forest. They went slowly, the horses' hooves mostly silent on the cover of moist dead leaves. Now and then they had to duck under a branch or detour around a thicket, but the trees were old, the shadow beneath them was too dense to nourish other vegetation, and so the underbrush was not thick.

At last they could see, from their half-hidden vantage point, the sheen of the setting sun on the darkening waters, gold on black, and the dragon silhouette of the long castle, crouching on its headland. Molly signaled for silence, and dismounted. As she had instructed them in camp, the others walked their horses to form a rough perimeter to ward against surprises: Jack to the south with Molly's mount, Hob to the north, Nemain in the middle.

Molly now paced through the forest from just north of the castle to just south of the castle, placing the metal tokens here and there at the tree roots, to guide corvids by day and owls by night to the castle. From these trees they would fly to castle eaves, roofs, buttresses, windowsills, anywhere they could see and hear what transpired within. Others watched the road, and the gatehouse, to see who came, and who went.

When all the tokens had been distributed, she took her horse's reins from Jack, swung up into the saddle, and led them back north, threading a way between the tree trunks, till they were able to come down onto the road, and make their way by moonlight back to the camp. They would spend one more night in the wagons, camped in the clearing, and then back to the inn to await word of the Blanchefontaine force's arrival.

* * *

That night, sitting about the campfire, well fed, mugs in hand—*uisce beatha* for Molly and Jack, brookwater for the younger couple—Molly tried to explain her watchers to Hob.

"How will they see the markers, Mistress, it being so dark beneath the trees?"

"'Tis not that they see them, but that they sense them, and the messages I have put into them."

"But, Mistress, they are just birds!" Hob objected.

"There are birds, and they have little wisdom, and there are those the Mórrígan has made captains of birds, and these may be spoken to, and instructed, and there are others . . ." Molly's voice trailed away, and she drank from the clay mug in her hand.

"And others . . . ?" prompted Hob.

She looked right at him. "There are times when I feel that the bird, like the raven in my dreams, is Herself, and aren't its eyes having a great distance behind them—the eyes no bigger than they should be, but . . . *ollmhór*—vast, immense—in some way." She drank again. "'Tis hard to put in words in Irish, much less English, and any road it's not that I'm understanding it myself. And that's all I'm saying on it tonight, and 'tis time we were all in bed."

CHAPTER 21

THE DAY AFTER MOLLY'S BAND had returned to the inn, Molly decided to have Sweetlove do a sweep of the little compound. Both Molly and Nemain could detect the traces of Sir Tarquin's sorcery that somehow emanated from his strange rodent spies, but it was faint—Sweetlove would discover them more quickly, even if she would not deal with them. In the process, of course, the inn would also be swept of its ordinary mice and rats.

They began in the outbuildings—the sheds, the stable. Sweetlove dashed about, wriggling into dark corners and crevices, dragging her victims out and shaking them till dead. Jack followed her with a sack and a cudgel, and removed the tiny corpses. Hob had his own cudgel, a blackthorn stick with a knob at one end. Then they moved on to the inn proper, where Joan was outraged to find several mice and a few rats hiding in secret nests underneath this and behind that in her kitchen and her pantry.

But no sinister agents of Sir Tarquin were found. Had they never been here, or had they escaped, somehow understanding the purpose of the terrier's hunt? Neither Molly nor Nemain could find any scent of witchcraft, however faint.

They stood in the midst of Adelard's tiny buttery, casks of new ale and some bottles of wine stacked against the walls. Molly looked around, hands on hips, and shook her head.

"Nay, there's nothing atall to be found," she said, perspiring a bit from the effort, tucking a lock of silver hair behind her ear.

"Mistress," said Hob.

"What is it, *mo chroí*?"

"There is the upper level," he said.

"*Och,* sure and I'm old and forgetful!" she said. She pointed at Nemain. "And you no better, young as the springtime that you are!" She said this with a laugh, for she was pleased that they had not encountered any of the strange creatures, and—having encountered none so far—did not really think that there would be any in the sleeping quarters above the common room.

They trooped up the crude and creaking wooden stairs, Jack carrying Sweetlove under one arm and the cudgel and sack in the other hand. The moment he set the ratter down, though, it was apparent that something was wrong. The dog sank where she stood into a crouch; a snarling growl began in her chest; her ears went flat back and her lips writhed away from her inch-long fangs, the skewed bottom fang giving her an expression of demonic ferocity. But for all that, she would not move, gazing fixedly at the back row of cots that Adelard rented to weary travelers.

Molly and Nemain crept nearer the cots. They looked at each other; Molly took her dagger from its sheath and Nemain did the same, producing an additional dagger from beneath her skirts. Molly reached down, one-handed, and flipped a cot out from the wall. There was a scrambling burst of sound, and five rats sprang forth and fanned out across the floor. Two were transfixed by daggers hurled by Molly and Nemain; an instant later a third was pinned by Nemain's second dagger, and Hob swung at a rat and knocked it stunned and sliding across the floor toward Jack, as though playing some game. The fifth rat was almost past Jack, when Sweetlove unexpectedly took a stand: she leaped toward it, landing in its path, her fangs clicking shut on the air as the rat scrambled backward, its escape checked for an instant. It dithered, apparently trying to decide whether to go right or left around the snarling terrier, or—it being almost as big as the dog and evil as well—whether to attack. As it stood with its hindpaws in one place and its forepaws, so much like tiny hands, dancing this way and that, its comrade came sliding up beside it, impelled by Hob's glancing blow.

Jack took a long step forward, raised his cudgel, and struck twice in rapid succession. The cudgel was what they called a loaded stick, the knob at the end hollowed out and filled with lead to increase the weight, and each stroke killed a rat instantly, the floorboards beneath producing a *boom* muffled only by the rodents' bodies, so that Adelard, waiting below with his family, thought that "inn were falling doon, sithee, like thunder it was, and just there above oor heids."

Later, over celebratory bumpers of sweet ale, Molly inclined to the somber. "For there's no telling what reports of our doing in this inn that these rat-fiends have made to those devils, Sir Tarquin and his witch-wife, and when we return to Chantemerle, it's Adelard and his family we'll be taking with us, for I swear before the Great Mother I'll not have them suffering on our account."

She drank again, but she was moody for the rest of the night, and retired early.

TWO DAYS AFTER THE RAT HUNT, Hob was making the acquaintance of Hawis's herb fritters, made with parsley and savory and marjoram from the inn's herb garden, and a bit of salt from the salterns by the coast, the batter fried in oil and served with honey from Mistress Joan's hives. Hob was thinking that Hawis had the gift of making simple food, familiar food, surprisingly good: some variation in the ingredients, or the length of time they were cooked, came instinctively to her, and the result was delicious.

Hawis, tending a pot of heated oil over a small fire on the hearth, scooped out a second bowl for him with a slotted spoon, and placed it shyly before him. To her, Molly's troupe was a miraculous irruption into her quiet life—a life she had not thought of as drab, till contrasted with these women who played music such as must be played at God's court.

Hob was waiting happily for the fritters to cool enough for his fingers when Timothy burst in the door and ran the length of the common room, skidding to a halt at Molly's table. The ruckus brought Adelard from the kitchen, wiping his hands on the cloth tucked into his belt, and Hawis swung the pot of oil on its iron arm away from the fire. The boy's narrow chest was heaving, and he tried to gasp out something of importance, but could not, and they all had to wait till he could obtain breath enough to speak.

"Master," he said to Adelard, "I were by Wat's field, and Mistress were gaan by me and said nowt, and didna deek me atall, nae sae much as ane look, and she seemin' all fey-like, an' her eyen verra odd-like, deekin' summat Ah couldna see, an' she ganged reet past me, an' ganged toward t' woods."

Here he stopped, taking in more air. Adelard was clearly puzzled, wondering what was happening; nor did Hob know what to think. Was the innkeeper's wife in some danger, or had the boy misunderstood? Nemain was looking to Molly to see what she thought, and Molly was plainly thinking hard. Jack had been eating as well, sharing every fifth bite with Sweetlove; now he stood up, still chewing, brushing crumbs off his hands, watching Molly for orders. There was a moment's tense silence, and into this silence Timothy said, low, hesitant: "And Ah'm nae sartain, but theer may ha' been someone, mayhap a woman, at the edge o' t' woods."

Molly blinked, and then leaped up; the bench she sat upon went over with a crash. She pointed a finger at Hob, then pointed to Jack. "Hammer! Run!" To Nemain she said, "Hazel staves!" The two young people ran toward the back of the common room, Hob first. He flew at the back door—a blurry impression of aged gray-brown wood, rough-textured—and banged it open, and then he was out in the warm spring air, running to the wagons. He dashed up the stairs of the main wagon; through the door and two steps to the war hammer in its wooden clips. He slapped it up out of the clips and was bounding down the stairs when Nemain emerged from the midsized wagon, with a hazel staff in each hand. He had a moment, almost immediately forgotten, when he noted how much older, how much more authoritative, Nemain looked holding the staves.

Then they were back into the inn through the rear door. No one was there but the terrier. They pounded down the long empty room and out the front door into the road, closing the door on Sweetlove, who showed every inclination to follow. The inn was on the northeast corner of the crossroads; Wat's field was on the southwest corner, bordered on the south and part of the west by forest land. Molly and Jack Brown, Adelard and his daughter, were already in the field and making for the woods, Timothy leading the way and pointing. Nemain sprinted for the field, going up and over the split-log fence like a deer, a leap up, one foot to the top bar and down again without breaking stride. Hob, with his longer legs, was right behind her, albeit less graceful in clearing the fence.

Hob caught up with Jack and passed him the hammer, and the dark man began to increase speed, intending to be first in case there was danger, but Molly, taking her staff from Nemain, called to him.

"Jack," she said, "stay behind us a bit, *stór mo chroí*, but not too far. I'm thinking 'tis more work for Nemain and myself than for you."

Timothy had stopped, and was pointing into the woods. Hob, trotting along, tried to see what the boy was indicating, away there amid the shadows between the tree trunks. Was that white shape, a little way into the forest, a woman, and was she . . . bent over something?

"Timothy," said Molly sharply. "Go back to the inn. Hawis as well."

Molly and Nemain still advanced, but slowed to a walk. They lifted their hazel staves before them, at arm's length, the wood held vertically so that the upper part was in front of their faces, constituting some kind of shield. What it protected them from, or how, Hob could only wonder: they did not share such things, things that pertained to their Art, with him, or with Jack, or indeed with any man, nor with most women.

They were coming to the tree line. The woman straightened unhurriedly, and now they could see that it was Lady Rohese. She sneered at them; she turned slowly; she moved away at no great speed. It was very dark under the canopies of the trees, though, and within a few steps she was lost to view. And now from behind separate trees stepped two of the wraithlike knights, with their underwater movements, and Jack increased his speed: this sort of enemy was his meat.

But Molly and Nemain were coming on relentlessly, and began to chant in unison, in Irish, and the knights turned as one and stepped into the forest as Lady Rohese had, and vanished into the gloom.

Now Molly and Nemain had come to the edge of the wood, and there, a few feet inside the forest line, lay Joan, collapsed on the ground. Her eyes were open, and she moved her hands and feet feebly, and she spoke, though not to any purpose. Hob, coming up with Jack, Adelard right behind, heard Nemain gasp. He crowded around her to see.

Joan had aged twenty years, her eyes sunken, her skin like parchment, her limbs thin, almost withered.

"Ochone!" said Molly, shocked. She knelt beside Joan, and just then Adelard came up, and saw what was toward, and gave a loud wordless cry, and buckled at the knees. Jack just managed to catch him, and after a moment he steadied, but began to pull at his hair, his eyes wide.

"Jesus, Jesus, what hae they done tae her?"

Molly stood up. "It's back to the inn she must go, and that as swift as swift can be! Jack, it's you must carry her, 'twill be the faster." She took Adelard by the arm and forcibly turned him around; Nemain took the innkeeper's other arm, and they began walking him back rapidly across Wat's field. Jack handed Hob the war hammer, went down on one knee, and scooped Joan up like a sleepy child, an arm under her shoulders and one under her knees. Her head lolled on his chest, and she said incomprehensible things in a hushed unhappy voice.

Hob and Jack made a swift march across the field; Hob opened the gate near the corner, and Jack went out into the road, almost trotting, up past the crossroads to the inn, where Nemain was already holding the door open.

As soon as everyone was into the common room, Molly looked around. Just now there was no one else at the inn: no traveler, no passerby, no villager, no guest. The first thing Molly said was to Hawis, who stood near the hearth, two fists pressed against her mouth, her eyes fastened on what had so short a time ago been her mother.

"Bolt the doors, front and back. Now, lass, now!" This last got Hawis moving, although slowly, as one in a dream, or a nightmare. Molly had Jack lay Joan on a table near the front doors, and bade Adelard and Timothy steady her, and guard her from rolling off the table, for she was still making random movements. Adelard looked stunned. Molly went back to the hearth, and stood, her hands opening and closing into fists. Nemain and Hob and Jack joined her.

She said to Nemain, "These people, it's we who are under their roof, and it's they who are under our protection. It's myself who swore to protect these innocents, and the Great Queen listening the while, and I'm not to be going back on it. It's myself who's after letting down my guard over them, and letting this *cailleach phiseogach* come nigh them, and here she's done this to that poor woman." She said something to Nemain in Irish.

"Nay, *seanmháthair,* 'tis too dangerous."

" 'Tis more dangerous to lose your way," said Molly, "and that's begun with the first step off the path of virtue." She put a hand on Nemain's shoulder and gave her a gentle push toward the back door, the innyard, the wagons. "It's not to be said that I'm an oathbreaker, not among men and women, not among the phantom councils of the Great Queen."

Nemain undid the bolt and went out the door. Hob was unsure what was happening, as was so often true when the women worked their Art. Jack was nothing if not stolid, but if Nemain was afraid for Molly, he was bound to be uneasy, and he did seem restless, limping about here and there. Molly bade Hawis to fetch a pillow, and then went to Joan, and arranged her on the table, and when Hawis reappeared, lifted Joan's head and slipped the pillow beneath it. Joan appeared to be worsening; her skin seemed darker, drier, her muscles more withered; striations began to appear beneath the skin of her face and neck and hands. Hob thought of the corpse in the rhine, and felt a shudder of distress, which he managed to conceal.

Here came Nemain, bolting the back door again behind her, trotting down the room to Molly, a ceramic flask and a stone bottle in her hands. She gave her grandmother the flask, sealed with wax. Molly took her dagger from her belt and pried the wax loose. Nemain had procured a birchwood cup, and was pouring *uisce beatha* from the bottle, a half cup. She put the bottle down on a table near the one on which Joan lay mumbling at the ceiling. Nemain looked at Joan and said, low, "She is failing."

Molly said through her teeth, "I will be pulling her up; by the Great Queen, *I will be pulling her up!*" She pushed Hob back a bit, saying, "Hob, *a chuisle,* stand back a pace; I'll not have you breathing of this powder." She poured an amount into the cup of Irish spirits. She held out her hand, and Nemain placed a spoon in it, and Molly stirred the cup. She looked into the cup a moment; she looked over at Joan. "*Bíodh sé amhlaidh,*" she said.

Molly drained the cup.

Hob noticed that Nemain had clenched her hands together, and the fingers were interlaced so tight that her knuckles had whitened. He had been growing used to the idea that nothing daunted Nemain, and though his betrothed strove to conceal it, he had not seen her this agitated since she was a little girl.

Molly began to breathe heavily. She put the cup down awkwardly; it clattered onto the table. She went back toward the hearth a bit, and began to walk up and down, slowly at first and then somewhat more rapidly. She swung her arms back and forth, out and back so that her arms came together and her hands gave a clap. She did this several times, as one who is overheated, pacing up and then down. Her hands went up, removed pins, and her veil came off. A few more pins and the thick glossy river of gray and silver that was her hair poured free down her back, well past her waist.

Hob remembered old Father Athelstan, the priest who had raised him, and his tales of the Christian martyrs, given to the lions by the old Roman folk, and the priest's descriptions of the iron cages with the lions and lionesses, pacing back and forth, looking out from the cage shadows into the bright sandy space where their victims awaited. Molly reminded him of those lionesses, striding back and forth in the narrow space between the two rows of tables, breathing more and more heavily, her face reddening, her breathing horribly labored.

Molly began to chant in Irish, striding up and down. Adelard and Timothy looked on, terrified to numbness, from beside the table where Joan lay mumbling in delirium. Nemain pulled Hob and Jack to the side of the room; Hawis had retreated to the kitchen doorway. Sweetlove, her tail tucked between her hind legs, crowded behind Jack's legs and peered out at Molly.

Molly was chanting, louder, louder; her voice, usually so musical, had grown harsh. Her hair by some force seemed to stand out from her head, increasing her leonine appearance. She began to run a few steps, turn, run back, her head thrown back, shouting in Irish, looking up at the ceiling. Hob had never seen her so out of control, her eyes blazing, her whole aspect like a demon, or like a goddess. She had left mere womanhood behind and was quivering with some force that rippled through her, troubling her breathing and her limbs.

She ran toward the fire in the hearth, skidded, spun, and ran at Joan roaring incoherently, Adelard instinctively taking a step or two backward as she approached. Molly gave a great whooping inhalation, clapped her hands together on Joan's cheeks, making the half-conscious woman open her mouth. Molly stooped like some savage lover, clamped her mouth to Joan's mouth, pinched the woman's nostrils shut, and blew into her lungs, a long, long, groaning exhalation; to Hob it seemed as though it went on longer than any human being could manage.

Molly straightened, inhaling gustily, and in a flash she had covered Joan's mouth and nose with a big white hand. She held it there for a long moment; Joan's eyes widened and rolled this way and that. Molly released her and Joan took a long breath on her own.

Molly staggered back; to Hob she croaked, "Bring me a chair till I sit down." She was panting and disheveled, and wobbling where she stood. Hob ran back with one of the few chairs the inn had, and helped her sink into it. Joan closed her eyes with a small groan, and soon began to snore lightly.

Molly said to Adelard, slurring her words, "Let her sleep; cover her warmly. If she's waking before nightfall, give her broth. Nemain, burn that cup. Jack, put me to bed."

Jack gathered her up as he had Joan, despite the fact that Molly was a much more robust woman than Joan, and carried her toward the back door. Nemain plucked the birchwood cup Molly had used from the table.

"And if she does not wake before then?" asked Adelard.

Hob and Nemain were starting after Jack.

"Bury her," snarled Nemain over her shoulder, her fears for Molly making her cruel. She tossed the cup into the fire and went out the door after Jack and her grandmother.

Hob turned about and showed his palms in a calming signal, at the same time making a reassuring face at Hawis, who had joined Adelard and Timothy. "She will be well," he said quietly to them, then turned and followed his flinty betrothed.

CHAPTER 22

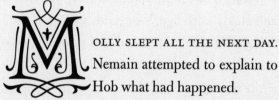OLLY SLEPT ALL THE NEXT DAY.
Nemain attempted to explain to
Hob what had happened.

"It's a portion of her *beatha,* her . . . vitality?
life itself? that she's giving that innkeeper's wife, to
put back what that witch stole from her, and she's
after stopping Mistress Joan from slipping away into
death, and now they're both needing to rest and
come back, for it's a dark border they've both almost
crossed, and a long way back, with food and with
rest, and the help of the Goddess."

At the mention of the Goddess, Hob duti-
fully crossed himself, but he was in no way as
wary of such speech as he used to be; in truth he
hardly noticed it anymore; and in his admiration for

Molly and love for Nemain it had ceased to matter to him.

Joan took nearly a week to recover, but her flesh rapidly filled out and moistened, her eyes no longer looked sunken, and she regained clarity and sense. She could remember things only as a sort of very bad dream, and shuddered, and did not wish to speak of it at first.

Molly, however, came in from her wagon on the second day and ate everything Hawis could think to put in front of her. "It's some strength I'm needing, and a wee bite to eat, for 'twas a great struggle to undo that witch's mischief, and myself no longer young, and my appetite turning poor and sickly with age," she said, sitting at the table with a bumper of ale in one hand and part of a leg of mutton in the other, tearing the meat off the bone with her strong white teeth.

THE SECOND DAY after Joan rose from her sickbed, she sat down by Molly and the others, and began to speak. "Ah ken Ah went oot tae feed t' hens, and then Ah'm thinkin' tae hear someone callin' tae me. Then it coom tae me that Ah were gangin' across Wat's field, and thinkin' tae mesel', 'Why'm Ah gangin' here?' and seein' t' wood coom nearer an' nearer, and Ah didna want tae enter, sithee, but Ah entered, an' gaed in just under t' trees, an' stopped in t' first shadows, and wonderin' why Ah were theer, but 'twas as if Ah were dreamin', sithee, and didna have ae control. An' then that woman coom frae behin' a tree, and she glowerin' at me, an', an' . . . Ah thought, 'What-for does she hate me sae?' for 'twas a look o' hatred, an' she took a step toward me, an' reached oot a han' tae me, tae touch me, tae touch m' arm, an' Ah didna want her tae touch me, sithee, Ah didna, but Ah couldna move. Ah didna want her tae touch me, an' Ah couldna move. Ah couldna move. Ye ken, Ah didna want her tae touch me."

Molly made soothing noises, for Joan was breathing more and more heavily, and her face was moist, and tears began to run down her cheeks.

"But she did, she put her han' on m' arm, an' her han' verra cowd, an', an' . . . Ah remember nowt, Ah remember nowt, Ah dinna ken what she, she did tae me, Ah—"

Molly put an arm around her shoulder, and murmured in her ear, and stroked her hair, and she became calmer. Molly gave a significant glance to Nemain, and a faint tilt of the head, and her granddaughter rose quietly and went out the back door to the innyard, where the wagons were, and reappeared with a little crockery jar. She pulled the stopper and placed the jar by Molly's elbow. Nemain went into the kitchen and returned with a mug of ale, half-full, for Joan, and a spoon.

Molly, with one arm still around Joan, working one-handed, tapped a bit of the contents of the jar—a dun-colored powder, as far as Hob could tell—into Joan's ale, squinting judiciously. She accepted the spoon from Nemain, stirred, and held the mug to Joan's lips. Joan, still upset, drank as though hardly aware of what she did.

After a bit Joan sighed, and her expression eased, and she said, "Och, weel, 'tis a' spilled milk, sithee." And she straightened up, and after a while she stood and went into the kitchen, and began to help Hawis with the cooking.

ADELARD CAME TO HOB a few days later, very nervous, and said, "Yon Mistress Molly has saved ma Joan, sithee, and she's a yem here whenever she needs un, but, but . . ." He looked over his shoulder, though Molly was outside and Nemain across the room by the window. "Tell me, young maister, be they witches? For 'twas fey doings that night, sithee, and Ah fear for our souls."

Hob looked at him and thought, *Molly will be saved before anyone I know is saved.* He gazed innocently into the innkeeper's face, and said, "Nay, it's by her special devotion to Mother Mary that she heals, and the Blessed Mother herself guiding her in everything." He clapped the innkeeper on the shoulder, and said, sounding much more mature than his years, "Be of good cheer, Goodman Adelard, you are in safe hands."

Nemain had glided closer, making no more noise than the house cat, and now she looked at Hob, and crossed her eyes at him behind Adelard's back, so that he had to struggle to be serious.

Later, when they were alone, she said to him, joking a bit, but only a bit, "It's everyone in the world you may lie to, Robert, but not to me."

"Never to you," he said with utmost simplicity, and for that she clasped her hands behind his neck, and gave him such a burning kiss that he could not speak for several breaths, fearing that his voice would quaver, and distracted by his attempts to master his disobedient body's inconvenient enthusiasm for his betrothed.

CHAPTER 23

TWO MORE OF THE WIZENED corpses had been found, much nearer the inn, and folk were once more keeping to their cottages. The evening was fairly well advanced, a cold rain was falling, quiet but steady, and despite the season there was a moist chill in the air. Adelard had built a small fire in the hearth to drive off the damp. Molly and her troupe sat at the north end of the large table, by the door to the inn-yard. Adelard was sitting with them, and Joan had just brought a beaker of ale for Jack. Sweetlove lay on her side by the fire, snoring peacefully. There came the sound of several horses and the rumble of carriage wheels, and Timothy went down the long room to the front door to see.

He opened the door, and stepped back in, his eyes very wide, his mouth drawn down at the corners. Through the open door they could see part of a carriage, with a glowing horn-paned lantern fixed to the end of the driver's bench; the driver's legs; a curtained window; and a knight in mail stepping to open the carriage door. Two knights came in, and Hob realized with a shock that they were of the group of peculiar knights that had accompanied Sir Tarquin to Chantemerle. They stepped to either side of the doorway, and in walked Lady Rohese, pushing back the hood of her traveling cloak.

Joan fainted immediately, dropping where she stood, and only partly caught by Nemain, which softened her fall but did not stop it. Adelard sprang up and, with Hawis's help, carried his wife into the kitchen. The terrier immediately ran behind Jack's chair and stood there, slightly crouched, her upper lip lifting and falling, baring and concealing her teeth, surprisingly long for such a small dog; from her came a faint groaning snarl, as though she wished to threaten, but did not dare more.

Behind Lady Rohese came two maids, and the whole party came up to the large table, and seated themselves at the end opposite Molly and her family. Molly sat utterly still and gazed at Lady Rohese with a complete absence of expression, and Nemain, her eyes on the newcomers, sat down again, very slowly. The rough-hewn chair beside Hob creaked as Jack sat forward, gathering his feet under him, his powerful legs tense and his right hand down by his dagger.

Lady Rohese, with her bizarre expression, fair and foul at once, sat for a long moment, looking into Molly's eyes. Hob had once seen two cats sit face-to-face in the alley beside the priest house, staring into each other's eyes with unfathomable meaning. Each had slowly come to its feet; backs were arched; at a signal known only to themselves they flew at one another in a squall of blood and screams of hatred. Now he felt himself in the midst of something similar: on his right Jack was coiled, watching the two knights' every move, but it was Molly and Sir Tarquin's witch-wife who held his attention: the air between them seemed almost to crackle with imminence.

The moment stretched on, taut as a harp string, and then Adelard crept out of the kitchen again, quickly spread a cloth over the table, and stood waiting to serve the party. Lady Rohese sat back and looked up at him.

"You are Adelard, are you not? I have heard good reports of your ale from my men. They are Scots," she said, and Adelard went dead-white, "and Scots know their ale. Four fine, strapping men—do you know them?"

"Theer's m-mony cam' through t' inn, m-ma lady," said Adelard, swaying a little from terror of those large, beautiful eyes, dark as the night, dark as the grave. "Ah dinna ken 'em all."

"Bring us ale, and them also," she said, turning away,

indicating the troupe at the other end of the table. Adelard scurried back into the kitchen; reappeared with birchwood mugs and set them out; scurried back for flagons of ale, cloths, and water in bowls for the guests' hands. His wife and daughter remained hidden in the kitchen. Once, Hob thought he heard a muffled sob, but only once.

One of Lady Rohese's maids was a side-glancing, furtive young woman, with a long nose and snapping black eyes, slender wrists, slim flexible fingers. These last were notably deft as she attended her mistress, pouring her ale, tying up a loose riband, handing her mug and napkin and washbowl, all without spilling aught. Lady Rohese sent her on an errand out the door to the coach, and she took the long way by the fire, which necessitated her passing between Molly's chair and the wall behind. She squeezed through the gap easily enough on her way out, but upon her return, a small jar in hand, she seemed to stumble and fall rather awkwardly against the back of Molly's chair. A moment later she was all apologies, brushing at Molly's shoulder and straightening the back of Molly's veil, while her mistress scolded her in a low but intense voice from down the table.

Molly nodded pleasantly enough at her, but her lips were set in a crooked half smile, and she looked significantly at Nemain.

The maid returned to her place, sitting at Lady Rohese's right hand, but a little behind her chair. Her mistress studiedly ignored her. Hob noticed that Molly and Nemain were not tasting their ale; indeed, each was toying with her mug, but each seemed to be unobtrusively watching the far end of the table.

After a short time the maid drew something from within her gown and, leaning a little forward, put it in her mistress's lap, below the table-line, out of sight. In a moment Lady Rohese looked down, and smiled. It was an unpleasant smile. She looked up and reached for her ale. Then she lifted her mug to Molly where she sat at the far end of the table.

Molly sat stone-faced for a moment, then drew the ring-pommel dagger from her belt—the two strange knights tensed and watched her hand closely. She took a generous lock of her hair and cut perhaps six inches from the bottom. She dropped it on the table in front of her, pricked her thumb with the dagger-point, and returned the weapon to its sheath, her movements rapid, her hands steady. She let a few drops of blood fall upon the hank of silver hair before her. Hob, watching Molly, heard the knights' chairs creak as the two relaxed and sat back again.

From her bosom Molly drew a little deerskin bag, put the moistened lock of her hair into it, then pulled tight the leather laces. She tied a simple knot, murmuring over it in Irish, so low that Hob could barely hear her voice.

"Do not be stinting yourself," she said, and tossed the bag unerringly down the table, so that it landed just beside Lady Rohese's mug.

Lady Rohese looked down at the deerskin bag. She did not raise her head, but her eyes sought Molly's face, so that she was looking up from under, and she began again to smile, a cruel delighted smile, and Hob crossed himself, thinking, *If it be that Satan smiles, then this is the shadow of his smile.*

Nemain had gone rigid; she stared at Molly, appalled.

"*Seanmháthair,* you—"

"Hush, child, all will be well." Molly was watching the other end of the table. Lady Rohese sat up very slowly, till she was straight against her chair back. She darted a hand into a pocket in the lining of her cloak and brought forth a cloth doll, with painted features and a long mane of silver threads.

Nemain drew breath with a sharp hiss. Hob was looking back and forth from her to Molly. He was unsure what was happening, but it boded no good.

Molly sat, still as a cat crouched in ambush, and watched the witch-woman at the far end of the table. Lady Rohese tore open the pouch strings and brought forth the bloodied lock of hair. At this moment, Molly sat back with a bleak smile, and took a sip of her ale.

Lady Rohese thrust the wad of hair and blood into a hollow in the doll, muttering to it the while, then turned swiftly in her seat and threw the doll into the fireplace. It fell on the topmost log and was afire at once, as though soaked in pitch: the mane of silver threads went up in a burst of light, and the cloth followed, and even down the table Hob caught the faint acrid smell of burning hair from within the doll.

Lady Rohese swung back and glared at Molly.

But Molly just sat and smiled at her. Molly's only discernible discomfort was a slight sheen of perspiration upon her forehead; she patted delicately at her face with a hand cloth.

"*Seanmháthair,*" said Nemain again, her voice anguished, her eyes wide with horror. Sweetlove, hearing the fear in Nemain's voice, shifted her feet, turned in a circle, and peeped around Jack again, alternating between whines and faint growlings.

Molly waved a hand at her granddaughter. "Away with your fretting! Would you ever be setting a kitten on a panther, and you thinking you'd have a panther-skin cloak on the morrow?"

Nemain nodded toward the head of the table. "Yet this kitten has claws. . . ." She turned back to Molly.

Molly sighed. "Nay, she does not. Look upon her, child."

Hob and Nemain followed Molly's gesture toward the other end of the table.

A thin stream of blood, like a dark little ruby-colored snake, slid from Lady Rohese's left nostril. She did not notice at first, and kept looking round at the fire, where the doll crisped and blackened till nothing of it could be discerned. Then she would look back, stunned, at Molly, who sat smiling grimly.

Lady Rohese suddenly put a hand out to steady herself, and with a panicky motion scrambled upright. There was a collective gasp. The white linen over her thighs was sodden red, and even as they watched, the stain spread downward with appalling rapidity: Hob realized that her lifeblood must be pouring out beneath her gown. There was a lock of Molly's hair that had not fit in the doll. The fear left Lady Rohese's face and she snatched at the gray wisp, her face a mask of frenzied malignance. But she could not seem to grasp it, and the outstretching of her arm had put her off-balance, and she toppled sideways, striking the table edge, her last frantic clutch pulling part of the table linen and its burden of mugs and bowls down upon her.

The maid sprang to her side with a shriek and knelt, and the other maid and the knights crowded about her and her fallen mistress. The maid sprang up again. She put her palms on her cheeks; she looked about distractedly. "Dead! Dead!" she cried. She looked at Molly, and her lips curled in a grim leer. "Sir Tarquin, Sir Tarquin! What will he not do to you!" she snarled.

Jack bent a little, put his hand on his dagger, out of sight, and Hob unobtrusively loosened his own new dagger. But the two knights, with their oddly detached manner, seemed uninterested in hostilities; they bent and cradled their mistress in their arms, and forming an impromptu litter, slowly shuffled their way to the door.

At this moment a trembling hand was placed on the

jamb of the kitchen arch, and Joan peered around the edge. When she saw what was happening, she broke into a vengeful smile, composed of equal parts glee and hatred. Hawis took her by the shoulders and tried to turn her back into the kitchen. Joan shook off Hawis's hands and went step by slow step after the knights, keeping a certain distance, but still with that savage grin of triumph on her face.

The maids scurried ahead, one opening the inn door, the other going out and holding the door to the carriage. There was a stifled exclamation of dismay from the driver as the knights came into his view with their burden. Through the open door Hob could see the knights placing Lady Rohese within the coach, and placing a robe over her body.

Joan crept down the room. She reached the door, and slowly, silently, swung it shut, and shot the bolt. She put both palms against the door and leaned on it, as though pushing, and she stared at the wood before her face, grinning, grinning. From the road outside came muffled orders, the jingle of harness, and a rumble of wheels, as the coach got under way.

SOME TIME LATER Hob made himself ask, "But, Mistress, what did you do to her?"

Nemain was sitting quietly beside him, looking drained.

"I'm after putting a spell of loosening on the drawstring," said Molly, "and a hidden spell it is, so that she should not be aware of it, though she saw it done, and myself doing it right before her eyes."

"That was when you said something over the pouch-strings, Mistress?"

Molly drank off her ale. She was in a mood to explain some of the mysteries of her Art to Hob, a rare thing, and Adelard and Hawis were upstairs making Joan lie down, with one of Molly's calming potions inside her.

"'Twas. She's fancying herself a grand adept, but 'tis Sir Tarquin who's to be feared in that marriage. There's a great deal hinges on whose will is the stronger in these matters, and I am not some novice at this."

She paused, and looked moodily into the fire, and poured more ale from the beaker on the table.

"My words were—I'll not be telling you the exact words, and any road they being in Irish, but 'tis this that they signi-fied—that whoso loosed those strings with evil intent would loosen the strings of their blood. You could have opened that bag, lad, and it would have been safe as mother's milk. But she opened it with evil intent, that she might burn me up with that doll. It's herself she was killing when she plucked at those strings."

Hob looked at the table and sighed. Every time he learned more about the two women in his life, the ground beneath his feet, so solid when he was a boy in Father Athelstan's care, seemed less substantial. But he yearned to know things, and he had to ask.

"And how was it that her spell failed, and you giving her blood and hair and she having the doll and . . ."

Molly looked at Nemain. "What would you be telling him, so that he's understanding it?"

Nemain shrugged wearily. "Nay, *seanmháthair,* I'm after thinking you were courting your doom myself. I'm knowing what you did, but it's something I thought would fail."

Molly turned to Hob. "It's a thing that is not in words, and there are secrets in it that you are not to know, but think on it in this wise: she's after attacking me, and I knowing 'twas coming, and the doll and the blood and the hair giving force to her attack. And my inward . . . call it *armor,* the armor of my will. 'Tis that armor that's stronger than the weapon she's hurling at me, and she's failing. But her armor, her armor—'twas too weak, and it crumbling like sand before that spell, and all the strings of her blood loosed in her body. But it's she who killed herself, with her evil intent."

Hob looked at her, the closest thing to a mother he could remember, and for a moment he had a vision of a world in which some people were inwardly as lions or pards, powerful in secret ways, and striving invisibly, and Molly not the least of them.

Outside the inn, the sky was growing ever so slightly light, so that the windows were beginning to become visible against the dark walls. Molly drained her mug again, and set it down with a thump. "Hob, *mo chroí,* go and fetch

Timothy; send him here, and then go up and ask Goodman Adelard to come down, for we must be closing this inn and fleeing to the castle. That maid's after having the right of it: Sir Tarquin will be coming for us. It's we who must be gathering our forces, for he's a giant of the Art, and from this night on he'll be burning for our destruction."

Part III

THE WICKED

CHAPTER 24

ALONG THE COAST ROAD, TURNing onto the upward way toward Chantemerle's outer gates, came four wagons: the three barrel-roofed caravans of Molly's troupe and a wain, drawn by two horses, with Adelard driving and Joan and Hawis on the seat beside him; Timothy rode in the back, on heaps of hay. They had locked the inn and fled to the castle just before daybreak.

Joan sat slumped against Hawis, who held her mother in her arms, a strange reversal of roles. Last night Molly had finally managed to calm Joan, still in a frenzy of fear and rage, mixed with a sort of vengeful gloating, engendered first by the reappearance, and then the death, of her tormentor. At intervals

Joan would peer into Adelard's face, and ask, "Yon's truly dead?" Finally Molly gave her a draft to drink, and bundled her off to bed for a short nap. Now she rested against her daughter, wrapped in a shawl, sleepy and unenthusiastic, but with a modicum of tranquillity.

Molly had reassured Adelard, just before they left the inn: "'Tis your Joan she'll be again, in time, friend Adelard, but not tomorrow. Give her to drink from this—a swallow only, mind—each morning." Here she handed him a clay jug stopped with Spanish cork. "'Twill ease her past the next days, and by summer's end she'll be well, but for now you must be tender with her, and patient."

Now, in the brightening morning, the valves of the gate swung open, the guards recognizing them; they rolled within; Daniel was sent for, and appeared soon afterward. The clerk bade Molly welcome courteously, if a bit hastily; escorted them into the stables; and as grooms unhitched the wagons and rolled them manually against the wall, went quickly over to Hawis and her parents, bowed, and stood talking and smiling graciously at them all, but mostly at Hawis.

Molly was looking back at Daniel Clerk, tall and keen of expression, with a certain elegance in the simplicity of his manner of dress, beaming down at the innkeeper's daughter, who peeped shyly at him and away again. Hawis did not seem displeased at his attention, and Adelard was positively jovial as he beheld his daughter and the young castle official.

"Hmm," said Molly.

Nemain stood beside her. "*Och,* aye," she said.

Hob looked from Molly and Nemain to Hawis and Daniel and back to the two women, unsure of what they meant. Then he shrugged and began to pull Milo toward the ramp, prepared for another battle of wills. But Milo, for an ox, had an excellent memory, particularly where his comfort was concerned, and he stepped smoothly onto the ramp and walked placidly upward, setting a good example for Mavourneen and Tapaidh, who were being led by Jack, a set of reins in each hand.

By the time they got the beasts settled and made their way down again, Jack and Hob found the innkeeper and his family gone, as was Daniel. The page Guiscard stood with Molly and her granddaughter, ready to escort them to the great hall. Jack got a chest with clothing and other necessities from the main wagon, and Nemain locked everything up, and they set off, Sweetlove at Jack's heels and generally underfoot, making their way toward the gate to the inner ward.

In the hall Sir Odinell greeted them, had them settled in their former quarters, and bade them attend him, when ready, in a tower room. He left Guiscard as a guide. A while later they had everything stowed, had quaffed off jacks of honey beer, and were ready to follow Guiscard along narrow passages, up winding stairways, to a door in a seaward tower.

Here, in a circular room with shutters open to the salt

air, the cries of gulls floating on their long narrow wings coming up to them from the shoreline, they found Sir Jehan and Sir Balthasar, newly arrived that morning, welcome sights in this time of peril. After a round of greetings whose restraint just covered a real warmth on both sides, Sir Odinell had them be seated at a large table, on which were flagons of ale, tankards, and nothing else, not even cloths.

Sir Odinell stood at the table and regarded the others. "I have some matters of urgency to impart," he said. "I have had communications from the De Umfrevilles, by privy channels. The reports of Sir Tarquin's doings have reached as far as London, and even unto Rome. Both the king and the pope have become uneasy with their creature, coming to the understanding that there is more to him than they had realized, and all of it worse than they had realized, and in short: they have begun to fear him, and what he might grow to be, away here in the North Country, with none to check him.

"I said they have *begun* to fear him, but in truth it is more: the pope, fearing deviltry, had an exorcism attempted *in absentia*—they had some articles of Sir Tarquin's clothing, and . . . Well, I do not pretend to understand these matters. Apparently all seven priests, and a senior exorcist was among them, were found in the chamber where the ceremony was conducted, and they were quite dead. And . . . horribly so.

"The king, for his part, sent a summons to appear at court in London, by the hand of Sir William filz Gerald, one of the foremost knights of the king's retinue and a mighty champion, successful in war and tournament, and he went up to Sir Tarquin to bring him down to London, and he had thirty men with him. The thirty were never seen again. Sir William was found sitting on a bench in a garden in Durham, hard by the cathedral, staring at the garden wall. He has said not one word since he was found, and cannot abide the sight of rat or mouse—he begins to scream and become unruly, and he is still powerful of body, and thus a trial to his attendants, for he must be kept confined, and attended.

"So word has been sent to my kinsman that the protection of church and crown has been removed. Since they fear him, though, we can expect no aid if we move against him; if we fail, they will pretend ignorance, so to avoid his vengeance."

Molly heard this with a grim smile. "Ah well, we shall not be interfered with, any road."

"We may move against him, then," said Sir Balthasar.

"Be said by me, he will move against this castle within the week," Molly said. "I'm just after saying—"

The room, bright with the last rays of the waning sunlight, grew a bit less bright: one of the windows was partially darkened, filled with a four-foot spread of black wings, a rustling as of silk, and then a large raven settled to the sill, snapping its wings shut. Sitting in the window, the late-afternoon sunlight falling on its back, the raven's feathers had a purple sheen. Sweetlove came to her feet beside Jack's chair, but the dark man put a big hand down to keep her still. Sir Odinell took a step toward the raven, hand raised to drive it back out, but Molly's voice came sharply:

"Nay! Let be—'tis a watcher of mine."

Sir Odinell stopped, retreated a step, looking curiously at Molly. "Your watcher, madam?" he asked.

"'Tis." She tapped the table before her with her fore-finger and the raven sailed effortlessly into the room, the silken rustling louder in the confined space, and came to rest before her. It cocked its head this way and that, looking about the room, and Hob felt, when its keen brown eye fell upon him, that it was more than an animal intelligence that was assessing him.

The raven turned back to Molly, and very deliberately dropped a white pebble in front of her. It bent to the pebble, moved it to Molly's right. Then it straightened and looked at her expectantly. Molly reached for a deerskin pouch that hung from her zone, the belt from which her dagger and pouches depended. She undid some thongs, and slipped the pouch free from the zone. She loosened the drawstring, and carefully emptied about twoscore black and white pebbles to one side.

The raven strutted over to the pile, cocked its head to look at the black stones, the white stones, each a flat disk about the width of a grape. The raven chose two black stones, strode back over to Molly, dropped them in front of her, cocked its head and looked at them, bowed and nudged them this way and that; walked back, rocking a little, to take up a white pebble, then back to Molly again. The large handsome bird, solidly built, with feathers of glossy black, kept walking back and forth to the pile of pebbles, and soon was arranging the white and black stones in a complex pattern on the tabletop before Molly's seat.

Sir Odinell crossed himself several times, and wore an expression of deep disbelief, as though he could hardly bring himself to credit what he saw, but otherwise the knights watched, fascinated. At one point Molly moved one of the stones, a question. The raven moved two stones in apparent response. Molly sat back, her expression somber. She looked down at the table, and became very still.

The raven took three strutting steps toward her, and tilted its head to look up into her face. Molly said something low to it in Irish, and reached out her hand. She slowly stroked the nape of its neck with two fingers, smoothing the ruff of feathers there, perhaps a half-dozen times. Then she murmured something else to it, and the raven walked to the table edge, spread its wings, and flew through the open window, out into the sea air.

The sun began to dip behind the mountains, far to the west, and outside the window the light dimmed, and dimmed yet more, and Molly sat in the darkening room, and looked at the stones, and said nothing. The three knights, Jack, Hob, even Nemain, sat in silence as well, fearing to interrupt Molly's thoughts. Finally she roused herself, took a deep breath, spoke in low tones.

"That *buidseach,* that . . ." Molly looked at Nemain and shook her head in frustration. *"Buidseach*?" she asked her granddaughter.

"Wizard," said Hob, with his excellent memory for things once heard, before Nemain could answer. Molly glanced at him in surprise; Nemain, sitting next to him, just patted his hand in approval.

Molly returned to her thoughts. Her face was very bleak. "It's something I'm after marking about Sir Tarquin the last time we were here, and Hob bringing it to my mind, so that I'm understanding the secret, and a secret it is, that's at his core. He is as mighty—and as evil—a magus as I have ever even heard of in tales. Such things are spoken of in shadowed places, but to think—"

"But what have you learned of him?" asked Sir Odinell.

Molly stood, walked to the window. The tower they were in stood at the lip of the promontory, and to its height was added the height of the cliff that fell sheer to the water. Molly looked out at the gray twilit sky above the gray booming sea far below. She came back and stood by the table. "It is best you know as little as possible. You have said you trust me utterly—now is the time for you to act upon that trust. My watchers have told me that he will move on us, and move at night, and 'twill be soon."

"I must bring the folk within the walls," said Sir Odinell. "We must prepare—"

"Nay, now it's your trust I must be having, and you must

heed me—it's a man he is who can rot the pintles of your castle gates with a word, this *draíodóir*; who can burst the iron bands on every door with a wave of his hand—and you yourself no more safe here now than on yon strand below."

"Then what—"

Molly was standing just across the table from the burly lord of this castle, and she was a big, handsome woman, erect, commanding, and she said to him quietly, "Hush, now," as a mother speaks to a frightened child, and the Sieur de Chantemerle sat back and fell silent.

"We're needing to meet him on the road, you and your knights and Sir Jehan and his people—come on him at night as he marches up the coast road. I'll be after attempting a glamour, and that concealing us from his ways of seeing through his Art. There's a fear to me that he is so strong, that it's all unavailing that my Art will prove, yet it's try we must. You to fall upon his men-at-arms and those ensorcelled knights of his—they are spellbound, yet aren't they mortal as you or I—and Nemain and I will deal with Sir Tarquin."

"You and—" Sir Odinell turned his eyes on Nemain, so young and so small—she would never be as tall as was her grandmother—and looked back to Molly, who said again, "Hush, now."

Molly looked around the bare table at the big grim men seated there.

"Be said by me, it's an enemy that's more powerful than any you're after facing in your lives; aye, even the Fox." This last was directed toward Sir Jehan. "Nor can you be about killing him." She leaned on the table, her palms flat to the wood glossy with beeswax.

"It's a thing I'm not wishing to say here, or anywhere outside my family—" Here she nodded at Nemain and Jack and Hob, sitting to one side. "It's trust from you I must have, and your tongues with all their questions silent—I will not say all that I know, 'twill only make things worse, but be said by me, he can kill any one of us, even Sir Balthasar, even myself, and nor can we kill him, not even Sir Balthasar, not even myself. But myself and my *gariníon*"—she gestured vaguely toward Nemain; she was so wrapped up in her urgent thoughts that she had lost the English word—"my, my—"

"Granddaughter," said Nemain, very low.

"—granddaughter," said Molly, "can between us trap him, and hold him, though we cannot kill him, and then, we having him trapped, I'm having a way to destroy him utterly."

There was some clearing of throats; Sir Balthasar spoke aside to Sir Jehan, very quietly, a tone of complaint in the knight's gravel bass. Molly raised both hands and brought her palms down with a bang on the table.

"You are lords of castles, and high men, but I am a queen on my own earth, and in this matter, be said by me, you are as children and I as your wise *seanmháthair*—"

"Grand—" began Nemain.

"—grandmother," said Molly. "And you to do what I say,

and no more, and no less; else all will perish at the hands of this *gruagh,* this giant of evil. 'Twill be a near-run race as it is, and nor can I be having the least disobedience to think about." She glared about the table, and those prideful high men, each with brightly burning soul, glanced down or aside, even Sir Jehan, save only Sir Balthasar, who looked her straight in the face and said, inclining his head toward Sir Jehan, "Madam, I am first his man in all things, but after that I am your man, as you know, and if he will follow you, as I think he will, that will I."

Sir Jehan raised his head. "I am your man in this, madam, and will do what you say, neither more nor less."

Sir Odinell, looking from one knight to the next and taking his direction from their trust in Molly, said, "And I as well, madam."

She gestured toward Jack and Hob. "These two will be protecting Nemain and myself from meddling by any who eludes your knights, but 'tis only ourselves who must deal with Sir Tarquin. I'm after seeing what he is, and calling to mind things I've heard from women older than myself, and feeling his power. It's a great magus he is, and it's the death of others that's giving him strength, he's drawing it from them—if you're coming nigh him, and he able to reach you with his hands, sure and he'll be killing you, even the mightiest of you, even Sir Balthasar, and him growing stronger on the instant, and that by the amount, the exact amount, of his victim's strength."

Sir Jehan spoke up. "Then we aid him by engaging him?"

"Aye," she said. "If he's killing a mighty warrior, it's that strength he'll be garnering to himself, and himself the more terrible because of it. Let us trap him, and drain him, and destroy him."

Sir Odinell sat silent till he was certain she was done speaking, then asked, "You can do that, madam? And yourself unharmed?"

"She can do that," growled Sir Balthasar from down the table. "Aye, and all else that is needful."

Sir Odinell said simply, "But *how* will you do that?"

"We'll be doing it, nor are you needing to know how," said Molly. "It's not a thing I could be telling you in a way you could understand, and any road, such knowledge is forbidden you."

She looked at the window through which the raven had gone.

"'Tis more than Sir Tarquin's doings that I've had from my little messenger tonight: 'tis guidance as well on what will be, and though it's by the one strand of spider silk that our safety is hanging this night, yet I'm of the belief that we will prevail."

TWO DAYS LATER the raven returned. Again it was late in the afternoon, and the castle just sitting down to the tables.

The raven came in at a window at the lower end of the hall, and flew the length of the room, occasioning an upwelling of comment and conversation. It sought out Molly at the high table, landing before her amid the trenchers and the goblets, and dropped a gray stone in front of her. She nodded, and the bird took to the air, circled the dais, and flew back down the hall and out into the light of the setting sun.

Molly looked around at the assembled knights and their ladies. "Eat now, and then arm yourselves," she said. "'Tis this very night."

CHAPTER 25

OB STOOD JUST WITHIN THE
shadow of the trees, stroking his
horse's nose, looking out and down
a bit at the grassy slope to the coast road, a ribbon of
bare earth winding along the shore. Beyond the road
was the scalloped coast of Northumbria: to left and
right the sea pushed into semicircular bays, while
ahead was the stony headland that divided them.
Beyond the rock-studded sands of the bay shores,
the German Sea shone like steel; the full moon, new-
risen, spilled a path of light along the wave tops.

Around him in the gloom were the half-seen
bodies of Sir Odinell's force, dismounted now,
everyone holding his horse's head, prepared to put
a quick hand to the animal's nostrils and a soothing

murmur in its ear, if necessary. The inevitable small sounds of such a force came softly to Hob's ear: the shift of large bodies; the muffled thump of a hoof as a horse moved in place; a faint jingle from tack and from weaponry; the rustle of chain mail and the squeak of leather; a rattle as a horse made water against the carpet of dead leaves beneath the trees. He was also aware of a strong odor of horse, spiced with the oil-and-tallow treatment used on saddles and boots, as well as the green scent of the forest. Over everything lay the salt breath of the sea.

Molly was near, with Nemain and Jack and Sir Balthasar. Sir Odinell, Sir Jehan and the knights of Chantemerle and Blanchefontaine, armed cap-à-pie with mail hauberks and coifs, armored gloves, greaves, and helms, were stationed to the north; to the south was grouped a levy of men-at-arms from both castles, in boiled-leather gambesons, some with pikes, some with shields and swords. The placement of foot soldiers and knights was based on information about Sir Tarquin's order of march, reported to Molly by her avian spies, and on her plan of attack, thrashed out with the three senior knights.

Sir Balthasar had provided Hob with a falchion, a sword that was not only short, which made it easier for Hob to wield, but also had a heavy drop point, the thick-backed blade functioning almost as an ax and compensating somewhat for the disparity between the lad's strength and that of a grown man. Jack of course had his crow-beaked war hammer

with him, and both wore leather gambesons. It had been decided that neither would carry shields, because they would
have to race after Molly and Nemain, and speed was vital in
the initial part of the attack.

The soldier to Hob's right discovered a lacing that had
come loose on his boot, and he moved away a little, so to
avoid being stepped on by his mount, and bent to tie it up.
The men-at-arms fought on foot, and the horses were used
only to bring them to the battlefield, and in fact were now
picketed to stakes in the ground. These rounceys were
not trained as were the destriers, the warhorses, and this
soldier's horse immediately, perversely, began to whicker,
hoping perhaps to start a conversation with the horses to
right and left.

A great bulk loomed up between Hob and the glimmer of
the sea, and he heard Sir Balthasar's grinding bass, address-
ing the unfortunate man-at-arms: "Quiet that fucking horse,
or I'll stuff its mouth with your tarse." There was a muffled
apology; the soldier turned to his horse, stroked a hand over
the velvet nose, and spoke very quietly in the restlessly flicking ear; and the grim mareschal went back to watching the
coast road.

For a time nothing happened. Hob would not dare to
move about, but he leaned over, the better to see the road
to the south, whence Sir Tarquin must come. A few feet
beyond, his view was blocked by a low branch, black on one
side, moon-silver on the other. On the branch was an indis-

tinct mound, perhaps a cubit high. A moment later the top of the mound swiveled, and two enormous eyes glinted in the moonlight. One of Molly's owls sat there, and farther along the branch were shapes that might be others. He and the owl regarded each other for a moment, and then the head turned smoothly back to the road.

More waiting. Hob began to think that some mistake had been made, although Molly rarely made mistakes. Yet the road was so empty, and the sound of the waves so bleak and lonely, that it seemed that nothing would ever happen on this desolate stretch of coast. Even as Hob thought this, there was a furtive movement in the shadows beside the road. He watched the spot where he had seen it, and there was nothing there but darkness, and then there was movement again, and into a small patch of moonlight between areas of leaf-shadow stepped a rat, and it raised its snout, facing toward the hidden war party, and its eyes had a blue sheen to them.

Hob controlled himself with an effort, and made no sound of surprise. He took a stealthy step forward and put one finger to Nemain's shoulder. She turned and looked at him, and he pointed. The rat was still there, nose quivering, eyes searching the shadows where the knights waited. Nemain nodded, and gave a low whistle.

The lump of darkness that was the owl launched itself into a long, shallow, soundless dive; the wings flew out in a three-foot spread to brake at the last instant; there was a moment's savagery, a muffled shriek, and the owl beat its way back to the limb, where it began to tear at its victim. Several more times owls drifted like dreams across the shafts of moonlight, stalled gracefully here and there above the ground, and bit and clawed Sir Tarquin's spies to death. The rats had been sent to scout ahead, to warn of just such an ambush; now none would return to report to the witch-lord.

Again there was a period when there was just the empty ribbon of road, the ceaseless swash of the waves. Then Hob saw the heads of the owls perched nearby swivel as one, looking to the south. The acute, the very acute, hearing of the brown owls had discerned the first warning of the approaching column.

CHAPTER 26

WHEN MOLLY HAD, WITH THE help of the lords of Chantemerle and Blanchefontaine, finished disposing the troops in under the eaves of the forest, she had taken the silver box from her saddlebag, and from it the ball of green ribbon. She and Nemain had gone a little past one side of the crowd of horses and men, and faced each other. The two women wore simple gowns of white linen, tight-sleeved, and pulled up through their belts and bloused over somewhat, in order to allow their lower legs to move freely in the coming battle. Molly had handed one end of the ribbon to Nemain, who stood in place; then she had walked backward, always facing Nemain, unreeling the ribbon as she went, muttering prayers in

Irish, till she had gone a little past the other end of the battle line. She had paused a moment, then she and her grand-daughter had simultaneously faced the sea, backed to the nearest low branch on either side, and knotted the ribbon to the trees. The women were thus behind a barrier of green ribbon, and the war party with them.

"'Tis like a wall, and we behind it, so that, mage though he be, he will not be perceiving us through the spells I'm after placing on that ribbon, nor will he be able to come at us till we are ready, and I cut the barrier." So she had told Hob, though to the knights and their men she said nothing of the sort, but only to stay behind the ribbon till she cut it.

Now Molly had seen the movement of the owls' heads, turning so easily on their flexible necks, and drew from within her cloak a small pair of silver scissors. She watched the road where it curved out of sight. The sea grumbled; the moon burned along the ridges of the waves. Around the bend came a double column of Sir Tarquin's bewitched knights. From this distance they seemed almost normal, but after a moment it became apparent that they did not speak to one another; they did not look to left or right; they stared ahead and moved only in counterpoint with the horses' movements.

There were perhaps a score of them, and one more in the lead, a big man, a very big man, nearly seven feet tall, with a hand-and-a-half claymore, an outsize Scottish sword, strapped to his back. Behind came two white horses, and they drew a carriage like a little room, with a door and two windows in the side that could be seen. Two lanterns—boxes of thin-scraped horn with candles inside—were set at the forward corners of the vehicle; a burly man drove the team, clad in a mail hauberk and coif, but no helmet, a mace in a slot by his side. Curtains of some sort were drawn across the coach windows, so that the interior was hidden.

It seemed to Hob that the carriage, inoffensive enough in appearance, yet radiated menace, and afterward he could never say whether this was so in truth or because he knew that therein must be Sir Tarquin. Behind marched, in poor order, the roughs and ragtag mercenaries that the mage had accumulated as men-at-arms, men who would not flinch at the evil they served, or that they were asked to do.

The eldritch knights passed the midpoint of the ambush; then came the carriage. When the first of the crowd of mercenaries had passed the spot where Molly stood, she snipped the ribbon in half with the scissors, and as the two halves fell to the ground, the men-at-arms surged forward, some with pikes leveled and some with drawn swords, running as silently as possible, as Molly had instructed them. In this way they covered much of the distance before the soldiers below were aware of them.

Sir Tarquin, however, was sensitive to them as soon as the ribbon was broken: the curtain on one window was whipped back, and the mage's face glimmered indistinctly in the shadowy interior. A word to the driver halted the carriage. A moment later he had flung open the door, and down he stepped to the ground, a tall saturnine man, wearing no armor but swathed in a billowing red cloak, the color just apparent in the glow from the near-side horn lantern. He peered up toward the forest. Hob felt, as he had on the night of the water-mirror, that Sir Tarquin looked right at him and at him only, although he knew this could not be true.

The men-at-arms of Chantemerle and Blanchefontaine had reached the bottom of the slope and jumped without pause onto the causeway, crashing into the disorganized mob of ruffians that followed the carriage, producing an instant uproar compounded of men yelling, the *clang* of swords, the *thuds* of pikes as they were driven into leather or quilt gambesons. Many of Sir Tarquin's soldiers were driven right off the road by the initial impact of the down-rushing pikes, the victims tumbling down the farther slope toward the beach, rolling over and over to a halt in the dunes, tangled in the marram grass with gaping wounds in their bellies, thrashing feebly, no more to rise.

As soon as the men-at-arms had begun their charge on foot, Sir Odinell, in nominal charge of the force of knights that included Sir Jehan and Sir Balthasar, signaled for the mailed riders to spread out; at once they began to advance at a fast walk, the knights instinctively slotting themselves in beside one another, forming a battle line. The dew had beaded up on the oiled rings of their chain mail, and when they emerged into the moonlight the dewdrops clothed them in gems, a line of jeweled knights.

Molly and Nemain snatched up their golden hook-headed weapons and trotted after them, effectively concealed by the line of knights and their huge destriers. Behind the two women came Hob, running lightly with drawn falchion, and Jack, making all speed with a furiously determined limp, his terrible war hammer in his big right hand.

Down below, Sir Tarquin's knights, at the first sound of the clash behind them, had wheeled their mounts and raced back along the road, splitting to either side of the coach and sweeping into the melee at the rear. The struggling men-at-arms from the two castles were now at a disadvantage, caught between the hammer of the eerie knights' charge and the anvil of the remaining mercenaries.

Sir Odinell gave the word to charge, and the knights began to canter, then to gallop, toward the rear of the coach. As the left wing of the knights' line swung toward the battle behind the carriage, Sir Tarquin stood revealed. His right hand was upraised toward Sir Odinell's riders, his left held a book. Was the book on fire? It seemed to be on fire—Hob could not decide: Hob ran, and kept fast hold on his sword hilt, and that was enough to take all his concentration. He was pounding, breathless, down the slope after Molly, and keeping his eye on the magus, the women, and the diminishing distance between them; everything depended on Molly and Nemain reaching Sir Tarquin before he became fully aware of them. To some extent all the rest of tonight's bloodshed was a battle of pawns; it was the women and the Sieur de Duncarlin who would decide the game.

Sir Tarquin made a sharp pushing motion at the air with the flat of his palm and voiced a piercing cry that seemed as if it would reach the clouds, so loud it was, and there were words in it, but not in any language Hob had ever heard, and a knight and his horse, caught in midstride, were dashed to the ground. They were knocked flat on their sides with a crash that overrode all the din of the fighting, so that Hob faltered as he ran and risked a glance to his right, to see what had transpired. Man and mount were dead, and Hob thought to see wisps of smoke curling up from under the knight's mail hauberk and the horse's saddle blanket.

Molly and Nemain were running full out at the mage, their shortened white gowns fluttering, their naked feet flashing as they sped down the grassy slope, their long unbound hair streaming behind them like two great banners, gray and red. The golden crescents at the ends of their spear shafts were flickering with glints of moonlight, and stretching, stretching out before them, seeking the wizard's throat. So intent was he on the forces from the two castles, and perhaps a little blinded by Molly's vision-tangling spells, that he became aware of the women just too late.

They closed the last few feet at a dead run and sprang

at him like two wolves attacking a stag. The crescents, one on each side, circled his neck and locked with a surprisingly musical *clang,* and the impact knocked the book from his hand—Hob now saw that it was indeed emitting little licks of flame, though it was not itself consumed by them, and it lay smoldering there in the grass, scorching the green blades.

Sir Tarquin drew breath but then plainly could not speak—a hissing groan, very faint, came from his mouth, and the close-fitting blades had already seared a shallow necklace of burnt flesh where they touched him. Hob had seen Molly silence another wizard with a binding spell, and had time in the whirl of action for the fleeting thought that she had impressed something of the kind into the golden metal.

Sir Tarquin seized a shaft in each hand and made as if to wrench them from the women's grasp, but as quickly let go with an expression of agony, and another hiss of pain, as his palms contacted the strips of metal that ran the length of the staff. There followed a period in which he tried various stratagems to free himself, including some time spent staring first at Molly, then Nemain, with an expression of intense concentration. Hob himself, normally insensitive to these things that Nemain and Molly felt so keenly, now felt some sort of pressure—clearly the mage was silently commanding them to release him.

Molly and Nemain, struggling against the weight of the

spear shafts and the immense thrust of the wizard's will, staggered a little in place, their faces set in expressions of strain and concentration. Hob whirled in a circle, making sure that no one came nigh his betrothed and her grand-mother. Jack was doing the same, the war hammer held at port arms, trying to keep the terrible struggle of the three adepts in sight, while making sure that the space around the conflict was kept clear.

The burly driver, who at first had run back to help in the battle behind the carriage, now realized that his master was in peril, and returned, lumbering up, in his hand the brutal mace, a short club ending in a lump of iron with six flanges sharpened to a knife edge. Jack Brown limped swiftly toward him, placing himself athwart the driver's path. Sir Tarquin's servant aimed a tremendous overhand blow at Jack's head, but the dark man threw up the war hammer: the heads col-lided with a piercing *clank,* and the driver danced backward, cursing, transferring his weapon to his left hand that he might shake his stinging right hand.

Jack's body might have been made from the gray-stone bones of the earth, and he showed no such distress. He shuffled forward, and as the driver managed to resume his grip on the mace, Jack swung his hammer over and down, the hammer side of the head smashing the flanged mace to the ground, the war hammer continuing back and up and over again, Jack deftly swiveling the head so the crow-beak side was leading, falling like a summer-night shooting star, punching a hole in the chain-mail links of the driver's coif, and thence through the roof of his skull.

Now the space around the struggling trio of Sir Tarquin and the two women was, at least for the moment, clear. Hob took up a position facing generally southward, turning his head constantly to keep everything in view. Jack put his foot on the driver's chest and wrenched the war hammer free. He raised it up again and plunged it into the grassy soil to remove what clung to it, then took up station facing north, his back to Hob. In this way they kept a circular field in view, ensuring that the women would be free to concentrate their efforts on the witch-lord.

Hob looked to his right, toward the forest; there was nothing there, nor had he expected anything, only that he wished to leave no quarter unwatched, in case there was some attempt to circle around by any of Sir Tarquin's men who might win clear of the melee. Then he looked left, to the battle, but there was little to be seen: the women moved their feet slightly now and then, readjusting their balance; Sir Tarquin could barely move for the sorcerous blades that held him trapped. His eyes bulged with rage, and with his silent struggle to break each woman's will. Every time the blades touched him there was a little blue spark or flamelet, and Hob felt the women were draining him, with the spears, with their resistance to his will.

To the south Sir Jehan was driving his horse between two of the enchanted knights. He had his iron campaign hand locked on his shield's bracket, and the reins loosely looped about his right wrist. In his left hand was a flicker of bright metal—the Sieur de Blanchefontaine had indeed recaptured most of the speed of his right hand with his left. Even as Hob watched, one of the knights fell away and slipped dead from the saddle, and Sir Jehan turned his ferocity on the other.

Beyond him, in the midst of a throng of enemies, Hob could see Sir Balthasar, like Death in Revelation, hacking and smashing an irresistible path through knights and men-at-arms, his horse biting at faces, striking with spike-studded horseshoes at the foot soldiers. The mareschal's face was dark with suffused blood; his arm rose and fell tirelessly; nothing stood before him. Hob saw him cleave another knight from his collarbone halfway to his heart despite the mail shirt he wore.

Hob looked left, then right again; he looked back at Jack. All seemed to be quiet nearby, and the melee behind the coach was drifting southward, but the men from Chantemerle and Blanchefontaine were clearly prevailing. He looked to the struggle by the carriage; Molly to the north and Nemain to the south, their backs to him, and Sir Tarquin facing him—Hob avoided looking directly into those eyes, a thing he knew could be perilous with wizards.

The mage now swiveled his burning eyes to the south; his left hand stretched out in the same direction, its fingers extended. Then his hand closed as on a garment, an unseen garment; slowly he drew the hand toward his side. Hob watched this with fascination and unease. The group remained in a kind of fidgeting stasis: the women would readjust their positions, setting their feet anew, and the wizard would attempt a small movement, flinching from the touch of the golden collar made by the locked blades. But otherwise nothing would have seemed to be happening, were it not for the expressions of intense concentration on the three faces, and a humming in Hob's bones, a feeling that there was a sound too low for him to hear, as power was matched to power between the women and the magician. It was a strong sense that there was a roaring and a shrieking that was inaudible to him, a feeling he could not begin to explain even to himself.

But outwardly there was little except the harsh breathing of three people in some sort of extremity. Then came a scrabbling from behind the carriage. The horses drawing the coach, that had stood so stolidly, now shifted and neighed, startled, as around the front of the vehicle came two of the mercenaries Sir Tarquin had assembled, Scots by the look of them and by their dress. They must have escaped the melee to the south by some means and crept along between the road and the sea, heading north, and, seeing their master beleaguered, decided to take a hand. They ran around the horses and toward the trio of adepts, but Jack moved to thwart them, moving at his fast rolling limp and drawing back the war hammer.

Hob started toward Jack and the Scots, but there was a movement just at the edge of his vision; by reflex his head turned toward the motion, and then he saw what the magus had summoned. The Scots perhaps were as insensitive to his commands as Hob, but the eerie knights, whom he had already compromised in an unholy fashion, were tied to him in some way, and now, unhorsed in the battle, bloodied but essentially whole, striding on long legs toward them, came the lead knight, an enormously tall man, clad in mail and bearing in both hands his claymore, the blade resting back on his shoulder. He was a narrow-built man, but one of those lean narrow men who are all sinew and flat muscle.

Now he broke into a run toward Nemain; his sword came off his shoulder and he lifted it high. It was one of those huge swords with a bastard grip, the hilt too big for one and too small for two hands, so that the swordsman held it with a hand behind the quillons and stabilized it with the other folded over the pommel and the remainder of the hilt. A powerful knight could sever half a horse's neck with such a sword, and now the knight plainly meant to strike Nemain with it.

Hob's fear for her safety, churning in his stomach all through this unnatural battle with a terrible and uncanny foe, was now brought to a crisis by this new and immediate threat to his betrothed; on the instant, by some alchemy, all this dread ignited into a sudden burning mixture of rage and hatred, and he spun on the spot, leaving Jack to his own devices, and ran full tilt to intercept the giant knight. The knight veered toward him and the claymore came moaning through the air toward Hob; the lad threw up the falchion to block it and the claymore tore it from his hand.

Smoothly the giant followed through, whirled the sword above his head, and returned the weapon with a whistling horizontal cut. Hob leaned back frantically and felt a line of thin fire run across his chest. The sword circled, went up and around and came back again, this time in a downward stroke that Hob, running backward, eluded by the width of a blade of grass.

The prodigious stroke buried the blade in the soft ground, but the knight's long arms immediately began to tug it free. The giant was in a crouch as he pulled his sword from the ground, and Hob, snarling like a badger, reversed himself, and ran at the knight. He leaped at the last moment, planted his left foot on the giant's bent thigh, and sprang upward, his right hand plucking his new dagger from its sheath at his right hip, the pommel up and the blade projecting from the bottom of his fist. His left hand caught the back of the knight's neck; the giant began to straighten, unwittingly helping Hob to ascend.

The long claymore was now useless because the lad was inside it, climbing, climbing, clambering up the knight as though going up a tree, one leg drawn up and the foot scrabbling for purchase in the man's belt. Hob's hand drew back, he saw the strangely emotionless eyes of the knight staring at him from either side of the helmet's nasal, and he drove the dagger into the knight's left eye until the increasing width of the blade caused it to wedge into the bones of the orbit—was that a blue flame or flash that Hob saw ripple up the blade?— and the knight began to topple backward, as a grandfather pine is felled, rigid, already dead, and Hob went down on top of him, and had to exert all his strength, cursing under his breath and still in a rage, to pull his dagger free, the steel so strongly embedded in bone.

He rose, breathing like the north wind, and turned. One of the two Scots who had thought to come to Sir Tarquin's aid was dead at Jack Brown's feet. The other had closed with Jack while he was disposing of the first man, and gotten inside the range of the war hammer, and now tried to stab Jack with a foot-long dirk, but the silent man, beast-quick, seized the knife wrist with his left hand, dropped the hammer, and gripped the mercenary by the throat.

As Hob watched, Jack, powerful Jack, held the tall Scot helpless and throttled the life from him. The Scot struck Jack again and again with his free hand, to no apparent effect, and the blows soon became feeble and erratic. After what seemed to the lad a long and unpleasant time, Jack let the body, purple-faced, eyes and tongue protruding, drop like a sack of peat to the ground.

Hob came to himself, quickly turning in a circle to assess the situation. No enemy threatened the women and Jack was picking up his hammer again. Hob cleaned his dagger on the grass and went to retrieve his falchion, but the impact with the claymore had notched and bent the blade, and Hob threw it down again. He pried the sword from the hand of the first Scot Jack had killed and resumed his post, his back to Jack and his eye alert for any enemies that might yet live.

CHAPTER 27

KNIGHTS AND MEN-AT-ARMS FROM the two castles began to straggle up from the south: all of Sir Tarquin's men were now dead. The young Sir Josce came riding up and without checking his horse's gallop swerved to ride between Sir Tarquin and the carriage. Seeing the mage trapped in the golden noose that the women held so steady, seeing an opportunity for advancement, for glory, the young knight urged his mount onward, steering with his knees, dropping his shield and drawing back his sword for a two-handed stroke.

The mage rolled his eyes toward the oncoming horse and rider, and flung up his left hand. A pulse of some sort ripped the sword from Sir Josce's hand, flinging it in an arc, trailing smoke, till it landed in the grass, smoldering. The knight, his hands numb, was carried past Sir Tarquin by his terrified horse. As he passed close behind the wizard, Sir Tarquin's right hand stretched out backward; his claws sank into the knight's calf; he gave a mighty wrench and Sir Josce was dragged from his saddle, the horse clattering away.

The mage's fingernails, so like claws, now crackled and smoked where they were embedded in Sir Josce's leg; there was a spark of blue and a report, and faint blue flame played about the mage's fingertips. To everyone's horror, the knight aged and withered before their eyes, while Sir Tarquin grew visibly more energetic, and the ring of burnt flesh about his neck partially healed itself.

Hob saw that the women's task had become harder, for they staggered a bit more as the renewed vitality of the wizard was felt, a strengthening of the invisible battering that his will was working on them, and that they were resisting—this in addition to the effort of maintaining the position of the golden lance heads. Sir Tarquin, newly robust, even tried once more to wrench free of the trap: he put a palm to a lance shaft again, but again was forced to release it immediatel. with a hiss of pain.

Sir Balthasar, furious at the foolish loss of the young knight and even more at the strengthening of the mage, wheeled his mount back and forth before the arriving knights and men-at-arms, directing them to withdraw several yards inland from the sorcerous struggle and settle there, the knights to picket their mounts. He declared, with pungent and even vulgar clarity, what would befall the wretch who disobeyed, and thereafter dismounted, but paced up and down before the growing ranks of men from the two castles, glowering at them.

Sir Jehan and Sir Odinell, as lords presumably exempt from this prohibition, dismounted and stood to watch closer to the struggle than their men, but no one else. Sir Odinell summoned one of his men-at-arms and gave muttered instructions, and shortly thereafter a party of three men made their way in a wide circle around the struggle and came up to the two white horses, unhitched them, and led them away, again in a roundabout fashion. Now the carriage offered no possibility of escape should the mage defeat the women's trap.

Everyone settled in to see what the hours of this terrible night would bring. The women were obviously weary, and yet Hob had been told that they could not triumph before dawn: that the evil magus could not be destroyed before that. The night was more than half-gone, but it was long before the dawn. The men-at-arms' horses that had been left tethered in the woods were now brought down to the grassy slope, and knights and soldiers saw to their mounts. The men drew wine and barley beer from their saddlebags and settled on the sward to await the workings of destiny, gloomy spectators at this little-understood event.

Jack, Hob, Sir Balthasar, and the two castle lords stood

in a loose line behind the women, preventing any least interference. Some way inland the natural rise of the land, and the tendency of the force to settle with their mounts in a semicircle, gave the impression of an audience on a hillside at a tournament, or a mystery play held outside.

If the women were weary, so was Sir Tarquin. Even the increased vitality he had stolen from poor Sir Josce was beginning to ebb. As the mage poured more and more of his energy into the struggle, that portion of his life force that he used to sustain the appearance of life was recruited to supply vigor to his limbs and his will, and his person began to suffer a certain degree of deterioration.

His skin became blotchy, and small lesions appeared on his face, and on his hands, and perhaps other areas hidden beneath his robes. Most perceptible was the odor of corruption: at first just a hint, as of a rodent that had died within castle walls, and then more and more intense.

At one point Hob turned his back on the static conflict to get a breath of cleaner air. Behind him he saw a silent host of men, sitting, squatting, down on one knee, but all watching, unspeaking, somber, attentive. The horn lanterns on the coach had begun to falter, and Sir Odinell had torches driven into the soft earth and lit, to illuminate the struggle.

After a while, as more and more torches were placed, the glow revealed the whole area of combatants and their witnesses, and reached a little into the shadow under the trees. There Hob could just make out a branch with the hunched shapes, the large round moon eyes, of two owls, further witnesses—and Hob was sure there were more that he could not see.

He turned back to the battle. Nothing had changed, but he could hear the tortured breathing of the women, and the wind from the German Sea, though diluting it mightily, brought further indications of Sir Tarquin's corporal decay. Yet he strove as sturdily, and glowered as terribly at the women, as he had done at the beginning.

Hob stood there, unable to help at all and in an agony of fear for his betrothed, and also for her grandmother, who had adopted him, or as near as made no difference. And as he stood there, forced to do nothing but brood on the situation, the brute reality of it began to be borne in on him, by the odor coming in wayward gusts to his nostrils, by the small disfigurations and peelings and spots of corrosion on the wizard's visible flesh, that Molly's assessment was correct, that what Hob had heard of Sir Tarquin was being made manifest here before him, that the mage's spirit had managed to persist in this crumbling mansion, this foundering vessel: this body that was long dead.

CHAPTER 28

S O THE WEARY NIGHT WORE ON. But no night is endless, however it may seem. Beyond the struggle, beyond the carriage, beyond the rock-strewn strand, far out where the German Sea met the sky, a pallor, thin as watered milk, began to seep up from the world's rim. Hob suddenly tore his eyes from the torchlit, silent battle, where Nemain had begun to shift from foot to foot to gain a moment's rest for each in turn, a kind of controlled stagger that was alarming in its suggestion of imminent collapse. He looked out to sea; he blinked and looked at the horizon from the side of his eyes; at last he decided that the dawn was struggling to be born.

Sir Tarquin had his back to the shore, but the

women, whose every rasping breath came clearly to Hob above the grumbling of the sea, faced east, and now they saw the paling of the night sky over the waters. They straightened; they seemed in some way enheartened, although plainly very weary. The light grew; the graying sky began to show hints of color; far out over the sea, the underbellies of clouds turned rose and gold.

Molly said something in a gasping voice to Nemain, who grunted agreement. A moment later the women took a great breath, threw back their heads, and gave a long, wailing call up into the sky, some word in Irish, the low-and-high voices of grandmother and granddaughter making a barbaric harmony, the cry going on and on, echoing from the rising land behind Hob, the fey music of it setting up a shiver along his bones, a stirring of some deep-heart animal self.

At last it ceased, and all was as before, yet there was a sense that some vast border had been crossed. Sir Tarquin, his now-rotting face a mask of malevolence, his lips drawn back from those disquieting incisors, showed no awareness of a change in circumstances, but Hob could see that the women stood taller, easier, had ceased to stagger in place.

The first hint of the sun's rim appeared, sending a path of fire from the horizon along the ridges of the waves, a fuse burning toward the rocks of the headland, the sands of the bays. With the dawn came a stronger breeze from the sea, bringing the odor of corruption from the magus more pungently to Hob. The men of the two castles had spiked perhaps a score of torches near the sorcerous battle. The dawn brought an etiolation of their golden light, and the dawn breeze made the flames flap and roar.

Hob stood and watched his beloved and her grandmother, and waited for the deliverance Molly had said would come with the daylight. The roaring of the torch flames in the sea wind increased, and increased, and was suddenly joined by a commotion from the troops behind them. Hob turned to see what was happening.

Above the woods where only last night they had waited in ambush, lit by the first level rays of the rising sun, a dark cloud swirled, and the bustle of its myriad wings was the source of the increased roar: crows and ravens—scores, hundreds; more, and yet more—so many that Hob could not put a number to them. He thought dazedly of Father Athelstan, who had memorized three of the four Gospels, reciting to him the incident of the Gadarene swine—"My name is Legion, for we are many."

The birds began to drop from the sky and settle in the trees. The trees grew black with them; the branches drooped with the weight. All the glossy black heads were being cocked this way and that, always to maintain a view of the conflict down there by the side of the road. The sun, catching their eyes, glittered in countless beads of darkest brown. And still birds were dropping into the trees. Every crow and raven south of the Tweed seemed to have come in answer to what Hob now realized was a summons: that cry from Molly and Nemain.

The men were all turning back and forth, trying to watch both the struggle and the arriving flock, and not a little frightened at the vast somber mob of birds perching, settling; every crow, every raven watching the scene below with curious eagerness, the tiny dark jewels flickering with each eyeblink. As strange as the sight was, stranger still was the utter silence; there was flapping as new birds arrived or as birds kept their balance on the thinner branches, but no call, no *caw* from the crows, no *cronk* from the ravens: only silence, tense and greedy attention, a sparkling cloud of miniature eyes returning the rays of the new sun.

Molly and Nemain began to sing. They sang the same melody, but one voice higher than the other. Hob had heard them sing like the angel choirs of great God, but this song, though beautiful in its Irish speech, had a dark strand in the long rise and fall of its melody, that—though Hob could not understand the tongue—somehow made him think only one word: *Death*.

As they sang, a crow rose from the trees, flew over them, circled out over the strand, and came forward again, alighting on the carriage roof. Now Sir Tarquin seemed to notice for the first time the mass of black in the trees, and rolled his eyes this way and that, and put his hands to the shafts of the lances again, which served him no better than before, for he snatched them away at once, wincing and shaking his hands.

The odor coming from him was now almost unbearable: the odor of carrion.

Two crows and a raven alighted in the grass near Hob. There was a roar behind him; he whirled, to see the whole flock taking to the air. The sound was deafening. The crow on the coach snapped open its glossy wings; two beats and it was on Sir Tarquin's shoulder. It leaned toward him, head bent sideways, and like a lover bestowing a kiss, bit a piece from the mage's cheek. Sir Tarquin gave a hiss; his eyes bulged; he glared at the crow and swung his clawed hand at it, but the bird almost casually sprang into the air and away. Molly and Nemain released the locks of their hooking lances and stepped back three, four paces, grounding the butts in the grass.

Sir Tarquin put one hand to his throat, stretched out a clawed hand and drew breath, ready to hurl destruction upon the two women, but just then the raven from the grass took wing and landed on Sir Tarquin's other shoulder. It darted at his face, and he was forced to turn from the women and swat at the black beak, so close to his eye. The raven flinched away; the mage's clawlike fingernails caught only air; and a moment later the vast cloud dropped with a thunder of midnight wings onto the evil magician, a black avalanche, the birds piling in an ever-increasing heap of darkness, fighting for a place at the feast, coming and going, alighting with empty beak wide and sharp and hungry and taking off again, each with a tiny particle.

The heap of black feathers seethed like a cauldron of ink brought to the boil.

And each bird did its work in utter, unnatural silence; there was neither call nor cry, only the storm of flapping, the clicking, shuffling, rustling blanket of birds over whatever was left of the magus. All the men on the hillside were also silent, their eyes wide and their lips moving in prayer; signs of the cross were made over and over, and many kissed cruciform dagger-hilts, caught in this unholy nightmare: afraid of bodily death, afraid of spiritual pollution.

One by one, the birds took their mite of flesh, and fought clear of the pile and lifted away into the sky. Slowly the huge struggling heap diminished, and diminished, and after what seemed a year of hideous activity, the last dozen of the feathered attendants of the dead sprang up, flicked broad black wings open, and beat up and away into the morning air.

There was a tattered red cloak, and some gray cloth, on the grass beside the road—the remains of the wizard's clothing. A few fragments of darkened ivory, no bigger than a thumbnail, stood out here and there amid the folds of gray and scarlet. At some point in the relentless destruction wrought by the birds, there was not enough left of Sir Tarquin's flesh to house his unnaturally sustained life. Upon the release of the rest of his body from the binding grip of his will, the long-thwarted forces of Time had rushed in and overwhelmed the structure of his bones; they had crumbled, and the birds had made off with all but these few small shards.

The carriage stood, its drawshafts vacant, and creaked a little as it flexed in the wind from the German Sea. The mage's book lay in the scorched grass, but its uncanny flames were quenched with his death. There was nothing else. The breeze lifted a corner of the red rag, just an inch or so, and let it fall, and lifted it again, and let it fall. There was no other movement, and but for the scraps of red cloth and of gray cloth, a few tiny chips of discolored bone, and the dead book, the ground before the mage's coach was utterly empty.

SEVERAL MEN had dragged a log from the forest to the space by the carriage so that Molly and Nemain, weary almost unto death, might sit and direct the movements of the men of Chantemerle and Blanchefontaine: there was still some work that must be done, and only the women knew what it was. They sat side by side, swaying with fatigue, and yet with an air of deep contentment, and Molly gave a string of orders to Sir Odinell and Sir Jehan and Sir Balthasar, and those high men went and had their men carry those orders out. The two packhorses, with saddlebags that Molly had prepared before they left Chantemerle, were brought up and tethered to the log. From one of the packs Molly had them bring a small cask of the *uisce beatha,* and cups for herself and Nemain, and the two women sat and drank, Molly heartily, Nemain sipping slowly.

Hob sat next to Nemain and put his arm around her and kissed her with the utmost tenderness, for he did not know whether she was in pain or other distress. She smiled at him, and then looked down and frowned. She put a hand to the slit in his gambeson, and the shirt beneath, and it came away red.

All at once she was on her feet. "It's off with that thing, *a rún*; I'm not to be losing my man before my wedding night."

"Nay, it's you should be sitting down, and resting, after you—"

But she was tugging at the laces of the gambeson, and so he began to help her, and they got it off. There was a line of red across his chest from one side to the other, and it had stained a broader band below the cut where his shirt had absorbed the bleeding, but it was a superficial wound, and Nemain was relieved. Hob urged her to sit and rest, but even he could see that the *uisce beatha,* and the consciousness of victory, had gone a fair way to ameliorate her fatigue—and she was young.

She went to the packhorses and came back with salves and powders and linen strips, and washed the shallow slice in his skin, applied pulverized herbs and a soothing salve, and bound all up in clean linen. She draped his shirt around him, and at last he persuaded her to sit down on the log, and to rest. He put his arm around her again, and so they sat while Molly directed these last stages of the cleansing of Sir Tarquin from the land.

Sir Odinell had sent riders to Chantemerle for wagons to remove the wounded; the castle was only a few miles up the coast, and now wagons with straw pallets began pulling up, loading wounded men, and heading north again. Gradually none were left but those who had escaped harm.

Not all the wagons were on errands of mercy: one was a supply wagon prepared the night before under Molly's supervision, and another was Molly's large traveling wagon. Sir Balthasar had thoughtfully ordered that two horses be harnessed to her personal wagon instead of Milo, and that it be brought down the coast, for he did not think Molly and Nemain in any condition to ride saddle horses, and he thought it better that they should be able to ride inside, and lie at their ease.

Now Molly, sipping at a second cup of the *uisce beatha* and working with a small group of Sir Odinell's men, had them bring forth from the supply wagon sacks of pig fat and a bottle of poppy oil obtained from Sir Odinell's kitchen, and toss some of the sacks in through the open door of the coach. A sack was opened and pig fat smeared around the outside of the carriage. Poppy oil was poured through the windows and along the roof.

A wooden shovel from the same wagon was used to pick up the ragged remnants of Sir Tarquin's red robe, and the book that now lay so quietly on the ground, and toss them into the carriage, followed by the shovel itself. The door was pushed shut, and four men took hold of the shafts and dragged the wagon down to the strand.

The tide was almost out. They stopped the wagon on the damp flat sand left by the withdrawing waters, and held torches to the bottom edges of the coach, and thrust torches in through the windows so that the curtains caught, and let the flaming brands drop to the carriage seats within. There was a *whoosh* as the fat and oil caught, and the whole structure was enveloped in crackling flame.

By the time the wagon had burned to ashes, the tide had gone out completely and was now returning, the advance edges of those waves that reached the shore spreading in a foam-white carpet nearer and nearer the smoking remains. At last the leading edge of the German Sea touched the ashes, hissing against those glowing embers still surviving. Thereafter wave upon wave invaded the ashes, soaked them in salt water, lifted them, bore them out and away to the deep.

SIR ODINELL AND SIR JEHAN stood together, watching the disappearance of every last fleck of ash. With them were a few others: knights, men-at-arms, and Hob as well—he had reluctantly left Nemain's side at Molly's bidding, to make sure the carriage was utterly destroyed. Sir Odinell stood holding a bloodstained white cloth to a minor wound on his forehead. He said, speaking to Sir Jehan but watching the waves arriving, the waves departing, "Christ be my salvation, I would not have believed it. You said she would cleanse my land of this filth. I would not have— I *did* not believe it, not then."

Sir Jehan, looking out on the silver immensity, said, "She is the sea, Odinell, the sea."

CHAPTER 29

T HE LORDS OF CHANTEMERLE AND
Blanchefontaine climbed back up the
slope to the road, Hob and the others
trailing behind, and thence to where Molly sat with
Nemain.

Hob went immediately over and sat beside
Nemain, putting his arm about her. She leaned back
against his chest, then sat up abruptly, realizing she
was pressing against his wound, but he pulled her
back against him, and thereafter they sat quietly.

Two knights had led up the white carriage horses,
and asked if they should be killed and burned, to remove any taint of the evil mage they had served. Molly
heaved herself to her feet and went to the horses. Between the intense fatigue of the struggle with Sir Tar-

quin and the *uisce beatha,* she was halfway to being drunk. Certainly she was as drunk as Hob had ever seen her, but the result was only an exaggerated caution in her movements.

She put a hand under one horse's jaw, looked in its eyes, patted its neck; then she did the same with the other. She stood back, and said, "Nay, there's no evil to them; it's only innocent slaves of evil they've been, and they not having an easy time of it, and it's setting them free that's the path of justice, and they to be slaves no more. Take off these bridles, and let them loose up in those woods we're after hiding in." This was done as she directed, and for years afterward it was noticed that white horses would crop up occasionally among feral Galloway ponies.

She sat down heavily on the log again and reached for the cup. Sir Jehan came over and put his right leg up on the log, and leaned in to speak with Molly, his right elbow resting on his thigh. The iron hand shone dully in the sun, save where the light caught the silver legend.

"Madam," he said low, so that only Molly on the one side and Hob and Nemain on the other could hear, "must we burn these knights of Sir Tarquin's household as well, or can they be given Christian burial?"

"Himself is no more; sure and his power is destroyed entirely. These knights were after being enslaved by him, and they being victims themselves in that way, no less than his horses. Christian burial—it's a priest you should be asking that of, but burning—nay, they're not needing it."

"And his castle? Should Odinell have it purified by the Church? Or is it safe as it is?"

"'Tis safe as it is, that castle. I'm just after telling you, his power is no more. As to letting the priests at it, well—" She took another sip, smiling to herself, looking into the cup. "Sure and it can do no harm."

SIR ODINELL, SIR JEHAN, AND SIR BALTHASAR were walking about the scene of conflict. Not far from where Molly sat they came upon the corpse of the giant knight that Hob had slain. In the daylight, stretched full-length on his back, one mailed fist outflung as though reaching for the hand-and-a-half hilt of the claymore, the knight seemed even larger than he had by the glow of the carriage lanterns. He lay there like a toppled statue, as long of body as Walking Rollo—for whom Sir Jehan had named his wolfhound pup— the Orkney jarl, who was too big for a horse to carry.

"By Saint Cuthbert! The size of this wight!" said Sir Odinell. "I saw you batter him from his horse." This to Sir Balthasar, who nodded. "How comes he here?"

Molly said, "That *gesadóir*'s after summoning him, with the hold he had over him, and the giant coming to aid him, coming on foot from the melee."

Sir Odinell paced alongside the body, and stopped. He looked along the corpse to the feet, and back to the head; he noted the congealed lake of blood in the left eye socket.

He looked over at Jack, sitting cross-legged in the grass near Molly with his war hammer across his lap, and looked at the crow-beak on the hammerhead. He indicated the fallen giant, and called to Jack, "You slew him?"

Jack, extending an arm that was the definition of brawn, pointed a thick finger at Hob.

"You slew this, this—?" Sir Odinell said to Hob, who nodded shyly. The three knights drifted over to the log, where Hob was made to tell his story, which he did as simply as possible.

At one point Sir Odinell burst out, "With a *dagger*? You slew him with a *dagger*?"

When he had finished, Hob found to his immense irritation that he was blushing, so strongly that he could feel prickles of heat on his cheeks.

Sir Balthasar pointed silently to the dagger he had given Hob, back in its sheath at Hob's side, and Hob just nodded. Sir Balthasar's habitual expression was so savage that one would have to know him to realize he was gazing approvingly at the lad, but Hob could tell. The knight said nothing. He went around behind the log and off up the hill to get the men ready to move, but as he passed Hob he clapped him on the shoulder. Hob thought to himself it was not unlike being struck with a mace, but nonetheless an unfamiliar emotion rose in him, which in a moment he recognized as pride.

Sir Odinell went to look again at the body, glancing back at Hob a few times. Sir Jehan set off up the hill in

Sir Balthasar's wake, but before he went he said to Hob in a quiet voice, "Sir Balthasar has an apt pupil, it seems: not yet fifteen, and fighting that outlander swordsman on Fox Night, and now you've come to be this giant's bane."

Molly started, as though at a barely heard signal; she turned blue eyes on Hob, unfocused with fatigue and strong drink, but also with a fey look that she sometimes had, when she felt that the future declared itself to her, and she said to Hob, "It's that name that men will be calling you, and they sitting around a fire, remembering this night we're just after passing through, and you a great man by then."

She looked away, toward the giant's corpse, although she appeared to be seeing something far distant. *"Robert the Englishman,* they'll be saying in Erin," she murmured. *"Giant's Bane."*

Sir Odinell wandered back from the giant's corpse and, inspecting Hob, said, still a bit bemused, "With a dagger."

Nemain, reclining at ease on Hob's breast, idly picking apart a tangle at the end of her scarlet hair, looked up at Sir Odinell—in her reckoning, in Molly's reckoning, he was her social inferior, she a queen and he but a Norman lord—looked up at him with leaf-green eyes, and smiled, a smile that suggested a cream-fed cat on a cushion, and patted Hob's thigh in a proprietary manner, and said only, "My man-to-be."

CHAPTER 30

MOLLY'S LITTLE CARAVAN LEFT Chantemerle quietly one morning at the beginning of August. The night before, it had rained heavily, the downpour roaring against the shutters, the wind from the German Sea hurling the drops against the castle wall. Hob lay snug in a seaward tower of the keep, and listened to the shout of the storm. The soothing contrast between the violence outside and the silence of the room, broken only by occasional crackling from the banked fire, urged him toward sleep, but it was warring with the excitement that roiled his heart—the day after tomorrow was his wedding day.

Eventually, though, sleep stole over him, and

then it was early morning, the rain had stopped, and Jack was opening the shutters. Outside the sky was still dark.

Molly wanted them to be on their way, and farewells had been said the night before. Some bread and cheese and a draft of ale, and the company was ready to take the road. In the stables, Nemain went about unlocking the wagons and restowing the locks, while Hob and Jack and Sweetlove waited at the foot of the long ramp. Grooms brought Milo and Mavourneen and Tapaidh down, the ramp boards booming under their mismatched hooves. Soon the animals were in their traces, Hob had Milo's lead rope in hand, and Nemain and Jack were up on their respective wagons, Jack with Sweetlove curled on the seat beside him. Molly called out, "Away on!" The wagons, in their usual order, trundled out of the stables and across the outer ward.

There was a bit of delay at the barbican—a delay almost inevitable, what with the usual opening of the heavy inner doors, the raising of the portcullis, the opening of the outer doors, the lowering of the drawbridge. This last would be done but once in the day, unless some threat emerged.

Hob led Milo through the gatehouse—into the dark echoing passage, where the clop of hooves was greatly magnified, and out again into the gray light of false dawn. They stumped down the slope, Molly leaning a little on the brake, to level ground; and Hob led Milo in a shallow curve to the left, heading south along the coast road.

Arrangements had been made the night before: Molly

had explained to Sir Odinell that they wanted to find some private woodland glade where her granddaughter and Hob—Squire Robert once again, when within Norman walls—might be married. The Sieur de Chantemerle, hearing Molly's requirements, had suggested a small clearing in the manor's woodlands, where Sir Odinell set up a camp at certain times of the year.

A nearby brook ran down into a rock-bound pool, where the knight and his guests, armed with six-foot hazel twigs to which were fastened horsehair lines, cast hooks into the chilly water. Flies made of colored silk, of partridge feather, of dove feather, enticed the fish to snap at the hooks, and Sir Odinell discoursed at some length on the subject, until Molly gently steered the conversation back to the coming wedding and the way to the campsite.

Lady Maysaunt had lamented the loss of an opportunity for a wedding at the castle, and had wept a little, and had supplied Molly with a large box filled with gaily colored ribbon, and flowers fashioned of ribbon, and heraldic animals fashioned of ribbon, all that Molly might decorate her wagons in a suitably festive manner. She had also offered to supply a gown, which Molly diplomatically refused; Sir Odinell had volunteered his chaplain's services to marry the couple, but Molly said smoothly, "There will be someone to officiate."

Now the wagons rolled southward, rumbling, creaking, with the grinding sea on the left and Sir Odinell's field land on their right. Here the flax and hemp had been harvested in July, and the fields were fresh-plowed for the planting of turnips by the knight's tenants, the rich dark furrows drenched with last night's rain. The sun rose, dripping molten gold into the pewter of the German Sea, and began to work upon the soaked fields.

A mist arose from the deep slits in the earth, as the heat of the sun torched the chill from the wet soil, and pulled water steaming from the ground. A layer of low-lying fog persisted for a time, and then began to burn off. They passed the side road that led to Adelard's Inn, and plodded on.

After a while the fields ended in a line of forest. A track led off at a slant toward the woods, and Molly directed Hob to turn off onto it. They entered the trees. As Sir Odinell had said, there was room for the wagons to pass, albeit with some bumping over roots and the odd stone half-embedded in the earth.

After not a very great while they entered the campsite, where trees and brush had been cut back, and the sun striking in past the canopy had nourished a carpet of grass. Molly had the main wagon drawn up at the far side of the clearing, close to the slope down to the brook, and the other two wagons placed along the near side, as far as possible from the large wagon, for privacy. The animals were loosely tethered and tended to, and while Hob and Jack gathered firewood and set up camp, Molly and Nemain, delving into the box

THE WICKED

of ribbons, decorated the main wagon, which was to be the couple's wedding chamber tomorrow.

A simple meal, with everyone perhaps a little quieter than usual, and then to bed. Hob lay awake a long time in the midsized wagon, the shutters open and the occasional hooting of an owl drifting in on the night breeze. Jack usually slept here as well, but tonight Molly had called him into the big wagon. Sweetlove lay, chin on paws, disconsolate, on Jack's bed at the other end of the wagon.

Nemain, who usually had a place in the main wagon with her grandmother, slept tonight in the little wagon. Hob thought of her, alone, so near, and a surge of desire made him turn this way and that, seeking comfort.

Tomorrow Molly would marry them according to the old Irish religion. Hob had been told by Father Athelstan that such old beliefs were of Satan, yet Molly was the most deeply good person he had ever known. Jack, that stolid cheerful man, a good if not very observant Christian, loved Molly and did not trouble himself with contradictions. The soldier, a man of action rather than introspection, did not fret about it: why should Hob?

There was no question of not marrying Nemain, but Hob would have liked something to ease his conscience on the question of his bride's pagan practices. Hob, as Nemain said, had always to "think three times" about what he was doing, and what it meant, and whether it was the right thing to do, either by the light of Father Athelstan's teaching, or by the light of Molly's teaching-by-example. Should Hob be guided by Jack's conduct; should he follow Jack's lead? In the darkness, broken only by a shaft of moonlight slanting through the leaves into the wagon, Hob clasped his hands and asked to be given a sign.

CHAPTER 31

THE NEXT MORNING THE WOMEN went down the wooded slope to the brook and followed it downstream. There they bathed in the pool formed by a rocky basin, in the dark cold water of the northland. They returned swathed in lengths of the undyed cloth known as blanket, laughing together at some murmured jest, to vanish within the main wagon.

Then it was Jack and Hob who made their way down to the water. The brook plunged over a gray slate ridge and fell in a sheet of silver six feet into the pool. At the other side of the basin, water poured out of the pool and away down the slope, running toward the east and, eventually, the German Sea.

Jack threw off his clothes and leaped in; immediately he began to scoop water over his brawny limbs. Hob stepped down, waded into the waist-high water, gasping at the shock of the chill. He plunged beneath the surface, hearing the rumbles and squeaks of the moving water. When he came up, Jack had retrieved the bar of soap that Molly had given him and was soaping himself. This was not their usual mutton-fat-and-ash soap: for this special occasion, Molly had brought out a bar of olive-oil soap, perfumed with thyme and lavender, brought all the way from Spain and bought at the Ely fair. When Jack was finished, Hob washed himself head to toe, sneezing a little at the unfamiliar perfume.

Back up the dirt path through the trees, cloaked in large squares of cloth, holding their clothes with one hand and drying their hair with the other. Hob had the sense that the day was like one of the dances Molly had taught them to play, beginning slowly but then increasing in tempo. Certainly his pulse was faster, and there was a growing impatience; his movements became quicker, his breath came more rapidly. When they came to the midsized wagon he bounded up the steps, Jack following with a grin.

Jack opened a shutter for light; from one of Molly's trunks he drew, to Hob's astonishment, a set of wedding garments for him: a green tunic and hose, green leather shoes, a woven belt dyed green. At the string-and-loop fastening, the belt swelled into a square, on which was embroidered an Irish endless-knot design in silver thread. Hob sat down on the chests, pushed together, that served him as a bed, and began to dress. He could hear the women outside, leaving the large wagon, laughing, talking, their voices fading as they made their way down the wooded slope to the brook again.

Jack, dressed in clean shirt and hose, but with his usual heavy belt, was, oddly enough, barefoot. He had Hob stand up and turned him around, inspecting him. "S'goorh," he croaked. It's good. For him this was a long speech, and an indication of his pleasure at the day. Jack picked up his goatskin drum, and they were ready to go.

They left the wagon, Hob in the lead, and he set off down the path to the pool where they had bathed. Perhaps two-thirds of the way down, a path branched off to the right. This led to the brook itself, some way upstream from the little waterfall into the rock basin that formed the pool. Hob became aware that Jack, right behind him, had turned off onto this side path and was gesturing for Hob to follow him. The lad retraced his steps to the fork and set off after Jack, following the soldier's lead.

A moment later he stopped, frozen. Jack's hearing was acute. When Hob's footsteps, padding along the dirt trail, ceased, the dark man paused, looked back, a question beginning to form on his face. Hob broke into a grin: he was *following Jack's lead*. Here was his sign! He set off again, a lightness, a happiness, spreading throughout his heart.

* * *

Jack and Hob came out onto the stream's bank, where the women waited. Molly stood barefoot in the middle of the little brook, and Nemain on the far bank. Molly held out her left hand, and Hob came to her. She positioned him, facing Nemain, on the near bank.

He gazed with something like wonder on his betrothed. Nemain wore a gown of green silk, a paler green than Hob's own garments, with an endless-knot border at neck and wrists, worked in silver thread; the gown was cinched with a belt of silver links. Her hair was unbound, and a mild but steady breeze that blew toward the falls fanned it sideways, a red flame flickering from behind the tree-green gown.

Molly, standing barefoot in the icy stream, with her hair in a thick silver braid down her back, had a silver goblet in her right hand. Now she began a prayer in Irish. Jack left his drum leaning against a tree, and stepped into the brook—Hob now understood why he had not put on shoes—and faced Molly, who handed him the goblet: he was, Molly had explained, the witness. Molly, still chanting, reached out to either side and, taking Nemain's right hand, placed it in Hob's. Around Molly's neck was a green ribbon; like Hob's belt and Nemain's gown, it had the endless-knot pattern of Ireland worked in silver. Molly now took this from around her neck, kissed it, and looped it around and around the young couple's wrists as they stood with hands clasped across the stream.

Molly had explained the ceremony to Hob the day before: the hands were clasped across the stream that the water gods might be witness to the marriage for all the gods, and Jack was the witness for all men and women. Now she half spoke, half sang a long prayer to those gods.

She turned to Nemain, but she had spent some time translating this part of the ceremony from the Irish, so that Hob could understand, and now she spoke in English. "From this day, you are to approach each other with awe and delight, and to lie with none else, and to be a tribe to each other, back to back against the wide world. Swear to this, by the water that runs between you, and by the gods, and they dwelling in that water."

"I so swear," said Nemain.

She turned to Hob. "Swear to this."

"I so swear."

For a moment there was no sound but the gurgling of the shallow brook as it ran over the smooth stones in its bed, the singing of the water: the voice of the water deities, witnesses for the gods.

She faced Jack. "Give them drink."

He handed the goblet to Nemain, who drank with her left hand, and reached the cup over to Hob. He took it left-handed and took a deep swallow: it was the *uisce beatha,* and burned down his throat.

Molly addressed Jack. "Witness, speak. Are they married?"

"Yerrh," Jack said from his ruined throat. Yes.

And with that, Jack Brown, man-at-arms, sometime Crusader, sometime mercenary, sometime shapeshifter, and the standing witness for all humankind, gave his assent, and so they were married.

CHAPTER 32

MOLLY UNWRAPPED THE RIB-
bon from their wrists, re-
tied them, Hob's left hand to
Nemain's right, and holding the other end, stepped
from the water, leading the couple—Nemain leaping
lightly over the brook to Hob's side—up the slope,
through the trees. Jack came behind, scooping up
his drum as he passed it. He took his bone tapper-
stick from his pouch and began tapping out a lively
marching rhythm with a skip in the middle. So it was
that they came to the large wagon.

Molly whipped the ribbon from their wrists
and shooed them within. Nemain closed the door
behind them, and they heard Jack's drum grow
softer as the older couple withdrew to the smaller

wagons and the campfire, leaving them alone at the far side of the glade.

Hob opened the shutters on the side away from the clearing, facing the wooded slope they had just ascended. A faint murmur came to them: the stream's chatter, drifting up-slope to them through the trees. Sweetlove, over by Molly and Jack's campfire, was barking at something; she fell silent suddenly, as though she had been hushed by someone. The room grew bright; the sunlight, shimmering gold and green through the clouds of leaves, fell mostly on Molly's big bed, a real bed with wood frame and leather webbing, goosedown mattress and large pillows, that Jack folded up against the wall in the mornings, and pulled down at night.

In after years, some of what happened was to Hob a blur, and some stood out in his memory, sharp and bright as one of Molly's arrowheads.

Hob turned back from the window; they contemplated each other. After a moment the corners of Nemain's mouth quirked up, the beginnings of that smile of pure mischief Hob remembered from her childhood.

"Oh, Hob," she said simply, meaning nothing and everything at once, and with quick clever movements of those slim fingers, she undid ties and ribbons, and let her gown slide to the floor. The sun struck in through the side window, a shifting dappled glow, filtered through the swaying branches, the wind-tossed masses of leaves, so that light and shadow moved over her body. Where the sun lit her, her pale, pale skin seemed to glow as though illumined from within.

He felt as though he could happily stand for a thousand days, and do nothing but gaze upon her, and lose himself in those large green eyes, but in two steps she came to him, laughing—"I wish you could be seeing yourself, and you looking like a man in his cups"—and began to pull at his laces. He started to help her, moving as one dreaming, and as he stepped from his braies he put a hand on her side, the skin at first cool and then the warmth of her blood rising to meet his burning palm, her side a yielding softness under which were the muscles Molly had trained for war.

He fell upon her then, enveloping her in his arms, bearing her gently down onto Molly's bed. They slid and rolled, a bit awkwardly, till they were fully on the bed: he did not want to release her, not for a moment.

He ran his hands over her, the gleaming milky skin, the mane of scarlet hair that poured down her back, the little patch of russet fur between her thighs, and the tips of her breasts, where the areolas, raised a bit like the caps of shy forest mushrooms, were tinted the pallid pink of the dog roses that grew throughout the North Country.

He kissed her everywhere, while she in turn, the young queen, explored her new dominion, entranced by the strength in his neck, the width of his shoulders, the depth of his chest.

Soon they fell to kissing and caressing each other,

laughing, teasing, and she showed him where to touch her, and how, and all laughter and teasing then ceased, and there was left only deep concentration, and at last she rolled to her back, lifting her hair to one side, graceful as a dancer, and with not a word seized him and guided him into her.

A period of slow movement, stately as the tide, and then she urged him to ride up on her a bit, so to bear upon her most sensitive part; she even introduced him to the idea of moving in slow circles, and it all began to go faster, and again faster, until she stopped him, and bade him lie still, and because he trusted her, trusted her completely—she was Nemain, his childhood friend, his fated wife—he followed her every direction, keen and attentive as any dog of the sheep-herding Scots, and soon she bade him move again, and he did, and stop again, and he did that also.

And at last Nemain had come to her moment, a lynx arrived at the rabbit's throat. She sank her nails into his back; she bit at his shoulder; she clamped upon him within, as if to milk the seed from him—and this proved to be the signal his loins had waited upon. One after another, inward gates flew open, and a sweet burning ran through him; his mind went silent, and his body grew taut as a drawn longbow. Like the sun above the rain-damp earth, he hung over her, and poured heat into her dark and secret places.

CHAPTER 33

ATE THAT NIGHT, THE TROUPE sat around a waning fire, watching the wood Jack had gathered slowly collapse into pale ash and glowing embers. The celebration had included music from the women's homeland, songs Hob had never heard before; a great deal of food; a fair amount of strong drink. Two logs were placed at right angles; the younger couple sat on one, and the elder couple on the other, with Sweetlove between them. The terrier was asleep with her chin pillowed on Jack's thigh, and her feet were fluttering: she was obviously deep in some running dream.

Conversation had ranged over every aspect of the summer's events, from serious discussion of the assistance the De Umfrevilles might provide Molly against her enemies back in Ireland, to merry reflection on Daniel Clerk's infatuation with Hawis, and what sort of marriage they might make. Molly—who was rarely wrong in such matters—thought it would be a good one.

Speech had gradually given way to a placid silence. Jack was working at the last bits of meat on a bone. Nemain had shifted herself and turned sideways so that she could assume what was becoming her favorite position, leaning back against Hob's chest. With one hand put behind him, he braced himself on the log; with the other, he was idly stroking stray wisps of hair back away from Nemain's forehead.

Molly was thinking her own thoughts, and now she said, somewhat obscurely, "Sure and that's done."

Hob, at ease and utterly content, asked, "Mistress, what will you do next?"

She looked at him, just the least bit unfocused. "Let me see." Molly picked up her mug of the *uisce beatha*. She had filled it again, and from this angle it looked to Hob a bit like the water-mirror: he could see the reflection of the moon in it, very small.

Molly began to gaze intently into the cup with its miniature freight of burning water and drowned moon.

Hob sat up straighter, now intrigued, and Nemain sat up as well. "Can you see the future in the cup, Mistress? What you will be doing?" he asked in a quiet voice, not wanting to distract her.

"Aye," she said, in a low voice.

"And, and what . . . ?"

Molly slowly reached out a hand sideways, a dreamlike movement, the loose sleeve of her gown falling away from her shapely arm, her hand reaching, reaching to the side, slowly, while she gazed with fervid intensity into her cup. Nemain put her hand over her mouth suddenly.

"It's after saying . . ." Her hand began to move quickly, and it captured Jack's earlobe without, as far as Hob could see, her looking to see what her hand was doing.

". . . it's after saying I am to finish this cup," she said. Jack was already beginning to laugh, a rusty gargling, to anyone outside the family a horrible sound. She held his earlobe between thumb and forefinger. "And then take this lad into yon wagon, and show him that in this wide world there are roads he has yet to travel."

Hob, now seeing that he had been toyed with, started to chuckle, and Nemain, who had been reddening and giving little choking gasps behind her palm, took her hand away from her face and burst into laughter. She fell back against Hob's chest again and leaned there, her peals of laughter echoing through the glade: the laughter of pure happiness, silver as the moonlight.

GLOSSARY OF IRISH TERMS

a chuisle	pulse, heartbeat (direct address; literally: "O pulse")
anmhas	hooligan
a rún	love, dear
Bíodh sé amhlaidh.	So be it.
bithiúnaigh	villains, scoundrels (sing. *bithiúnach*)
buidseach	wizard
cailleach	hag *or* witch (as Molly is using it; can also just mean "old woman")
cailleach phiseogach	sorceress; charm-worker
do-dhuine	wicked/inhuman person
draíodóir	wizard
drochdhuine	evil person

gariníon	granddaughter
geis	a supernatural command or obligation to perform a certain action, or a taboo that forbids a certain action
gesadóir	enchanter, spellbinder
gruagh	giant
Mavourneen	my sweetheart (Irish *mo mhuirnín*)
meirligh	outlaws, bandits (sing. *meirleach*)
míolachán	low/mean person
mo chroí	my heart
ochone	an exclamation of sorrow; woe (Irish *ochóin*)
scian	knife
seanmháthair	grandmother (literally: "old mother")
spalpeen	rascal, layabout (Irish *spailpín*, itinerant laborer)
stór mo chroí	treasure of my heart
uisce beatha	whiskey (literally: "water of life")

Glossary of Archaisms and of North England Dialect Terms

a'   all

ae   any

ane   one

brast   burst (archaic past tense of "burst")

Christ-money   the thirty pieces of silver paid Judas
                    (later modified to "criminy")

clerk   pronounced "clark" in the English
                    manner; one who could read
                    and write (from "cleric," because
                    churchmen could read and write
                    where most could not); Daniel's
                    occupational nickname, not his
                    surname (but eventually the origin
                    of the surname)

coney	a rabbit, *but also* loose woman
coom	come
cowd	cold
craic	entertainment, esp. conversation, good company
deek	to look at
didna	did not
dinna	do not
dole	pain, grief, sorrow
eldritch	strange, eerie, unearthly, weird
enow	enough
eyen	eyes
filz	Norman French, "son of"; compare French *fils*; gave rise to names starting with "Fitz": Fitzgerald, Fitzroy, etc.
gaan	going
gae	go
gang	walk
gie	give
giglet	a giggling girl, *but also* lascivious woman

God's hooks	the nails used to crucify Jesus (later modified to "gadzooks")
guid	good
hinny	a term of endearment: "honey"
jarl	Norse title, comparable to "earl"
mair	more
men of their hands	men proficient with weapons
mickle	much
mort	a great deal, a great many (literally "death"; a mortal amount)
nae	no
nout beast	a member of the cattle family (var. of "neat," as in "neat's-foot oil")
oot	out
pard	leopard, panther
rede	counsel, advice
sae	so
St. Cuthbert	c. 634–687; Bishop of Lindisfarne; patron saint of Northern England
sartain	certain

scran	food
sennight	a week ("seven-night")
siccerlike	such, suchlike
sithee	"see thee"
	As a question: "Do you see?" "Do you understand?" *As a command:* "Look." or "Look here." as in "Look, I'm willing to . . ."
sooth	south
spelk	a splinter; hence, a skinny person
summat	something
tae	to
tarse	medieval slang for "penis"
thae	these; those
theer	there
the noo	now
unco	strange [*adj.*]; very [*adv.*]
wean	child ("wee ain," little one)
weel	well
whisht	be quiet (imperative)

wight	a human being; any living being
yawp	hungry
yem	home
yon	over there, yonder; *but also as pronoun:* that [one]

Acknowledgments

Here in this quiet corner at the back of our book, dear reader, I would like to pause a moment to thank those who have made the writing of *The Wicked* such a pleasure.

First, my editor, Emily Bestler, for her excellent comments and questions and for her unflagging enthusiasm, and the staff at Emily Bestler Books. My gratitude also to my hawkeyed and insightful copy editor, Jaime Costas. Thanks go to my agent, George Hiltzik, for his efforts on behalf of Molly and Co., and also to my special friends Patricia and Michael Sovern, for their unfailing support. Thanks as well to my *mareschal*, Micheline Tilton, for sharing her horse wisdom, and to those who've helped introduce others to Molly's adventures, both in this book and in *Something Red,* including the staff of the elfin but mighty Rosendale Library, guided by director Wendy Alexander.

I must also thank those early readers whose enthusiasm

for *Something Red* and for *The Wicked* heartened me through the long process of seeing these works into print, among them my longtime reader Susan Holt; my friends and neighbors Susan Blommaert and Polly Pen; the always ebullient Yvette Lee; and, for his partisanship and encouragement, the incomparable teacher, erudite author and translator, fine calligrapher, and dear friend, Ronald Christ.

And finally, for all she has done for me, my love and devotion to the Fairy Bride, Theresa Adinolfi Nicholas.

> *"Doulce chose est que mariage."*
> —Christine de Pizan (1364–c. 1430)

About the Author

DOUGLAS NICHOLAS is an award-winning poet whose work has appeared in numerous publications, among them *Atlanta Review, Southern Poetry Review, Sonora Review, Circumference, A Different Drummer,* and *Cumberland Review,* as well as the *South Coast Poetry Journal,* where he won a prize in that publication's Fifth Annual Poetry Contest. Other awards include Honorable Mention in the Robinson Jeffers Tor House Foundation 2003 Prize For Poetry Awards, second place in the 2002 Allen Ginsberg Poetry Awards from PCCC, International Merit Award in *Atlanta Review*'s Poetry 2002 competition, finalist in the 1996 Emily Dickinson Award in Poetry competition, honorable mention in the 1992 Scottish International Open Poetry Competition, first prize in the journal *Lake Effect*'s Sixth Annual Poetry Contest, first prize in poetry in the 1990 Roberts Writing Awards, and finalist in the Roberts short fiction division. He was also recipient of an award in the 1990 International Poetry Contest sponsored by the Arvon Foundation in Lancashire, England, and a Cecil B. Hackney Literary Award for poetry from Birmingham-Southern College. He is the author of *Something Red,* a fantasy novel set in the thirteenth century, as well as *Iron Rose,* a collection of poems inspired by and set in New York City; *The Old Language,* reflections on the company of animals; *The Rescue Artist,* poems about his wife and their long marriage; and *In the Long-Cold Forges of the Earth,* a wide-ranging collection of poems. He lives in New York's Hudson Valley with his wife, Theresa, and Yorkshire terrier, Tristan.